For Ernst & Esther
With love & best wishes
Jon

SHAKEDOWN

By the author of

The Fountain Pen Conspiracy

The Mullendore Murder Case

SHAKEDOWN

BY
JONATHAN
KWITNY

G. P. PUTNAM'S SONS

NEW YORK

SBN: 399-11915-9

Library of Congress Cataloging in Publication Data:

Kwitny, Jonathan.
  Shakedown.

  I. Title
PZ4.K987Sh [PS3561.W54]   813'.5'4   76-51436

PRINTED IN THE UNITED STATES OF AMERICA

For (in order of appearance)

I. J. KWITNY
DOUGLAS LANGDON
BURTON LEE
LOURDES NISCE
JEROME PORUSH
STANLEY BIRNBAUM
JHOONG CHEIGH
ALAN AISENBERG
SAUL ROSENBERG

NOTE

The author wishes to thank for their generous reading time and helpful advice on the manuscript Martha Kwitny, David Thaler, Ellen Levine and former FBI Agent William F. Higgins Jr.

PART ONE:

THE SCHEME

CHAPTER ONE

Everybody used to be a newspaperman. Me too.

But most reporters leave because they're looking for money. I was still looking for justice. Money is what you want after you discover that justice is unavailable. For me, the discovery came late.

I had gone to work for the FBI, assigned to the Quincy Corporation case, which you probably read about in the papers. It was a mess—Michael Carmody's biggest job. And I will tell you the whole story, including the stuff that didn't come out in the newspapers, or in court, or anywhere else. Such as how Hezekiah X. Portaquil got shot. And who wound up with the four and a half million dollars. And why Quincy and the FBI and all those banks and insurance companies and their lawyers and even the Mafia oouldn't find it.

My God, how everybody wanted that money. They just didn't understand Mickey Carmody.

My name is Franklin Scanlon. People call me Frank. I think I did understand him. If those other guys had known Mickey as long as I had, then maybe all the strange characters he led us to wouldn't have confused them. Certainly nothing would have surprised them. Maybe they would have beat me to the four and a half million. At any rate they would have known that Mickey could turn almost any situation into money: other people's love, or hate—even his own.

I already knew, for example, that he was married to Sybil Manwaring, a good-looking honey-blonde neurosurgeon out of Yale Medical School. She operated only at the best hospitals, then came home every night to a gun-toting hood whose ostensible occupation was part-time truckdriver. Of course, Sybil was looking for something in her men, and truckdrivers like Carmody and Donald O'Neil had it, and I guess FBI agents didn't. You wouldn't know just looking at her, just chatting, what caused it. I did learn along the way that she was brought up poor. But somewhere that woman developed an anti-establishment streak.

Then there was D. C. "Fud" Peerce, the biggest banking tycoon in Caliquatta, Tennessee. The stink of the backwoods still smelled on his clothes. Wall Street didn't know what to make of him. But I can tell you that Fud's bank used to earn a lot of its money financing illegal moonshine stills. Then Mickey Carmody showed Fud how to empty the vaults at Morgan Guaranty.

And of course I could hardly forget Sara, Mickey's stewardess friend. How can I describe her? Fetching. Innocent. She insisted that Mickey was the only man who ever talked her out of a key to her apartment. They were that close. And yet she not only didn't know that Carmody had a wife, she also didn't know about Barbara, the other mistress he was living with. And she would scarcely believe me when I told her. She, too, played a vital role in the Quincy deal.

Carmody walked many worlds. Tracking him down, you found yourself wondering one day whether you were going to get laid and the next day whether you were going to get killed. The same guy who brought all those classy chicks into his orbit was busily conning the New York mob, not to mention the Bardell brothers down in Crockett County, Tennessee. There were five Bardells, every one of them six foot two or better, and four of them had been convicted of moonshining on various occasions. Seldom did a judge find the courage to send them to prison for it. Ellis Bardell sat for his interview with me playing with the shotgun slung across his lap. Sure I was an FBI agent. I had a revolver under my arm. So did the two revenue agents whose buckshot-filled bodies had been found rotting on Bardell property. In the third century of our independence, it's hard for a northerner to believe that moonshine wars are still a way of life down there. But Carmody adjusted quickly to strange situations.

The day that Old Man Quincy and his Wall Street lawyer called me out to the corporate offices in Westchester, they were still trying to fit the Quincy caper into the mold of their average embezzlement case. Four and a half million dollars in checks, written, taken and cashed. Only somebody inside the company could have done it, they figured. Just find out who.

Well, they could have examined their books forever as far as I'm concerned. The Quincy caper began long before those checks were written. And it was pulled off by one of the great criminal geniuses of our time. I have no doubt that Mickey Carmody by now could have swindled the President out of Air Force One and the Secretary of the Treasury out of the Fort Knox bullion cache had not Mickey, for all his genius, also been more than slightly nuts.

CHAPTER TWO

1

Walter Fakazzi looked at his watch for at least the thirtieth time in as many minutes. He pushed his heavy body away from the big Caddy and resumed his slow pacing down West End Avenue. Just before the entrance at 800 he looked up. He located the fourteenth floor without having to count. He had counted before. Mick Carmody, won't you please come down?

Fakazzi shifted his gaze back along the street to the Caddy. At least this time he had found a legal parking space. Usually when he waited for Carmody here he had to double park and couldn't leave the car. The nearest pay phone was at Ninety-Sixth Street, a three-block walk. He wished Carmody would find a broad with a more conveniently located apartment.

Fakazzi headed down West End to the pay phone. It was one of the open stalls that were replacing the traditional booths all over town. At first Fakazzi hadn't liked them. No privacy. But then friends told him the stalls let in traffic noises and the traffic noises interfered with the wiretappers. He thought of all those cops straining to hear over the truck roars and it pleased him.

Fakazzi had called the girl's apartment fifteen minutes ago, and ten minutes before that. Both times the line was busy. This time he finally got a ring.

"Hello?" It was a man's voice. Carmody's. Shit, Fakazzi thought, the dumb stewardess had given over her apartment pillar and post. She was even letting Carmody answer her telephone. Seven years the men had been friends, nine months they had lived together in Green Haven prison, and Carmody still amazed Fakazzi.

"Listen, Mick, it's 3:30," Fakazzi said.

"Wally?"

"I been trying to call for a half-hour. The line's been busy."

"I been on business. Relax."

"We told Richards 3:30." Fakazzi fidgeted nervously in the phone stall. It wasn't his role to tell Carmody what to do. On the other hand, Fakazzi had a relationship with people like Vincente Ruggiardo—Mr. Richards—that an Irishman like Carmody could never understand.

"I can take care of it," Carmody said. "He'll wait. I'll be down in half an hour."

Fakazzi's heart sank. "You know your business, man, but I know Richards. He don't want to wait. For Christ's sake finish with your business now and let's get going."

"I've finished with the business. I just haven't finished with the fucking. Now relax." The phone clicked dead.

Fakazzi was tempted to call Richards's house and say they'd be late, but he knew he shouldn't. He walked back up West End to the Caddy, eased in behind the wheel and began reading the *Daily News*. It said the cops were looking for a B & E man who had accidentally awakened a young woman in Queens and wound up shooting her. Bad planning, Fakazzi thought. He'd never had to fire a gun on a break-in. But maybe the *Daily News* didn't have the story right. The only time the *News* had written up one of Fakazzi's jobs they got it wrong.

2

The big car wheeled across the George Washington Bridge and followed Route 17 toward Ridgefield. When Fakazzi drove in a hurry he spent half his time scanning the rear view mirror for cops.

"Slow down and watch the road," Carmody said. "We don't need to get crashed. Or arrested. What I've got for Richards he won't mind waiting for." Carmody had settled his six-foot, one-inch frame beside Fakazzi in the front seat, where he usually sat when the two of them were driving alone. When someone else was along, especially a woman or somebody who might help on a deal, Carmody sat in back with the guest and Fakazzi wore his chauffeur's hat.

"Christ, that bitch can move her mouth," Carmody went on.

"Sara?"

"You gotta believe it. Man, I wish I could get you some of that action."

"I do all right," Fakazzi shrugged.

"It's not like with some girls, you know? Some girls would go for stuff like that. With a friend and all. But this Sara's class."

Fakazzi didn't say anything.

Carmody went pensive. "You know, I'll bet I'm the only one she's giving it to? Bet she wouldn't do it with two guys. Not within a month of each other."

"Jesus, Mick, have you got a deal for Richards yet? I mean, you don't understand. This is our ass. Three weeks ago he gave us this pigeon and we still haven't made contact. Three weeks is a long time to a guy like Mr. Richards."

"If Richards is as big as he's supposed to be, he ought to learn to think size, not speed. That's why he came to me, right? I think size. Keep it to sixty."

Reluctantly, Fakazzi slowed the car again. "He came to you because I told his people," Fakazzi said. "I been tellin' them for months. You know, they didn't want to do it at first. Not when they heard you was friends of Bill Connally."

"Connally's a prick."

"Whatever he is, he sure made a mess out of trying to cash the T-bills they gave him. He lost the T-bills and almost had a family member doing time."

"Dealing with me and dealing with Connally's two different things," Carmody said.

"It better be. Shit. This is my ass."

"Wally, my boy, I am gonna pull him a deal like he never saw before. Like nobody ever dreamed of before. I am gonna make millions off that crumby eighty thousand dollar pigeon of his. I mean it man, millions."

"Fine. Richards' people just want their eighty. This guy owes all over town. They come to Richards for enforcement, the guy's supposed to get his arms broke. Maybe his head."

"But this time Richards gave him to me because he knew I could turn it into money. Lots of money. What's the point of having some guy killed who could make you a million bucks alive?"

"Man, I know that. That's what I been feeding them. But the people who run Richards' games, they don't know that. They just can't stand the sight of this guy walking around now. You gotta understand. I knew Richards growing up in Brooklyn. He s like an uncle to me. Shit, he's like an uncle to a lot of people. He gets treated with respect. He don't like to wait."

"Wally, you know what this is?" Carmody reached into the side pocket of his sport coat and held up a key.

"It's a fucking key," Fakazzi said.

"It's the key to the fucking mint, my boy. It's Sara's key. The key to Sara's apartment."

"Can't you get your mind off cunts long enough to talk us out of this? We're gonna be almost an hour late to see Richards and we haven't touched the pigeon yet."

"Wally, use your imagination, man. We're gonna pull off this job from that apartment. With this key. It's a clean phone, Wally. I got a lot of long distance on this one, and it's a clean phone. With a stewardess the bill's already full of long distance. Ours will slip right in. No taps, no traces. And she flies four days at a stretch."

"You're gonna use that girl's apartment while she's gone, huh?"

"Man, why do you think I like to pick up stews?"

3

The car pulled up in front of an old frame house on a large corner lot. There were high shrubs camouflaging a steel fence. The house was well maintained and freshly painted. There was a veranda running around two sides and a large garden at one end of the yard.

Fakazzi rang the bell and was surprised when a woman opened the door. A servant he might have expected, but this woman was older, well-dressed.

"We're looking for Mr. Richards," Fakazzi said.

"I'm Mrs. Richards," the woman replied, still holding the door open only enough to look through.

"Uh . . . my name's Walter . . ."

"Walter Fakazzi . . . and Mr. Carmody?"

"That's us," Fakazzi said, then decided it wasn't the right way to talk to a cultured person. "That's who we are," he corrected himself. Carmody was right behind him and customarily did all the talking for them on business, but Fakazzi was the go-between here and everyone was depending on him. He felt uncomfortable.

Helen Ruggiardo opened the door wider and stepped back. "Mr. Richards went in for his nap. He said you gentlemen could wait in the living room."

Fakazzi started in, but Carmody grabbed his arm. "Oh, that's all right," Carmody said loudly. "If he's asleep we'll come back later. When do you think he'll be up?"

Fakazzi looked at Carmody, appalled.

Helen Ruggiardo said, "I think you had better wait. When Mr. Richards finishes his nap he often leaves the house on business."

"We don't want to get in your way sitting around the living room and all," Carmody said, still practically shouting.

"Mickey, let's just do what she says," Fakazzi pleaded.

"No, no, we'll catch him some other time," Carmody went on. "Let me leave my number and maybe he could give me a call when he's free. Or maybe he'd want to drop by sometime when he's in New York."

"I suggest you stay, but you do as you wish," the woman said.

"Well, we'll leave him to his nap. I guess he'll always know how to get in touch with Wally here."

"Don't leave just yet, Mr. Carmody." It was a voice from another room. "I'm coming out."

"That was my husband," the woman said. "I think you might like to wait now."

"Well, as long as he's up," Carmody said. Fakazzi's normally dark face was ashen. They followed the woman in and Richards appeared almost immediately. He was dressed in a shirt and unrumpled slacks, bedroom slippers and a dressing robe.

"It's good to see you again, Walter," he said, shaking Fakazzi's hand. "And you must be Michael Carmody."

Carmody took the hand. "Listen," he said, "I'd be embarrassed as hell if we woke you up. After all, we were late."

"I understand," Richards said. "You must be a very

busy man. Why don't we go into the den to talk?"

They followed Richards through double doors into a paneled room and watched him close the doors, leaving his wife on the other side. "I'm sorry I'm not dressed so I could show you the garden. The tomatoes are really exceptional this year. Can I offer you a drink—some Scotch?"

"Scotch'll be fine," Carmody said. Fakazzi nodded.

Richards's hair was greying, but Carmody guessed that 20 years earlier Richards had looked a lot like Fakazzi did now: swarthy, clearly Mediterranean in background, thickly muscular without being really big. Carmody himself, tall, blond, blue-eyed, with Robert Redford good looks, made quite a contrast.

"How have you been, Walter? Is your mother still living on Avenue Q?"

"Yeah, she's doing fine."

"I do miss the neighborhood. And I miss your father. Let's see, it's been two or three years, hasn't it? Since he passed away?"

"That's right." Fakazzi felt dreadfully unsure of himself.

"And you, Mr. Carmody. I understand your wife is a doctor. That must be very interesting."

Carmody relaxed on the sofa with his drink and crossed his legs, ankle over the knee. "Yeah, she's a neurosurgeon, all right. Can you beat that?"

Richards smiled back. Fakazzi couldn't believe it. Carmody was getting away with behavior no one else would have dared. He appeared to be charming Richards.

"Of course, we're kind of separated now," Carmody went on.

"That's too bad," Richards said. "Well, I suppose I should get right to the point. I don't want to waste you gentlemen's time. This man, Stanley Timmons, owes my business associates a lot of money. I turned the matter over to you several weeks ago, and I'm anxious to know what you're going to do about it."

"This guy Timmons, he's the assistant treasurer at Quincy Corporation," Carmody said.

"Whatever he is," Richards said, "he still likes to play cards and shoot craps. And he's had very bad luck at both."

"Quincy's a big outfit," Carmody went on. "They're traded on the New York Stock Exchange. They've got projects all over the country. If this guy helps run their finance department, there's probably more than a million dollars a day going through his hands."

"And you think you and he can get away with some of it?"

Carmody beamed like a little boy getting out of bed his birthday morning and wondering what presents were waiting. "There's bound to be a way," he said.

"Why not a very simple way?" Richards asked. "Why not have him just write out a check to cash and cash it?"

"Who would cover for the money?" Carmody replied.

"Let him cover for it. Out of his salary. Or let nobody cover for it. Let the stockholders of Quincy Corporation cover for it. Who the hell cares?"

"I care," Carmody said. "I don't want to go back to Green Haven." He paused to emphasize his authority. "No banker's going to accept a big check just made out to cash. This has got to be done carefully. We're going to have to go over procedures, find out who handles their vouchers, who handles their checks, where they do their banking, what days of the month the money comes and goes. I've got to have time to learn their whole accounting system."

Richards frowned. "The man owes $80,000. I question the amount of time that's worth. Especially since I know how we could get the money out of him if it came to that."

"Fuck the $80,000! This guy handles millions. The least I ought to be able to hit is a few hundred thousand. With a little luck, who knows?"

"Suppose I agree," Richards said. "How long is it going to take you?"

"The first thing I wanted to do was make sure I had a bank ready. So that when Timmons comes up with the check, or whatever it is he's going to give me, I have some place to turn it into cash."

"When will you have your bank?"

"I think I set up the deal this afternoon, as a matter of fact," Carmody said.

"In New York?"

"You're very curious about how I operate, aren't you, Mr. Richards?"

"Yes, I am." He turned and walked behind the desk. "But I'm less worried now than I was. You know, some friends of mine had a bad experience with a friend of yours, Bill Connally."

"Me and Connally's two different people," Carmody snapped.

"I understand that," Richards said. "I like you. If you want to keep your banking secrets to yourself, go ahead. Maybe it would be better if I didn't know."

"My bank is in Circle, Montana," Carmody said. "There's a bank president out there who's in trouble. The same way Timmons is. This guy invested in a lumber business a few years ago. He put in a lot of his own money, he put in more of the bank's money, and the lumber business didn't do so well. So he started screwing around with his taxes, and then his bank's books, and now he's in trouble. He needs cash. For the right percentage, he'll do what I ask him to."

"How do you find people like this, Mr. Carmody?"

"I have friends. Lots of friends."

"I'd like to meet some of them some day. Tell me, if

you've got your banker set up, when are you going to be ready to meet our friend Timmons?"

"I'm ready now."

"Good. I'll fix it up for tomorrow. Do you have a place?"

"I told you, I'm not living at home now. What about his house?"

"That's out. He's a family man. Suburbs. Four kids. You certainly can't meet him at his office."

"Then what about lunch? A nice business lunch. Jim Downey's on Eighth Avenue and Forty-Fifth."

"Is that the nicest part of town you can find?" Richards asked.

"Quincy's doing some work back behind the Port Authority bus terminal. I've seen their equipment there. If he needs an excuse to be in the area, that'll give him one. Besides, I like Downey's. It's a class place."

"Then he'll be there." Richards smiled, obviously liking the way Carmody seemed to think of everything. He waved his glass at Carmody, who returned the gesture and they drank.

"One more thing," Carmody said. "Money. If I hit this guy the way I think, you could be reading in the papers about a lot of money. Now, this guy owes you $80,000, right?"

Ruggiardo was silent, the smile gone.

"Well, if the deal works out," Carmody went on, "I'll triple it. You get up to $250,000 if the money's there. If there's less than $750,000 we split what there is. A third for you, a third for me and a third for expenses, the banker's cut and so forth." He was waiting for Richards to react, but getting only an icy stare.

"Mr. Carmody," Richards said finally, "I get half of everything."

"No way. This is going to take a hell of a lot of work, and if I hit it big, I hit it. Besides, there are going to be other people to pay off and I'm going to have to take care of it. A quarter million's a fair share for supplying the pigeon. Without what I can do, all you've got is a stack of bad markers."

Richards walked away from his desk and stood over Carmody. "People have told me about your work, and it's impressive, Michael. I've seen your press clippings and I know what you can do. That's why I invited you in. I've even enjoyed your front up to now. But you must realize your bounds, my friend, and you have reached them. We won't argue about this. I get half. I always get half."

"Now, wait," Carmody started.

"We won't argue," Richards said coldly.

Carmody glanced at Fakazzi, whose eyes were pleading with him. Fakazzi's face had whitened again. Carmody looked back at Richards and said nothing.

"And don't try to hold back on me," Richards said, barely whispering.

"You've got to understand there could be a time lag," Carmody said. "I don't know how the money is going to be coming out yet, but it could be hot. We might have to store it somewhere."

"You make sure I know where. And where you are."

"And how will I know whether the meeting's on for tomorrow?"

"It's on. You show up at Downey's at 12:30. The table will be in Timmons' name."

"How can you be sure he can make it?"

"Michael, I can be sure."

CHAPTER THREE

1

I first encountered Mickey Carmody five years ago, long before the Quincy swindle, before the much-publicized Christmas Eve shoot-out and the killings. Back when I was naive. An idealist. A newspaperman.

I became what is popularly called an investigative reporter through a strange combination of good fortune and bad taste, which, when I could look back on it, had a lot to do with my ultimate decision to quit the newspaper game. It was my first summer out of college and I had taken a reporting job on *The New York Press*. The *Press* was a tabloid that had limped along for many years, last in the bitter competition for the city's afternoon newspaper readership. The typewriters were in miserable repair. Only the sports department was authorized to spend money traveling out of town after stories. And the staff used to joke that you needed a requisition from the publisher to sharpen a pencil.

Still, the *Press* had hung on, often by methods nobody

ever told us about in journalism school. If we didn't hire the best reporters, if our stories often were rewrites of news that appeared in the morning *Times,* if the rewrites occasionally were spiced with quotes that had been invented by the rewrite man, and if the headlines frequently promised more than was in the text, nevertheless we had the toughest, most determined delivery truck drivers in the city. In afternoon newspaper competition, trucking counts for a lot. Being first on the newsstands or having a little mud splashed on the competition can carry you a long way.

The summer I joined up, there was a brief flurry of excitement about changing all that. In fact, people said that when I (and two others) were hired out of journalism school at more than minimum scale, it was part of the flurry. The economy was booming and two competitors had just been driven to the sidelines by a typographical union strike. Our publisher, an aging dowager named Henrietta Jenkins, was overcome by visions of quickly doubling our circulation and becoming a respectable leader of the journalistic establishment after all these years of sleaziness. Some of the more experienced guys on the staff were told to dig into this or that possible source of corruption. One was even authorized to go all the way to Albany in his pursuit.

In the reshuffling of assignments occasioned by this brief elevation of company ambition, and by the summer vacation schedule, I was given to cover the civil courts. This was a job considered so petty that when the reporter at the more colorful criminal courts found an inconvenient number of sensational trials or arraignments going on at the same time, I was supposed to dash one block north through Foley Square at the jingle of a telephone and back him up.

But no active courthouses, even civil ones, are dull. Anybody who thinks they are shouldn't be working for a newspaper. In those thick docket books, in those rows of file cabinets, lie the makings of a careerful of five-column banner headlines—even best-selling novels. Like a sheik looking for oil, a courthouse reporter needs only the will to break ground.

I am not claiming credit, however, for unearthing the big scandal that broke under my byline that summer and suddenly turned me into an investigative reporter, thereby leading me to Mick Carmody and changing the course of my life. Let the record reflect that the big New York highway scandal of 1970 was uncovered by Arthur W. Rosenstadt, who had been covering that civil courthouse diligently for *The New York Times* for 18 years.

But the venerable *Times* wouldn't allow Art Rosenstadt the same free rein that the *Press* gave me, a kid just out of college. If he had been able to run quickly with the ball he found, Art would have won a Pulitzer prize. He might then have been assigned to the Washington bureau, or maybe the Sunday News in Review. Instead, he's still laboring on in that courthouse.

What happened was this: For my first few weeks I had been phoning in a lot more stories than were being published. Like Art Rosenstadt, I wasn't content to sit in the pressroom playing poker just because there wasn't a good trial going on somewhere. (Besides, I didn't have the money for those games.) Unlike the *Times*, however, the *Press* wasn't interested in news that was merely important. It also had to be sexy. So the stories I was turning up weren't making the paper. Instead of being recognized by my editors for showing spark, as I had intended, I was becoming known as something of a pest who was constantly phoning in useless copy.

So I laid off the searching for small stories. But I hung around the clerk's office anyway, talking to the young women who worked there and waiting for something big to develop. I couldn't help but admire the way Art Rosenstadt would come in, obtain file folders and sit for hours taking notes from them.

Suddenly it occurred to me that there was something strange in the way he was taking notes mostly from *old* file folders. Normally we were interested either in cases that had just been filed or in cases that were about to come to trial, which would have been sent up to a judge's chambers and wouldn't have been lying around the clerk's office. Why was Rosenstadt looking at all those closed cases?

There was this girl who sometimes waited on him who had red hair and always wore big-lensed, blue-tinted glasses. I decided to approach her and see if she could help clear up the mystery. I remember it was the day after the All-Star Game because the small talk I started up with her was about Aaron's home run the day before. "What's an All-Star Game?" she had responded. So I decided to get right to the point.

"Do you have any idea why that *Times* reporter is ... looking at all those closed cases?" I said.

"I guess he's just interested in highways," the girl in the blue glasses answered.

"Highways?"

"Sure. He keeps asking for old condemnation suits."

"What's a condemnation suit?"

"When the highway department wants to build a road, they have to file a suit to take the land away from the people that own it. Listen, when the other reporter comes back I'll tell him you're interested and maybe he can explain it to you."

"No, no, don't do that," I said. "I mean, don't bother him. I was just wondering if there's any way to find out what cases he's been looking at so I could see them myself."

"Sure," she said. "All the request slips for cases have to be filed in here." She held up a wooden box full of three-by-five request slips.

"Show me," I said.

The girl in the blue glasses let me stay well past closing

time that night, after everybody but us and the janitors had gone home. I bought her pizza and told her she had the prettiest hair I had ever seen, which was not far wrong. I didn't try to lay a hand on her. The next night we snuck in beer.

By the morning after, I was ready to talk to Arthur Protter, the city editor. Protter had been around for 20 years, running the budget-minded rewrite operation that our publisher called a newspaper. Our city room was to the *Times* city room what a bucket shop is to Merrill Lynch. Now, however, with all this talk about investigative reporting, Protter was as if being reborn into the profession. Suddenly he was back in the pursuit of dreams long set aside. He quit smoking, beamed greetings at reporters (in place of grunts) and talked in apparent seriousness about winning a Pulitzer prize that year.

"Mr. Protter," I told him when he answered the phone—everyone else called him Arty, but I was just out of college and thought I ought to be polite—"something's going on at the state highway department. The *Times* has spent the past four weeks or so pulling out the files of condemnation suits. They're obviously onto something."

"Yeah?" he said. "Well, why don't you go through the files yourself?"

"That's what I've been doing the past couple of days, Mr. Protter."

"Yeah?" he said. "Well, why don't you have the story?"

Protter would never be able to understand that there were some stories that couldn't be researched in a few hours. His idea of the thorough, blanket investigation that would bring in the Pulitzer was to allow a reporter to spend all day at something. Here I had spent two days, and there wasn't a line of copy to show for it. A few years later I would be able to laugh at this attitude, but what's a twenty-one-year-old reporter to say to his first city editor?

"Well, sir, it's not easy to understand exactly what's been happening. But the *Times* seems to be looking at land condemnations in the area south of Greenwich Village, mostly about two or three years ago."

"Hey, that must be the land for the expressway everybody's been protesting about. The one that would run through Washington Square Park."

"Well, yes, and the strange thing to me is that a lot of this land seems to have changed hands just about a year before the state condemned it. Now it looks like quite a coincidence that all these people would have sold their property just before—"

"That's not a coincidence," he shouted. "That's a scandal!"

"Well, that's what I was thinking, sir." My hands were so sweaty the phone was slipping out of them.

"Who's been buying up all this property?" Protter demanded.

"Well, it looks like a lot of different people. But there is one real estate firm that seems to be involved in a lot of it. Tipman, Weistholer and Solomon."

"Shit, that's not Paul Weistholer, is it?"

"Well, yes, I think that name was signed on some of this stuff." I began flipping through my notes.

"Don't you know who Paul Weistholer is?"

"No, Mr. Protter. But I'll find out."

"He's the goddamned assistant majority leader of the state senate. You've broken a hell of a story. Now get in here and write it. I'll send somebody else down to cover the civil courts."

It was then that I understood for the first time that he wasn't angry at me. He was shouting from joy.

"Well, don't you think we ought to check it out some more?" I said.

"What's there to check out?"

"Well, we ought to get some specific examples, look up the deeds, find out what prices were paid, see if any other politicians were involved, talk to some of the people who had their land bought out . . ."

"Hell, no. That would take a couple more days, wouldn't it?"

"Frankly, sir, I think it might take more like a few weeks."

"We can do that later. We'll run follow-ups every day. You just come in here right now with what you know and let's get into print before the *Times* does."

2

The first three pages of the next day's *Press* contained some of the most clever devices I've ever seen for covering up a lack of information. From the morgue, Protter dug out a couple of old aerial photos of lower Manhattan and had a staff artist draw the proposed highway as an ugly swath down the center.

One photo covered the top third of the front page. Then came the big black headline: HUGE HIGHWAY SCANDAL BARED. *Weistholer's Role in Loss of Millions.* Below that was a shaded box with the word "Exclusive!" etched out in white. Next was my byline, "By Franklin Scanlon," and the story, printed in 10-point type so that it would look much longer than it really was.

If anyone had tried to analyze that story he could easily have shown that the conclusions rested mostly on faith. Facts were scarce. Irregularities and nefarious deals were suggested by mention of what was possible; there was little proof of what actually happened.

But we knew the story wouldn't undergo such an analysis. Before the critics could respond, we would have smoked out *The New York Times* and the *Times* would prove our allegations for us. Which is exactly what occurred. They started running highway scandal on their front page the next morning, and later, when the public hearings were held and the indictments came down and

Weistholer and his friends did their few months in jail, the *Times* in its modest way tried to take the credit it deserved for exposing the mess. So we put posters up in all the subways inviting anyone who believed the *Times*'s claims to come to our offices, where we could prove by the dates on the newspapers that *The New York Press* broke the highway scandal.

With our spacious graphic displays and 10-point type all I needed was a few new facts every day for another scandal story with the big "Exclusive!" tag over it. And every morning the *Times* would come out and say, in effect, "Yes, you can believe what you read last night in *The New York Press* because here's the proof we've assembled." With that kind of back up, pretty soon the TV newscasters were relaying even our most unsubstantiated allegations. On Channel 2, Ellen Fleysher began providing her own, more thorough reports.

I was so busy that three of my stories had appeared before I even had a chance to take the girl with the blue-tinted glasses to the movies. We stopped by my apartment afterwards for a drink, and as soon as we got in the door I just kind of sensed something and held out my arms. She fell right in. Later, when we were getting up, she said, "Gee, when you just kept looking at those files the other night I was afraid you didn't like me."

CHAPTER FOUR

1

Stanley Timmons drove quickly down the Henry Hudson Parkway and found himself on the West Side. He parked on the roof of the Port Authority bus terminal, not knowing the garages in the area, and walked up Eighth Avenue, where the whores were already in their gauntlet. He decided it was an appropriate part of town for what was to take place. He also decided to get to know the subcontractor for the Quincy work behind the bus terminal, just in case somebody saw him down there. Maybe a few questions on the phone about expense vouchers, maybe even a luncheon at Downey's.

Then he saw the black limousine double-parked in front of Downey's, a uniformed chauffeur holding the door. There must be some respectable people here, Timmons decided.

A couple got out of the limousine. The man was blond and athletic, rather resembling Robert Redford, the actor, except taller. The woman was dark-complexioned, attractive, stylishly dressed. Timmons watched them enter the restaurant, wondering if perhaps it actually *was* Robert Redford. Downey's was famous as a haunt for show people.

Seconds later Timmons was inside giving his name to the *maitre d'*. "I'm meeting a stranger. He'll ask to sit at my table," Timmons said.

"That's your party—they've just arrived. Mr. and Mrs. Carmody."

Timmons was stunned watching the couple who had gotten out of the limousine. They were making their way to a rear booth, but at every few tables they would stop and exchange greetings. Men would stand up beaming, shake the blond man's hand, slap his arm and hug his companion. A woman stood up and kissed him.

Timmons had reserved a table for two expecting that privacy would be essential, but the couple he was watching settled into a booth that could hold six. Before Timmons could get to it, another man had settled in and begun talking.

The blond man looked up. "Are you Stan Timmons? Hi—I'm Mickey Carmody." He rose, grinning, and pumped Timmons's hand. "Say, this is Barbara, and this here's George, who's a broker and trying to sell me on some little stock nobody ever heard of. Hey—" he turned to the other man, George, who also grabbed Timmons's hand—"this here's Stan, and he's treasurer of Quincy Corporation."

"Assistant treasurer," Timmons corrected.

"He must know all about these stock things," Carmody went on, talking to George. "Why don't you try to sell him some of that horseshit?"

Barbara gave Carmody an approving laugh, then flashed a smile at Timmons. "You know, I remember Quincy Corporation," she told him. "I used to sell real estate in Westchester. That was before I met a good man." At that she squeezed Carmody's hand, and suddenly Timmons noticed that she was holding his own hand, too. "My firm put together a couple of shopping centers you built."

"I never knew you made that kind of commission," Carmody said.

"Well, I never got into your league, honey," she told him. "I'll let you make the money from now on." Her fingers were still on Timmons's hand.

A waiter came. Barbara ordered white wine. Timmons asked for scotch.

"Give him Johnnie Walker Black," Carmody said. "And make that all around for the men here."

George nodded.

"So, George," Carmody said, "tell Stan here about this deal you're trying to get me into." George seemed reluctant to respond.

"Stan, you do any securities buying for Quincy?" Carmody asked.

"A little. Mostly Treasuries. We don't put corporate money into commons."

"You ever heard of"—Carmody turned back to George—"what's the name of that outfit again?"

"Earth Systems Research," George said.

"Where's it located?" Timmons asked, trying to sound interested.

"Headquartered in Miami," George said.

"Oh, hell," Carmody broke in with a laugh. "That company's headquartered in some file folder in old George's office. Just like—what was the name of that last one you ran up?—come on—oh, hell, come on, you can trust Stan here. Tell him how you guys ran up that other deal—Financial Engineering?"

"Science Engineering Associates," George said, quietly, as if he'd rather not have said it at all.

"Don't be shy, for Christ's sake," Carmody said. "You

guys must have taken down close to a million bucks by the time you got through with that." He turned to Timmons, grinning. "They started out at forty cents a share, right? The stuff was worth nothing—some little corporate shell of a bankrupt company they picked up out west somewhere. But they got George here, in his little bucket shop in New York, and some guy out in Houston and a guy in Denver, and they get to trading this stock back and forth among themselves, up a little every time, and they're calling their own deals into the sheets and they ran that damn stock up close to ten dollars. And they're calling people up and saying look at it go. They had suckers all over the country buying that crap—"

Suddenly George couldn't restrain himself from the story. "It wasn't crap," he interjected. "We had Walston positioned with 35,000 shares. We had Merrill Lynch in there—"

"They had Merrill Lynch," Carmody laughed.

"Got Walston in the first time around two, three dollars a share. Then every time it went up a couple points they took more," George said. "Hell, the stuff had already gone up almost ten times what we started at. This guy out in Denver, he was talking about this contract they were going to get to farm the ocean floor. See, they had some kind of diving suit they had invented where you could stay down there for days and not get the bends. It was some kind of valve you attached—"

"Jesus," Carmody said, doubling up over the table. "Farming the ocean floor. They had guys really believing this shit."

"We had a guy out there really said he had this valve," George said, as if he still did believe. "Some engineer. Hell, they start getting those contracts, they could have cleaned up. Gone big."

By now even Timmons was laughing. They were on their second drink, Carmody had ordered them all steaks and Timmons had stopped worrying about when they were going to proposition him.

George still carried on, seemingly offended at the way Carmody was recalling their stock killing as if it were a fraud. "Come on, Mickey," he said, "I got you out at seven or eight. You must have made ten thousand or more on the deal."

"Tell them about the daisy chain, George," Carmody said. "That's where you really cleaned them up."

"Well, it was really Mickey's idea," George said to Timmons and Barbara, who was politely struggling to contain her amusement. "Mickey says, you make money on them going up, you can make even more on them going down. When the stock starts down, it goes fast, and you get these guys where their average buying price on the way up is showing a bit of a loss and they're getting kind of worried. You know, normally, you try to tell them, well, this is all temporary, you know, some guy had to unload, there were margin calls, you know, it's all going back up."

"So I tell George," Carmody said, "all this talk about it's going back up again, you're not going to make any more money on that. Nobody's going to buy more of the stuff when it's already showing a loss. All this 'going-back-up' bullshit does is keep them from getting too mad at you for awhile. So why not hit them again? Clean them up a second time on the way down? All you got to do is tell them the news is *really* bad, and you get them to sell short."

"Well," George said, smiling slightly himself now, "we started calling up our clients and telling them, frankly, look, this diving thing, the guy can't get his patent. It doesn't look like it's going to come off. The S.E.C. is sniffing around, the company is going to have to make some kind of announcement soon, and when they do, the stock is going to go through the floor. So why don't you let me sell you short the same number of shares you had long, and you make up going down for what you lost by not selling at the peak?"

"So they do it," Carmody laughs, and slaps the table.

"So we're buying back like crazy at a dollar or two a share," George said. "I got to really coax these guys out west, because they don't want to do it. They say, we've got our money, what are we giving it back for? But I tell them, I know this guy, Mickey, you just do what he says, it always comes out all right." There was no more trace of embarrassment in George's account. He was having as much fun with the story as Carmody was. "So we're buying like crazy at a dollar or two a share," he said. "The clients are selling short, thinking they can buy it back later for nothing because of course it's worthless."

Barbara shrieked. "Only you had all the stock!" She slapped the table, laughing hysterically. Timmons still didn't quite understand.

"A month passes," George went on, "and there's no bad news. There's no announcement. And all of a sudden they're looking in the sheets and the damn stock is going back up again. Well, of course it's going up. We've bought all the stock back and we're trading little bits of it. But these guys sold short, see. The damn stock goes back up to five, six dollars a share, and they've got to buy to cover those shorts. But they got nobody to buy it from because we own it all."

Now Timmons was laughing, too. He understood.

"We had a couple of guys in California, well, at least one of them actually went bankrupt over this deal," George said. "But of course the real money came from Walston and Merrill Lynch. They had to pay. I mean they had no choice but to send us another check for a hundred or a hundred fifty thousand."

"The guy at Merrill Lynch lost his job over that, didn't he?" Carmody offered.

"Damn right," George said. "I would have fired the son of a bitch if he had been working for me."

Suddenly, in the midst of the laughter, they became aware of a young woman with long, straight cinnamon hair standing by the table, her green eyes fixed on Carmody. "You going to tell me what the joke is?" she asked him.

"Judy, honey," Carmody said with a touch of forced cheer. He reached an arm around her waist to draw her to him. "Glad you could make it. Sit down."

"I thought you and I were going to have lunch together, the way you've been promising." She was talking to Carmody as if no one else was there.

"We are, honey. This is lunch. Sit down and have a drink and we're going to get a steak for you."

She looked at Barbara and then back at Carmody, as if to ask what the other woman was doing next to him.

"Hey," Carmody said, standing up in the aisle, "this is Stan. Stan's the treasurer of Quincy Corporation—they're one of the biggest construction companies in the United States. Stan's a very important man and he and I are working on a big business deal together. Now you sit right over here next to Stan, and we're all going to have lunch together. Hey, I know what you like—a whiskey sour, right? Straight up?" He took her hand.

She nodded and sat down obediently by Timmons, while Carmody placed her order with a waiter. "Hey, you know George, here, don't you Judy?"

Before Carmody had even sat down again some people called out from a table across the room. Barbara waved and slid out from the booth. "Let's go say hello," she told Carmody.

"We'll be back in a minute," he said to the rest of them. He laid a hand on Judy's shoulder and gave her a smile as he left. Timmons noticed she wasn't smiling back.

As soon as Carmody and Barbara left, the table was silent. Finally, Timmons turned to Judy and George and asked, "Who is this Mickey, anyway? I mean, what does he do?"

"Oh, he's a doctor," George said. "A neurosurgeon. He works up at Cornell Medical Center."

"Oh, crap," Judy said. "That's not true. Mickey isn't any doctor."

Timmons turned to George, who said, "Well, that's right. He just likes to pass sometimes, you know?"

"That's his wife who's a doctor," Judy said. "She works up at Cornell."

"I thought his wife said she sold real estate," Timmons said, puzzled.

"No, she's a brain surgeon," Judy said. George nodded.

"Well, what does *Mickey* do?" Timmons asked.

Judy and George both smiled slyly as if, independently, they had just enjoyed a private joke.

"Well, " Judy said finally, "he's just Mickey."

"Yeah," George said.

Timmons was bewildered. He saw Carmody and Barbara coming back to the table from across the room. When they were a few feet away, Judy excused herself and went over to Carmody. Barbara sat down.

Carmody and Judy were whispering privately, but Timmons clearly heard him tell her, "Honey, Stan is very important to me. It means a lot of money. I've got to see that he's happy. I couldn't ask just anybody to do that. I'm counting on you to keep him company and save this deal."

"But—" she started to say.

"I know it's not what you expected," Carmody told her. "But this deal came up and I'm counting on you to save it for me. I'll make it up to you. I promise. I'll owe this whole deal to you. Besides, Stan's a great guy."

She nodded.

At the table, Timmons turned to Barbara. "I thought

you told me you were in the real estate business. George, here, says you're a doctor."

"Oh, no, I'm not a doctor," Barbara laughed. "That's Mickey's other wife. I mean his first wife—well, actually, I think it's his second wife. Anyway, they're getting divorced. We're"—Mickey was sitting down next to her again and she grabbed his arm—"just waiting for the divorce to go through, aren't we, honey?"

Carmody smiled bashfully and looked down at his drink. Judy stared at Barbara with obvious hatred. Then, as if resigning herself, she turned to Timmons, smiled prettily and put her hand on his arm. "So you're in the construction business," she said. "That must be exciting."

2

The steaks were large and tender. Carmody took care of the tab. Never once did they talk about what Timmons was going to have to do to come up with the money he owed. Then, while the waiter was pouring coffee, Carmody suggested that he and Timmons excuse themselves and talk at the bar for awhile. George said he wanted to go, but they saw that his departure would leave Barbara and Judy alone at the table. At Carmody's suggestion, George agreed to stay.

Carmody brought Timmons to stools at a deserted end of the long bar, and ordered more Johnnie Walker Black for each of them. "So, who signs the checks at Quincy Corporation?" he asked, without bothering to warm up to the subject. "You?"

"No."

Carmody's face sank.

"We have a check-writing machine sign them," Timmons said.

Carmody perked up. "Doesn't anybody have to countersign them by hand?" he asked.

Timmons shook his head. "The machine countersigns them all by itself."

"Oh, shit!" Carmody gasped. He almost leapt off the barstool.

"You need keys to operate it," Timmons said.

"Do you have a key?"

"Yes—well, there are two different keys. But I can get them."

"I got to go up there and see that machine," Carmody said.

"Well, now, how do you propose to do that?"

"Just go up to your office with you and have you show me the machine. Exactly how it works. And I want to see your books and your bank statements and your checks— some cancelled checks and some blank ones—and—"

Timmons was frightened. "But you can't just walk up there in the middle of the day and start doing that. There are people there."

"So we don't go in the middle of the day."

"Well, just when do you propose to go?"

"How about two o'clock Saturday morning?" Carmody suggested.

"But how are you going to get in? The place is locked up."

"We'll get in. I got a friend, a guy named Walter, could pick the lock on Fort Knox if he wanted. We'll find a way in."

"Well," Timmons said, "I've got a key."

"Stan, my boy, why didn't you tell me? Listen, don't you worry. If somebody finds us up there, we'll think of a story. But who the hell is going to be up there at two o'clock Saturday morning anyway? Probably not even a watchman."

"The watchman goes off duty at four," Timmons said. "On weekends there won't be another one come on until eight."

"Hey, you really got your thumb on that operation,

don't you? All right, we'll make it at four instead of two. Listen, Stan, don't look so worried. You and me are gonna make millions off of this. Forget that crumby $80,000, or whatever it is you owe. You and me are going to make enough extra off this to keep us going for years. You like Las Vegas?"

"Yeah."

"Go there often?"

"Just a couple times."

"Been there this year yet?"

"Last fall. This spring."

"Well, listen, Stan. Next spring, when all of this is over, you and I are going to get together in Las Vegas and we are going to blow that town open. Really hit those dice tables. You shoot craps, don't you, Stan?"

Timmons nodded.

"Well, just you wait. We'll get us out to Las Vegas, get us a couple of babes—listen, you got nothing to worry about."

Timmons looked up from his scotch and into Carmody's face. He knew he was being sold a bill of goods. But the bill of goods was a bargain. He thought about his markers around town, and about the man they called Willie Shutters who could cripple people with his hands. He thought about his life at home and his job. He hated them. "I'm in," he told Carmody. "I'm in one hundred percent." Then he looked back down at his drink.

"I'll get everything planned out," Carmody said. "Just as soon as I see your operation. I got a banker out in Circle, Montana, all set to go on this deal. He'll cash any kind of respectable lookin' paper we can give him. You ever been out to Circle, Montana?"

Timmons smiled. "Can't say as I have."

"Well, maybe you better pass it up this trip. Just leave that part of it to me. We got to protect you."

Timmons nodded.

"You know, we got some pretty tough guys we're going

to have to deal with here," Carmody went on. "I mean those guys you got us into for that eighty thousand. You know, you wouldn't want to mess with some of those guys."

Timmons knew.

"Well," Carmody went on, "I just want you to know"—he unbuttoned his jacket and slipped a hand under his left armpit. Timmons could see him raising up the butt handle of a gun from its slip holster. "Now, Stan," Carmody said, "that's a .38 S and W. That would stop just about anything. So if you and I ever get in any trouble, you can count on me having that to protect us. Okay?"

Timmons nodded. He felt more afraid than ever. "I understand," he said.

"All right. Now, I been cruising your place up there in White Plains. There's an A & P four-tenths of a mile directly north of the northern boundary of the Quincy property. You know the one I mean. Now, there's a back road just behind that A & P. It's a public road, not A & P property. Now, you and I will meet there at four a.m. Saturday, right? By the time we walk down to your plant, that will give the watchman plenty of chance to pack up and get gone. Okay? Now, don't foul me up, Stan. Four o'clock."

Timmons was nodding. Carmody put his arm around Timmons's shoulders and they walked back to the table, which was stony quiet.

"Hey," Carmody said to Judy, "Barbara and I have a little shopping to do on foot. Why don't you take Stan here in the limo and show him around, maybe show him your place, or ride back up to White Plains with him when you're done?"

"Okay," she said meekly, and then, as if having reassessed her attitude, tossed Timmons a smile.

"I've got my car here at the Port Authority building," Timmons said.

"Up to you, Stan," Carmody replied. "At least I'll have Walter drive you and Judy back to your car, and one of you can take her home. I'll tell Walter to be back here to meet Barbara and me around five or so. Maybe we'll take in a movie. You do as you like."

Carmody reached out a hand for each woman to help them out of the booth.

"What about this Earth Systems deal?" George said. He was seated between the women. "These guys have really got something going in Miami. They can come into a strip mining operation and clean it up so there will be trees growing there in a few years. They got brochures and everything."

"Coal's really going to be big in the next few years," Carmody said. "The market's really gong to go for anything that will clean up coal mining and the ecology and all that, right, Georgie?"

George realized he was being mocked and stayed silent.

"How much will you let us in for?" Carmody asked.

"We're going on the sheets at $2. You can come in at $1.80."

Carmody smiled. "How much did you pick it up for, a nickel?"

"You can come in at $1.60," George said, "but that's the limit. These guys in Miami don't want no more partners. Even at $1.60 I'll have some explaining to do about you, but I owe you."

Carmody turned to Timmons. "Stan, I'll bet we can get in for a buck." Then he said to George, "Stan and I are going to talk about it and we'll let you know. Right, Stan?" He had his arm around Timmons again. Then they were all up and walking out.

On the way, Timmons recognized a man he had noticed earlier standing at the far end of the bar by the door almost the whole time they were there. It was Carmody's

chauffeur. And as the chauffeur saw the procession coming and turned to lead them out, Timmons realized that
the man had been drinking Cokes and quietly observing
everyone who entered or left the restaurant.

CHAPTER FIVE

Fortunately, I did not have to see Arthur W. Rosenstadt again after the highway scandal stories started running. I would not have been able to bear it. I didn't have to go back to the courthouse again, either, even to see the files. Julie—she's the one in the blue-tinted glasses—would bring them to my apartment at night and massage my feet and make us herb tea while I took notes.

Having proven my ability to make headlines while none of our older reporters had come through—even the one who was expensed all the way to Albany—I was appointed to be what is known outside the trade as an investigative reporter, or, as it was referred to by my jealous colleagues, a Green Beret.

I wrote a series of articles on the land holdings of prominent Mafiosi. Land records were easy to check, it's just that in most cases nobody had ever bothered before.

Women were attracted by what they saw as courage. "Aren't you afraid that one of them's going to kill you?" girls used to say. "I get so worried for you when I think about it," they'd tell me.

"Well," I would shrug, "I have to do my job."

Actually, nobody ever threatened me. I have no reason to believe that any of the mobsters I wrote about even saw my stories, much less was inconvenienced by them. Not even to the extent that Paul Weistholer was. It wasn't until a year and a half after the highway scandal stories ran that Weistholer even had to relinquish his position in the State Senate. Then, a few weeks after he began serving what was supposed to be a five-year prison sentence, he developed "heart trouble" and they let him out. He's still running his real estate business on Fifth Avenue and doing very well. But at the time of the prison sentence he was talking poverty. The government never went after all the profits he had made trading illegally on inside information about where a new highway was supposed to go.

This lack of effect was disenchanting me with the newspaper business. At the same time, I was becoming more and more enamored of the power I saw in the FBI agents I had started swapping information with. We'd go out drinking, and I'd hear their stories of crimes solved, men arrested. And this was my frame of mind when I first encountered Mickey Carmody.

Actually, it was uptown drinking with FBI agents that I learned all was not as it should be in the state bank examiner's office. Two of the agents I was closest to were complaining about the lack of progress in a case they had worked on. They were disinclined to go into details in front of a newspaperman, but it became clear from what they said that the case involved political corruption and a lot of money. I did as much as I could to indicate that I was interested without seeming to press them.

Finally, one of them, Bent Morrison, suggested I look into some bad check losses that had occurred the previous June. "Just look at some banks in Westchester County," he said. "Westchester Trust Company. First State Bank of White Plains. Scarsdale State Bank. Just look into them." He wouldn't explain further.

One thing about the *Press*, it had a good library. I could send up the names of the banks and 10 minutes later a copyboy would come around with little tan envelopes stuffed with clippings of old newspaper articles, not just from the *Press*, but from every New York paper. I guess the publisher figured that a good library was a lot cheaper than a good staff.

The *Press* paid little attention to Westchester County, but the banking incidents I was looking for had been covered in several small items in the *Times*. Eight Westchester banks had lost $50,000 to $60,000 cashing bad checks. The details weren't in the *Times* articles, so I called up officers at several of the banks. In each case, a man had walked into a branch office with a personalized check drawn on the account of a major customer of the bank. In each case the major customer did his business primarily with another branch. In each case the man who walked in off the street offered identification indicating that he was the major customer, and the checks were cashed. And in each case the man presenting the check for $50,000 or $60,000 was not the major customer at all, but an impostor. He had never been identified.

I called up Bent Morrison and went over what I had learned. He seemed impressed. But I told him it didn't make sense all by itself, and I pressured him for more details.

"Think," Morrison said. "The guy who did it, how could he have obtained personalized checks from all those big accounts?"

"I don't know," I said.

"Well, he could have bribed an officer in each of those banks."

"That's an awful lot of bribing and an awful lot of crooked bank officers," I said. "You'd think somebody would have turned him in when he went around making propositions."

"Of course. So it didn't happen that way, did it?"

"No." I kept very silent waiting for him to say more.

"Look," Morrison said finally. "Who had access to the accounts of all those banks?"

I didn't say anything. Eventually he was going to have to tell me.

"God damn it, Frank. What did all those banks have in common? They weren't national banks, were they?"

I went down the list. "They were all state banks."

"So find out who the fucking state bank examiner was. I'm not going to tell you any more." He hung up without even a good-bye.

It took me several days to discover that a bank examiner named Edward Spencer had been through six of those banks in the months just before the bad checks were cashed. And it took a couple of more days before I finally got an officer of one of the banks to make sense out of what happened.

Off the record, he told me that Edward Spencer was the son of Martin Spencer, the state comptroller. Pretty clearly, Edward Spencer had walked out of the banks he was examining with sample checks from leading customers. The checks were cancelled, just sitting around in the accounts waiting to be mailed back at the end of the month, and Spencer had taken them home. He had allowed an accomplice to reproduce the checks in blank, and then he had returned them to the banks.

Why was a young bank examiner from a wealthy family abetting a fraud? Nobody knew. But his father was a protégé of the governor, and was considered a likely candidate for that office himself someday. So it was politely agreed that his son wouldn't be prosecuted. A quiet resignation from the bank examiner's office had been arranged, and Edward Spencer was now on an extended tour of Europe. According to the bank officer who was filling me in, the FBI even knew the name of the con man who had cashed the bad checks. But the crime was under state rather than federal jurisdiction, and state authorities were having no part of a prosecution that might involve a Spencer.

So I did a little more checking around, and went back to Bent Morrison with what I had learned.

"Who was the guy who cashed the checks?" I asked, after I had related my story across our favorite bar table.

"Michael Carmody," Morrison said. "He's a real artist with bank jobs, forgeries, that stuff. He's pulled big deals before, but never anything like this. God, I never heard of anybody pulling anything like this. He took down nearly half a million dollars."

"How did he get the bank examiner involved?"

"Somehow he just charmed himself into Spencer's life. Lined him up with a couple of gorgeous girls. Introduced him to some ballplayers."

Ballplayers? That sounded like a *New York Press* angle. "What ballplayers?" I asked. "How did Carmody get ballplayers in his camp?"

"No need to bring their names into it. They didn't know what he was up to. He just charms people. Always the life of the party. Always a lot of beautiful girls. Always spends a lot of money. It works on all kinds of people. He seems to know just about everybody he's interested in knowing."

"There must be some way you can touch him on this," I said.

Morrison shook his head. "Essentially, those bank jobs were state crimes. Oh, if the U.S. Attorney here was really aggressive, wanted to step on the state's toes, he could work the federal insurance angle. But that would be reaching and we don't reach."

"And the state's D.A. is covering up the case to protect Spencer?"

"That's not what he'd say if you asked him. He'll say there isn't a strong enough case against Carmody, especially with the Spencer kid over there in Europe."

"But you think the case is strong enough."

"I think it's one of the strongest fraud cases I've ever seen. Hell, we've got half a dozen eyewitness identifications, handwriting analysis—they're protecting Spencer."

"Well," I suggested, "what about the other two swindles?"

Morrison looked surprised. "What other two swindles?"

"There were two banks that got taken the same way as the rest, but Spencer never went into them. White Plains Trust and First State Bank of Yonkers. Each of them was inspected by a different examiner. And I don't think the examiners had anything to do with the bad checks."

"Why?" I had Morrison hanging across the bar table.

"Because I talked to the two guys whose checks were used. The guys who supposedly went into the bank and cashed a $50,000 check, only it wasn't really them."

"What did they tell you?"

"That their houses had been broken into. They didn't notice any checks missing at the time, but later on they figured that that's how it must have happened. Somebody broke into their house, picked up a check and used it at a branch bank. Maybe the burglar even got some kind of identification from the house, too."

"Why would Carmody have bothered with break-ins when he had Spencer in his pocket?" Morrison asked.

"I don't know. Maybe this was before he had Spencer. Or maybe Spencer didn't examine enough banks for his liking."

"Well, even so," Morrison said, relaxing back in his seat, "we couldn't pin those burglaries on Carmody after all these months. Where's the evidence?"

"But if we could pin them on him, or others like them, then the state could prosecute him without involving Edward Spencer, right?"

Morrison thought, then shrugged. "Presumably. But that can't happen."

"Yes it can," I said. "I went a little further than just talking to the banks and their customers. I started calling around police departments in Westchester County to see if anybody had been picked up for stealing checks out of people's houses. I found a case in Scarsdale last April. That was two months before Carmody, or whoever, went on his big check cashing spree. A guy was arrested on the grounds of a rich house at four a.m. There was evidence of a break-in, and there were personalized checks in the guy's pocket that had come from inside the house."

"You really dug into this, didn't you?" Morrison was impressed.

"Yeah. Except, unfortunately, the guy who was arrested wasn't Carmody. And the police didn't make much of it. There were burglary charges filed, the guy posted bail, and nothing's happened in the case since."

"What was the guy's name?"

"Walter Fakazzi."

"No shit," Morrison said.

"Mean anything to you?"

"Carmody's bodyguard. Friends for quite a while."

"There you go, then," I said.

"Come on." He grinned. "It's interesting, I'll grant you that. But just because Fakazzi got arrested on a break-in and he knows Carmody, how do you prove to a jury that Carmody swindled eight banks out of half a million dollars?"

"Well, I went a little further," I said. "If the deal worked so well in Westchester County, why wouldn't Fakazzi or whoever it was try again? Only he wouldn't do it in exactly the same place, would he? He'd move. So I tried calling around Long Island."

Morrison could tell from my expression what was coming. "Where did you find it?" he asked.

"Oyster Bay. Just a month ago. Same deal, same Fakazzi. Out on bail again. But presumably he's got them lying around, waiting for the big cashing spree."

"Or better yet, Carmody has them. We can get the Nassau D.A. to put a tail on Fakazzi. When they catch him at Carmody's place they can get a warrant to search it. Fakazzi's place, too. My God, Frank, you may have found a way to get this guy!"

I shrugged.

"What did you go to all that trouble for?" Morrison wanted to know. "It's not that big a story for you."

"I wanted to impress you guys," I said.

So that's how Mickey Carmody and Walter Fakazzi wound up in Green Haven prison. There weren't any big bank robbery charges, of course. All the state could pin on Carmody was a few counts of receiving stolen property—for the checks they found in his apartment. He might have walked away on probation, but they discovered he had served a brief stretch for armed robbery back around 1960, which convinced the judge to lock him up again. Fakazzi had the two break-and-entries against him and had done probation for other offenses.

So they got a few years each, and were paroled early (a lot of parole boards treat you as a first offender unless you've served actual prison time within the past ten years). Nobody ever found the four or five hundred thousand dollars they had taken down from the banks. Fakazzi and Carmody never admitted the bank jobs or said why they were stealing the checks.

But I was feeling great about the whole thing anyway. I had solved a crime. I got to meet Carmody, and even though he wasn't confessing to much in the way of specific misdeeds, he does like to talk, and I got a good piece into the *Press* about the life of an eccentric hood. It was one of the last pieces I did for the paper. My FBI friend Morrison was really hot on me, got me together with the agent in charge of the New York office, and they offered me a job with the bureau. How could I refuse?

CHAPTER SIX

1

Stanley Timmons heard a child cry, no doubt one of his own. He was disappointed in himself because for a moment he actually cared what was the matter. He had told himself that today would be different.

He sat up in his bed and looked over at the empty twin next to it. The covers were thrown back. His wife had gone to dry the tears of his eight-year-old daughter, the spoiled one whom everyone still called the baby. He looked across the wall-to-wall shag at the gold-trimmed bureau, the dressing table, the heavy gold-trimmed wall mirror—if a phony French antique bedroom set cost $3,200, how much would a real one cost?—at the shirred curtains, which weren't really a good match for the shag, and at the pink tiles in the shadows through the door to the master bathroom. Good-bye to all that.

He left the grey suit jacket on the hanger and put on the new black-and-white hound's tooth jacket instead. It matched the grey suit trousers. He made it downstairs to the orange juice without confronting anyone. But then he heard the voices upstairs and felt another twinge of guilt.

After 48 years of probity, cynicism did not come easy. Where, he wondered, was the exhilaration he expected? Well, perhaps today really wasn't the break after all. Perhaps the break had come before, on the first day he had lied to his wife about the card games at night or to young Tom Quincy about going to the doctor's office instead of to the track. Perhaps the break still hadn't come. Perhaps it wouldn't come until he actually did whatever illegal act it was that they were planning for him.

Or perhaps it wasn't a clean break at all. Perhaps Stanley Timmons was becoming his own man in the same slow manner he had become society's. If you lived a certain way for long enough, then that was the way you were. Stanley Timmons could not look back on the one day that he had become respectable. Perhaps venality was just as gradually arrived at.

When he finished his orange juice, he went back upstairs and kissed his wife and both daughters. In the garage, Ralph Timmons, 18, was already at work, sealing the lower gasket on the engine of the Kawasaki. Timmons watched him a minute.

"Hi, Ralph."

"Hi." The youth fitted the next section of the cylinder head down over the bolts and his father watched for another minute.

"How's it going?"

"Should have it done by Saturday." Ralph never looked up.

"If you'll need a hand lifting that engine block back onto the bike, let me know. I'll be home Saturday afternoon."

"Thanks, Dad, but Jim's coming over in the morning. We've got a race at noon."

Timmons got into the Electra 225, the one the kids called the deuce and a quarter. In another year Ralph would be going to college—a second tuition to pay. By then Timmons might be on the lam, maybe in Vegas or L.A. Ralph would get by.

Timmons drove directly to the Merrill Heights Municipal Building. As usual, there were few people around to say hello to. The only important office in the building that opened at 8:30 was the treasurer's, and that was to accommodate the work schedule of Stanley Timmons, whose name had been on the treasurer's door for 12 years.

Harvey Knox was waiting for Timmons when the door opened. Knox was the treasurer's clerk, the civil servant who tended to the town's needs all day when elected officials like Timmons were off making money in the city. For quite a few months now Timmons had been spending noticeably less time at the treasurer's office. Harvey Knox, like everyone else, assumed it had something to do with Timmons's health problems. There was some sort of nervous condition that Timmons had been seeing a doctor for, and Knox had heard the gossip that the doctor was a psychiatrist. He assumed that was why Timmons didn't talk about it.

In truth, Timmons had indeed gone to a shrink a few times that spring. Even young Tom Quincy knew that. But the shrink wasn't the real reason Timmons had been away from his desks more frequently of late, and young Tom Quincy didn't know that. Fortunately for Timmons, people didn't ask you about your psychiatrist.

"Max Harrison called again yesterday afternoon," Knox said.

"Well," Timmons answered. "I've got the checks and vouchers to go through this morning."

"I told him you'd call."

"I've got to get out of here in an hour."

"People are going to want to know at the council meeting next week."

"I've handled these books 12 years without outside auditors. I don't know why I've got to start fooling around with outside auditors now.

"Merrill Heights became a Class B community June 30," Knox said. "Law says we've got to have auditors."

"I'll call him at nine."

At nine o'clock he called Max Harrison at the division of local government in Hartford. Harrison was upset that Timmons had settled on a local auditor rather than a large, established firm. Timmons tried to stall him off. He didn't have any dishonesty to hide. But he was under tremendous pressure from local accountants who were his neighbors to give them the work. And one of these local accountants had on two occasions steered clients to the Quincy Corporation for construction work, which had been a definite help to Timmons's career. Whatever Timmons decided now, he was going to catch hell either from the state or from his neighbors, and so he was trying to avoid deciding anything before the day he could simply leave this town and this job and this problem behind and start a new life. Somehow he finally got off the phone and promptly forgot whatever it was he had agreed to.

Timmons began the routine matching of bills and vouchers. Knox almost never made a mistake, but if he did it was Timmons's responsibility to catch it. Timmons began to ask himself how long it made sense to stay conscientious in one job while he was plotting grand larceny in another.

A few minutes before ten, the deuce and a quarter wheeled into its reserved parking space at the Quincy Corporation's international headquarters, a modern, block-like four story building in White Plains.

2

In his office, Stanley Timmons faced for the second time in a morning a pile of checks, each one paper-clipped to a voucher that authorized the expenditure of the money. Once again he began to examine them to make sure each expenditure had been properly authorized by the proper department to pay a legitimate bill. This time, however, there was no space on the checks for his signature. The Quincy Corporation paid several thousand bills a month and no one was expected to sign his name that often, not Stanley Timmons and certainly not young Tom Quincy, the executive vice-president and treasurer and Timmons's supervisor. The checks on Stanley Timmons's desk this morning had already been signed—by a machine that bore a rubber facsimile of the handwritten signature of Thomas S. Quincy Jr.

At 10:30 a.m., Timmons's secretary, Barbara Adams, entered the office and left a large brown envelope on his desk. She didn't have to tell him what it was. Every month the envelope came from Morgan Guaranty Co., Quincy's bank, stuffed with the cancelled checks Quincy had written last month and a statement, perhaps a dozen pages long, itemizing the checks and listing Quincy's balances. The old checks would be reconciled with the statement of balances by several accountants working under Timmons, the same men who assembled the vouchers and prepared the new checks. Timmons would glance through the work before assigning it, and would inspect it again when it was done. Then he would report to young Tom Quincy and they would determine how much money Timmons would deposit in the Morgan Guaranty account.

At 10:40 Timmons called Miss Adams into his office and instructed her to put the brown envelope from Morgan Guaranty in her files. He would not have time to go over the bank statement before his luncheon appointment in the city. Some time next week, perhaps. . . . Miss Adams was used to these delays. So was young Tom Quincy. The delays weren't exactly a good idea. But Stanley Timmons had been an employee in the Quincy finance department for 22 years, and had been head of that department for seven years, and there had never been any trouble with the bank balances.

At 11 o'clock Miss Adams buzzed him on the intercom. A Mr. Fitzgerald was there to see him from the American Business Machine Corporation. Timmons checked his calendar. Fitzgerald indeed was expected this morning for his semi-annual visit, and Timmons had overlooked the appointment. The American Business Machine Corporation supplied Quincy with the mechanical crutches for its accounting system, most importantly the ABMC-2000 check writing machine. Timmons recognized the visitor immediately. It was Fitzgerald's third such inspection since taking over the job.

"I know you're busy," Fitzgerald said, sticking his briefcase under his left arm to shake Timmons's hand, "but as I've explained before, these little check-ups every so often protect both us and you against anything going wrong. Let's start with a look at your 2000 unit."

The check-writing machine stood approximately four feet high. Its chunky central chamber housed what looked like a small printing press, visible through a sealed glass enclosure. On either side were long trays, one feeding into the machine, the other out of it, so that the 2000 as a whole somewhat resembled a robot with a bubble head, extending its arms to either side.

"Now, you know, the two keyholes on the front of this," Fitzerald said, pointing, "are one big reason the ABMC-2000 is the most secure check-writing apparatus in the world. Right now you're sabotaging that security by leaving the master key in the machine when no one's using it."

"But the machine requires a second key before it can operate," Timmons said. "And there are only five of them." In the past, Timmons had made sure that the master key stayed in his desk on the morning that Fitzgerald came so the inspector would be happy, but there had been too much else to think about today.

"Where are the other five keys?" Fitzgerald asked.

"Exactly where they were during your last visit." He pointed to the cubbyhole offices along one wall. "Mr. O'Donnell has one, Mr. Pinkerton has one, and Miss Bralove. I have one, and of course there is a duplicate in the safe."

Fitzgerald was writing on a pad he had taken from the briefcase. "The safe is kept locked?" he asked without looking up.

"Most of the time."

Fitzgerald looked up. "But it looks like it's open right now." He walked across the room to the safe, Timmons following.

"We're doing some checks today and the accountants need access to the books," Timmons said.

"Why isn't a person kept in charge of the safe to handle the books and keys and whatnot when they're needed and make sure they're returned?"

"We've talked over your suggestions before. Mr. Quincy is aware of them. Frankly, someone to watch this safe full time would be a waste of a salary and would slow down everyone in the office."

Fitzgerald was crouching, looking through the safe. "There's an open petty cash box in here. And the stationery."

"The safe is a convenient storage area," Timmons said, struggling to keep his voice polite. "We're cramped for space."

"So people are used to going in and out of the safe."

"At times."

"And where is the duplicate key to the 2000?" Fitzgerald continued to sniff around, his head in the open door. Timmons fought off an urge to slam it shut.

"The key is in the bottom of the cash box, under the tray," Timmons said.

Fitzgerald reached a hand in. "And the cash box is not kept locked."

"Mr. Fitzgerald, neither the cash box nor the safe are products of the American Business Machine Corporation."

Fitzgerald stood up and apologized. He was a security officer for the ABMC, but they were still in the business of selling machines and this was a customer. "I'm not trying to interfere in the internal affairs of the Quincy Corporation," he said. "I thought you understood my job, which is only to protect you from loss by fraud or error. And, of course, also to protect ABMC, because we have a big liability here. We've guaranteed this ABMC-2000 to be fool-proof. But only if you follow directions. I'm here to make sure that you know those directions."

Fitzgerald walked back to the machine. "May I have your key, please, Mr. Timmons?"

"It's with my secretary and she's away from her desk right now." Actually, the key was lying out on the corner of her desk, where it customarily did, but Timmons didn't want to go into that. Fitzgerald's inspection was taking long enough as it was.

"Why does she have the key?"

"Because I'm out of the office sometimes and people may need to use the machine. She returns it to me at the end of the day. In fact, here she comes now."

Miss Adams was approaching along the corridor from the elevator, holding a cardboard tray of coffee in styrofoam cups. Tucked under her right arm was a package wrapped in brown paper. She set the cardboard tray on a desk near the machine and delivered the brown package to Timmons.

"Did you want her to get the key now?" Timmons asked. Fitzgerald was being jostled by a dozen men and women reaching for their coffee and apportioning the milk, sugar and stir sticks.

"Let me just point out a couple of more things to you," Fitzgerald said, easing his notebook away from the coffee and milk. "The counter on this machine reads 470, and it's not yet 11:30 a.m. I presume that means that this number is still there from the checks you wrote yesterday, and that you haven't reset it today because you haven't started writing checks yet. But the counter is supposed to be reset to zero at the end of every business day. The counter is the way you make sure that the number of checks run off doesn't exceed the number of payment vouchers authorized. Without the counter someone could run unauthorized checks through this machine and cash them, and you wouldn't know it until the bank statement came back a month or two later."

Fitzgerald was staring at Timmons, waiting for a response, but Timmons just stared back. The truth was, they hadn't reset the counter in more than a year. If it said 470, that was a random number that came up after the machine had reached 9999 and gone back to 0000 of its own accord.

"And the most important thing—" Fitzgerald said, and walked around behind the machine. With his hand he traced a line from the glass bubble that housed the printing apparatus, down the eject tray, which also was covered by sealed glass, and into a wire mesh box at the end of the tray. His hand went to the rim of the wire mesh box and smartly flipped up the lid.

"—This is the crowning element of the 2000 system," he said, "the locked check box, which means that once a blank check is fed into the machine nobody can get it out again except with a key—preferably an executive from a different department who can compare the number of checks in the box with the number on the counter and then with the number of vouchers. But you refuse to lock your checkbox. This was on my report six months ago, and it still hasn't been remedied. With this checkbox unlocked, the check counter is worthless."

"Mr. Fitzgerald, the number of people we'd need to

carry out all your precautions—" Timmons stopped in mid-sentence. Thomas S. Quincy Jr. was approaching. Secretaries, clerks and accountants stopped stirring their coffee and began to appear busy. Young Tom was the boss's son and Mr. Quincy Senior's heart attack six months ago only underscored in everyone's mind that young Tom was destined to replace the founder, chairman and president of the company.

"I didn't know you had someone with you, Stanley," Tom Quincy Jr. said. "Could I see you for a minute when you're through?"

As Quincy turned to go, Fitzgerald stopped him. "Perhaps this is something you ought to hear, Mr. Quincy."

"I don't think it's necessary to bother Mr. Quincy about this," Timmons said.

But Quincy seemed interested. "What's the problem?" he asked.

"Mr. Quincy, Mr. Fitzgerald," Timmons said nervously.

"I represent ABMC," Fitzgerald said. "We make your check-writing equipment. I know you're busy, but you're paying a lot of money to us for this system because it's the most advanced concept in check-writing security there is. But when you don't follow the safety procedures, you're not getting the benefits you're paying for."

"What seems to be wrong?"

"Well, in the first place," Fitzgerald said, "the master key is being kept in the machine so that anyone with a second key can operate it. And the second key is in an open safe. The counter isn't being reset properly, and most important, your check writing box isn't locked, which means anyone could—"

"Mr. Fitzgerald, let me break in here," Quincy said. "I think I remember all this from what you told us last year. We had long talks about it, Mr. Timmons and I, and even my father. We value your machine very much, but to follow all your rules we'd have to hire several more people. We'd have to add to the duties of a vice president in some other department who's got more than enough to do already. It would hold up our whole accounting operations. We depend on people being able to get into and out of that safe when they decide it's time to write checks or make book entries."

Fitzgerald stayed meekly silent.

"You see, in a lot of ways," Quincy went on, "we're still a small company despite all the money we handle. Stanley Timmons has been here as long as I have—more than 20 years, isn't it, Stanley? He's like a member of our family. He knows these people, watches them. And I'm in here every day myself."

"Well," Fitzgerald said.

Quincy smiled and held out his hand. "Now we're very happy with ABMC, and we think we are getting our money's worth already."

Fitzgerald left. Timmons tried to conceal his relief. Whatever these hoods had in store for him, it wasn't likely that Fitzgerald and his security precautions would help.

Quincy put a hand on his shoulder. "The reason I stopped by was to let you know we've landed two of the Long Island contracts we've been working on. One of them's the new corporate headquarters for Continental Brands."

"Congratulations," Timmons said.

"The other one's for some Long Island Railroad bridges. You'll be hearing more later. The thing now is that I want to be ready to start subcontracting fast if the clients are ready ahead of schedule. I want you to start converting Treasuries as they come due and put the money in the Morgan account. The five million we're holding there isn't enough of a cushion."

"What do you want?"

"Well, there's probably not going to be any new spending until fall sometime. But I want you to work up so we've got a minimum, say, by August 1, in the Morgan Guaranty account, a minimum of say, eight million dollars."

CHAPTER SEVEN

1

So five years ago, I helped put Mickey Carmody and Walter Fakazzi in Green Haven and I joined the FBI.

From the very first there was a tension; I suppose if I had been fully sensitive to such things, it might have prepared me for the confrontation that occurred this year over the Quincy investigation. At any rate, my very first assignment was to a major white collar crime case. I got the evidence they needed for a conviction, and also found links to other large frauds involving some supposedly reputable businessmen. So I managed to build assignment after assignment on my own, all in the area of prolonged investigation of complicated financial crime.

I got along just swell with the federal attorneys to whom I turned these cases over for prosecution. But, as I say, there was resentment within the bureau itself. I never got the petty bank robberies. I never had to serve summonses. I was less than enthralled by pistol practice. I never had to chase down routine data for local police. I never had to make petty arrests on cases developed by other agents. (Ninety-nine percent of all arrests are sheer boredom. The other one percent, people are shooting at you. None of them are any fun.)

Coming up with your own assignments and running them out on your own, of course, isn't the normal life for a Fibbie, especially one without the law or accounting degree that old J. Edgar said all his agents would have (even in Hoover's day, *that* wasn't true).

Not only was my relative independence unpopular with other agents, but there was even an undertone of resentment among the assistant agents in charge, the supervisors. Bureaucracy is bureaucracy, even in the FBI. What kept things bearable, looking back on it, was my close relationship with Bent Morrison, my frequent partner, who supported me or at least played liaison between me and disgruntled superiors until things cooled off. Also, of course, it helped that I so often came through with successful investigations and got letters of commendation from the U.S. attorneys.

Not that I always won my arguments. In fact, my biggest defeat involved Mickey Carmody. I can look back on it with some satisfaction because it's clear now that I was right. As I said earlier, Carmody and Fakazzi were back on the street after about nine months. People think you have to serve a full third of your prison sentence before parole, but you don't. You get time off your sentence for every day that you don't stick your dinner knife into one of the guards, and more time off for helping the state bake cheap bread for its institutions. So parole eligibility comes at one-third of a much reduced sentence. It works out to about a fifth of what the judge gave you.

A year or so after Carmody was sprung I came across his name in an S.E.C. report. The Securities and Exchange Commission issues public reports when it takes action against stock frauds. All the action amounts to is a court injunction prohibiting the guilty parties from carry-

ing on with the fraud. The S.E.C. can't file criminal
charges or even make the crooks give the money back to
the victims. And the injunction normally comes long after the swindle is finished anyway, so the crooks usually
don't suffer at all.

Sometimes, however, the S.E.C. turns its files on a
stock fraud over to the Justice Department for criminal
prosecution. And since financial crime was my specialty,
I made it a practice to read through the S.E.C. reports every so often to keep up to date on what was happening.

Just a few months after he was out, Carmody had gotten involved in a stock issue for an outfit called Science
Engineering Associates, which claimed it had a patented
device that would let you plow 40 acres on the bottom of
the Pacific Ocean without getting the bends.

I never cease to be amazed that there are people around
to buy this junk stock, but there always are. Sometimes
professional people with more income than business
sense, sometimes even business people seeking that elu-
sive 1000% return on their money. Sometimes, as with
Science Engineering, the suckers include a big invest-
ment and brokerage concern or two, so the loot is extraordinary. When a firm like Merrill Lynch or Walston gets
involved in a fraud, it doesn't mean they're crooked; it
just means they're so big that all a real crook has to do is
get hold of a couple of employees in a branch office and
he can make a lot of money before senior management
catches on. Every once in a while it happens.

S.E.C. reports seldom make it entirely clear how a
scheme works. But among the six men enjoined in the
Science Engineering case besides Carmody were stock-
brokers from New York, Houston, Denver and Los Angeles (all of them had their brokerage licenses suspended
for six months) and two other guys from Denver who apparently were the "executives" who ran this purported
business. I called up a local S.E.C. investigator I knew
and asked him about the case. He remembered interview-

ing a New York broker named George Bender, who was working in a bucket shop downtown—you know, one room, four customer reps and 12 telephone lines, that sort of thing. The investigator had subpoenaed some records from Bender, but the case had finally been handled out of the S.E.C.'s Denver office, and that was where everything had been shipped. As for Bender, my friend didn't really know where he was. The bucket shop had closed down and thanks to the license suspension Bender was, you might say, out of commission for six months.

But I knew Carmody liked to brag, and what did I have to lose by looking him up? Besides, I hadn't seen Carmody since before he went away, and if I was going to be handling fraud for the FBI I had already been far too long without checking what Mickey Carmody was doing.

The Carmodys weren't in the phone book, but when I drove out to Baldwin on Long Island and found the roomy brick split level where they had lived before, Dr. Sybil Manwaring—she practiced under her maiden name—answered the door. She was a good-looking woman, blond like her husband and in her early thirties. It was afternoon already by the time I arrived, but she said she had just gotten up after having spent most of the previous night in emergency surgery. She wore a rather slinky houserobe. She remembered me and invited me in to share some chicken salad and coffee before she left for the hospital.

Mickey had moved out for good a few months earlier, she said. He had wanted to reunite with her after his parole, and so, despite her doubts, she had let him move in. He had always been good with the children, she said, and they needed a father. Besides which, she still kind of loved him. They had met back in 1966 at a delicatessen he was managing for some friends. She was still in medical school at the time. She said she didn't know he had served two years back around 1960 on an armed robbery charge—not until his record came out at his sentencing hearing in the stolen check case.

Anyway, he hadn't been into guns and such things when she was with him—not to her knowledge, at least. He had opened a delicatessen of his own in Brooklyn shortly before they were married. He couldn't keep his mind on it, though, and closed it after six months. Mickey couldn't really keep his mind on anything, she said, except a series of wild business deals that she never fully understood.

But she did understand he always had plenty of money, more than could be explained by the delicatessen, or his off-again on-again work later as a truck driver. She insisted that she never probed into his affairs or questioned him when he bragged about this or that big killing. She had her own life at the hospital, her own finances, and she was glad that they could respect a certain part of each other's lives as private. He was a good provider, always fun to be with, he loved good times and was considerate of her during her two pregnancies and was a most attentive father.

They had been married about five years, she told me, before she knew he was into anything illegal. Of course, she had always been suspicious of some of his friends— some of them spoke and acted the way gangsters do in movies—but then Mickey had always had all kinds of friends. They'd go to restaurants or parties and he would introduce her to prosperous, cultured business and professional people who seemed to be his pals, too.

During the months of hassling with the district attorney's office over his guilty plea and sentencing for the stolen check case, the veneer over his business life had been slowly stripped away. It hurt to find out that he had lied to her so often, that he had a prison record he never told her about and that the children would eventually learn their father was a criminal.

She agreed to take him back after his parole only on his promise that he'd stay clean and avoid his old friends whom she now knew to be crooks. He failed to keep these promises, so she threw him out. It wasn't a moral judgment, she said. She really didn't mind that he stole. After all, she said, the victims more or less deserved it; they were the kind of people who had life easy and had the money to lose. She and Mickey both came from blue collar homes where the parents had separated and there was never much money around. In fact, she admitted, they still shared some good laughs over the way he could run through the security precautions of supposedly astute patrician businessmen. The truth was that Sybil Manwaring, for all her remarkable conventional attainments, probably always had a renegade streak in her.

What really bothered her, besides not being able to trust Mickey anymore, was that she didn't want the children exposed to the kind of world it seemed that Mickey would never be willing to leave. Some of the people around Mickey were into far worse things than pulling the wool over the eyes of pompous bankers. Some of them even carried guns.

And with that argument—that the children shouldn't be exposed to these things—Mickey actually agreed to leave. He still visited them regularly, and she approved of that. But she had to stay vigilant about the hoodlum friends he sometimes still tried to bring by. And it bothered her that he remained so jealous of her own life. She knew now that he had a capacity for violence, and wondered if she could ever feel independent enough of him to pick up a new marriage.

The houserobe she was wearing was yellow and was wrapped to make a low V in front. At one point she dropped a piece of chicken salad down that V and started to reach for it. I was giving her mental encouragement, but apparently she decided there was no graceful way to make the retrieval and gave up. It certainly started my mind to work, though, on top of the remark she made about how lonely it sometimes was since Mickey had left. I began to think there were a lot worse ways I could spend the afternoon, both from a pleasurable and a professional intelligence-gathering point of view, than in bed with this woman. She had mentioned that the children wouldn't be home from school for a couple of hours yet. I'm sure she sensed my thoughts.

But as soon as she finished lunch, without a word to me, she rose, went to the wall phone and dialed. In a voice quite loud enough for my hearing, she identified the other party as "Mother" and instructed her to come right over. "I'll see you in about 20 minutes then," she concluded. Then she turned to me and announced that she was about to dress for work, so I would have to go.

Well, I decided I was really better off anyway, quashing any seductive impulses toward a woman whom Mickey Carmody was seriously jealous of. After all, I knew—even if Dr. Manwaring didn't—that Mickey had been carrying a gun for years.

I did ask her, on the way to the door, what she might know about a company called Science Engineering Associates. Vaguely familiar, she said. But then Mickey always had some deal or other going. Yes, she remembered something about underwater farming, but not much. Ask Mickey. She gave me the address of the brownstone he was renting in Brooklyn Heights, and said if he wasn't there, he'd be coming to the house in Baldwin around six to stay with the kids until she got home.

I thanked her and headed for Brooklyn Heights. Mickey wasn't in, but Walter Fakazzi was.

2

I had never talked at length with Fakazzi as I had with Carmody, but he remembered who I was, and wanted to know right at the doorway exactly what was up. I said there was nothing formal on, and nothing at all involving him. "I just want to talk to Mickey about a stock deal he might have heard of, a company called Science Engineering Associates."

Fakazzi studied me for a minute. I suspected he knew the name, but he also knew the rules. "You better talk to Mickey about that," he said finally.

"When's he coming home?"

"Don't really know when he'll be back here. You might catch him tonight at the house out in Baldwin."

"Mind if I wait for him here awhile?"

"I'm leaving soon. Got to go up to Queens to see my kids."

"Need a lift?" I asked. "I've got my car."

He studied me again, then shrugged. "Thanks. But I'm not gonna tell you nothing."

"I know. If Mickey's trusted you all this time, he must have a reason."

Fakazzi looked behind him into the room as if to make sure there was nothing to hide, then swung open the door all the way. "Come on in," he said.

One look told me that Mickey had another nice place, although so far he hadn't got around to furnishing it fully. Maybe he was short on cash—which would be bad news for the Federal Reserve System—or maybe he just wasn't planning to stay there long.

"You guys living together here?"

"Nah, just Mickey full-time. Here, sit down." He motioned to a chair. There were only three or four pieces in the room, but they were nice. There was one of those polished parquet wooden floors you see sometimes in New York brownstones, and a Navajo rug. Mickey had good taste.

"I don't hang out no special place these days," Fakazzi told me. "Since the old lady threw me out. I stay here sometimes, sometimes back with them. And I got an aunt

I stay with sometimes. I really like it back home best, you know? I miss my kids a lot. But. . . ." He shrugged.

"Sounds like you and Mickey got the same problem with your wives," I said.

"Yeah. That's what prison does to you. The women don't like us around our own kids when we get out. It really fucked me up good. They ought to think about that before they send you away, you know?"

I wanted to tell him that maybe he should have thought of it before he stole the checks, but I didn't. He went into the other room and came out a few minutes later with a clean shirt and his hair combed.

On the drive to Queens I asked him, "You think there's a chance you and your wife will get together again?"

He shook his head. "Truth is," he said finally, "she found another old man while I was in. That's what hurts most, you know? You go there sometimes and you know something's going on. Used to be she was your woman and now she's not."

"I'm sorry," I said.

"Sometimes there's even the other guy there, too. Nobody says nothing or anything, but you know what's going on. And you got to take that in front of the kids, too. They can tell what's happening, you know? Kids shouldn't see their father like that."

"I know what you mean," I said.

"You know Mickey, he won't stand for it. Just—Sybil's scared to do him like that."

"You think they're going to get together again?"

Fakazzi smiled. "Nah. I mean, Mickey, he thinks so. He thinks a woman's got to stay loyal while the kids are growing up. Maybe—I mean, Mickey pulls off a lot of things, but I think women's got a mind of their own. Especially Sybil. You know, if my wife can do it, hell, there's a woman went to medical school. What's gonna keep her, you know?"

"You got a point," I said.

"You married?"

"Nah," I said. "That's one I've stayed out of so far."

"Must be kind of rough. I mean, the FBI don't like you guys shackin' up or nothin', I hear."

I had to laugh. "You know the bureau pretty well. Used to be an agent?"

"Nah." He laughed, too. "Just things I hear."

"There was a little heat once. But not bad. Just dumb, you know? But I get by. You working now?"

"Off again, on again. Got this trucking company. Like, I'll go there tonight and shape up. Maybe I'll get a trip, maybe not. I go a couple times a week."

That left a lot of nights off for second story work, I thought. "What about Mickey?" I said.

Fakazzi laughed again. "You better ask him about that."

3

Fakazzi seemed surprised and pleased that we had gotten on without trouble. He wasn't the type to elaborate, but his "thanks" when I dropped him off seemed genuine, rather than perfunctory, and he even added, "see you around again sometime, okay?"

Fakazzi was caught in a transitional world he didn't quite understand. On one side was the gangland paradigm he knew so well, where cops like me were to be treated contemptuously at all times. On the other side was the con man's world where Mickey lived, where the crooks and the cops palled around in between jousts, like ballplayers from rival teams enjoying a drink and a few laughs together after the game.

In a way, I shared Fakazzi's distrust of that kind of camaraderie. Carmody was a professional, incorrigible crook, a dangerous man both to property and perhaps

someday to persons. I was uncomfortable driving out to
his house to shoot the bull for awhile, but that's the way
it worked. If I went up to his door with a cold stare and a
subpoena and started reading him his Miranda rights, he
could say nothing. If I came informally, he'd know that I
could never use what he said against him in a case. He
might tell me almost anything, except where I could get
the evidence to prove it. And that's pretty much what
happened.

We played around with his kids for awhile until their
bedtime. Then he broke out a couple of bottles of beer,
apologizing that his wife didn't keep imported brands on
hand. "So you wanted to talk about Science Engineering," he said, remembering my opening speech an hour
earlier. Then he laughed. "That was a hell of a deal, all
right. You know, you guys are out of it?"

"How do you mean?" I asked.

"The S.E.C. did the investigation. No Fibbies
allowed."

"Then you got nothing to worry about. Tell me how it
came off."

"Seriously. You don't believe me. Justice got the case
from the S.E.C. four or five months ago. It's already been
indicted—in Denver."

"You're right, I didn't know," I said. For one thing, the
S.E.C. hadn't told me when I called them, damn it. It
might have been sporting if they'd mentioned that the
case was already under indictment. "You're not a defen-
dant, I don't suppose," I said. "Or I would have heard
that."

"No way. They just got the two guys in Denver. The
guys who ran the outfit."

"Nobody else?"

"Nope. All they had for evidence was the brochures,
the prospectuses, that stuff. False and fraudulent. You
know, the guys who ran the company had to know it was

bullshit. How are they gonna prove the brokers knew? I mean, that's the only other people they got, is brokers, and how you gonna prove something against them?"

"How did you get involved?"

"Ah, not me," he smiled.

"Come on. I saw your name on the S.E.C. release."

"I held some stock, that's all. You know how those S.E.C. things are—they don't have to prove anything, all they got to do is allege it and it's on file. The Justice Department's something else. They got to convince a jury. Well, they studied the case, every scrap of it. And they didn't indict me. Because there was nothing there. I bought some stock, I sold it."

"Bet you didn't take a loss," I said.

Carmody laughed. "You guys can check it all out in my income tax return this year. You probably will anyway. Sure, I made some money—not as much as I should have, though, I'll tell you that. Hell, if I had taken my fair cut of the money I made for those sons of bitches—they packed in a fortune. You know, I hear there may have been more than a million. You know they got Merrill Lynch in it, don't you?"

I nodded, smiling.

"And Walston," Carmody said. "Merrill Lynch, me and Walston owned that stock. That's pretty good company, right?"

"Yeah. Except they lost their shirts and you turned a profit."

"Well—I'm smarter, right?"

"Probably so, Mickey." I meant it. "What do you mean you deserved a bigger cut?"

"You know what they were doing? How it worked?"

"A stock run-up, I suppose."

"Yeah. But do you know what they did to those schmucks on the way down? They got them short, way short. The schmucks were thinking they could bail themselves out when it goes down further, you know? Only instead of going down, the guys who are playing with this stock get it to go up. So there are the schmucks, they've got to buy the damn stuff back to cover their shorts, and who are they going to buy it from? They've already sold it all to the guys who are playing around with it and can charge anything they want for it."

Carmody laughed out loud, and I couldn't hold back a smile myself. It *was* funny. "That's what you guys call the daisy chain, isn't it?" I asked.

"Yeah," he said, surprised. "How'd you know? Anyway," he repeated, "I hear they may have got more than a million off that deal."

"But not you, though."

"Hell, no. Nowhere near. Maybe twenty, twenty-five thousand tops. You'll see it on my income tax."

"Why do you say you deserved more?"

"Oh, hell, Frank. You don't think those assholes could have thought of that short sale business by themselves. They never heard of the daisy chain before. Where'd you pick it up, anyway?"

"I guess I get around," I said.

"Guess you do. Anyway, I never made any money on that. I made it on the way up."

Carmody was so persuasive that for a moment I almost believed him. I had to keep telling myself that Michael Carmody would never set up a device for earning so much money and then let other people keep it all.

"I wouldn't have told you as much as I did if the case wasn't closed," Carmody went on.

"It can always be re-opened," I said.

"Nah. They made their decision. The feds out in Denver. They're not going to let you re-open it. You got no new evidence. Even if you did, I'm not notorious enough they'd take the case out of Denver and give it to you. You still don't believe me, do you?"

I didn't.

"Bureaucracies don't operate like that," he said. "I know your own organization better than you do."

"Maybe," I said.

"See for yourself."

4

I wrote a memo to the special agent-in-charge, asking for the investigation to be re-opened. I told him I knew from Carmody's own mouth—although the admissions could never be used in court—that Carmody had been a principal in a conspiracy to defraud investors, including two major Wall Street firms, of perhaps more than a million dollars, and that the conspiracy undoubtedly involved use of the federal mails and interstate telephone wires, plus interstate travel in furtherance of the conspiracy, plus violation of section 10(b)5 of the Securities Act of 1934, any one of which would give us jurisdiction. I noted that the case, as developed by the S.E.C., had been looked at by the U.S. Attorney's Office in Denver, and perhaps by our own office there, and that a decision had been reached to indict only two of the conspirators who had fronted the operation, and they only for the substantive securities act violations.

If the case were broadened to take in the conspiracy, I said, I felt confident I could obtain usable evidence not only against Carmody, but against three or four brokers around the country whose work had been indispensable to the success of the scheme. And even if the search for evidence should fail, I concluded, a reopening of the investigation would be worth the try because of the size of the scheme and the continued threat to commerce posed by the schemers.

Two weeks later, no response. I went to see the special agent-in-charge. He said the request had just been denied. The U. S. Attorney's Office in Denver had its case all set for trial and didn't want to jeopardize what seemed like a sure thing by reopening an investigation into what was essentially the same crime.

But had the F.B.I. office in Denver looked into it, I wanted to know.

I was told we are part of the Justice Department, all working for the same organization. The Denver decision had been approved by the fraud unit of the department in Washington. The FBI didn't override a decision of the U. S. Attorney General's office.

I wrote another memo. Carmody was an exceptionally dangerous man, maybe the best freelance fraud artist in the country. There wasn't a doubt in my mind that even as I had been talking to him, even while I wrote these memos, Carmody was involved in some scheme or other of his own conception that might cost the public hundreds of thousands of dollars. After all, when he stole money, half the loss was written off on the victims' income tax payments, and much of the rest was covered by insurance causing an increase in premiums for everyone. If we could nail him on the Science Engineering matter and put him out of circulation again, perhaps for a few years this time, it would be of incalculable benefit to the public. And at any rate, it was absolutely essential that we try.

My formal reply, a perfunctory denial, was a long time in coming. My real reply took less than a week. My friend Bent mentioned to me one day that just as a matter of friendly advice, I had better let go of this Science Engineering thing—it was really getting to be a sore point with the special agent-in-charge. I knew Bent had been put in an uncomfortable position, probably against his wishes, and I didn't press him on what had happened. It wouldn't be the last time he would be in the middle, between me and the Justice Department, over the issue of Mickey Carmody.

As for Carmody himself, he won that round. But I was

to get some satisfaction later when I found out that—although my action was unwitting at the time—I caused Carmody a significant bit of trouble in his planning of the Quincy caper. It involved this banker out in Montana.

CHAPTER EIGHT

1

If Mickey Carmody was blind to the pitfalls of arrogance, he was well aware of what his temper could do to him. Right now he was struggling, so far successfully, to control it. What he wanted to do was burst into the house and pistol whip this son of a bitch O'Neil until it was clear that the woman O'Neil knew as Sybil Manwaring was still Sybil Carmody under the law. She was still living with Mickey Carmody's children and they weren't to see her screwing around with other men. O'Neil would learn that if he wanted to fuck Mickey Carmody's wife he'd have to do it in his own house and still get Sybil home in time so that it wouldn't be obvious they had spent the night. And even then he'd better be looking over his shoulder because Mickey Carmody still carried a .38 and didn't believe in taking shit from anybody. . . .

Carmody squirmed uncomfortably behind the wheel of his Ford (the limousine was back at the rental agency for the weekend) and tried again to control himself. He had been parked a few doors down from the house in Baldwin for more than two hours now, ever since he had driven past and seen O'Neil's car. The lights were still on both downstairs and in the master bedroom. They had been on all along, and there was no sign of anyone coming out.

One reason why Carmody knew he had better not burst into the house right now was that the cops had already spotted him and questioned him. He was suspicious-looking, all right, parked carefully in the shadows between two streetlights in a residential section. But there wasn't much they could do when he showed them his driver's license and car registration, all stating clearly that he was parked practically across the street from his own house.

The smart thing to do was wait. Tail O'Neil. See where he lived, where he worked. From what Carmody had been able to wheedle out of his wife and son, O'Neil drove a truck, and sometimes at night. Perhaps a lot could be learned before sunrise.

The problem was that Carmody had to meet Timmons in White Plains at four. There was no overestimating the importance of their business and Timmons was so dumb he might lose his head if the police approached while he was sitting out there waiting. Carmody had to show at four. On the other hand, watching O'Neil's car parked in front of *his* house, where *his* wife was, and with the bedroom light on, was driving Carmody crazy.

Suddenly he saw two shadows moving behind the living room window shade, and then the front door opened. A sliver of light, then two figures. Carmody studied them intently as they stood on the front porch, apparently talking. They didn't even kiss. The man just turned away, and when he was halfway down the walk they waved at each other. Carmody tried to remember. He hadn't seen any shadows moving in the bedroom. Maybe. . . .

The man got into his car, the headlights went on and

the car pulled away. Carmody started his engine, waited until the other car had gone a block, then began to follow, without headlights. When they got to the Sunrise Highway there was some traffic. Carmody turned the lights on. He followed O'Neil down the highway to Freeport and then on the Meadowbrook State to East Meadow. They were on side streets now and Carmody's headlights were off again. There was a development of small, relatively inexpensive houses. Was this guy O'Neil living in a house? Maybe married? Carmody got a laugh out of the idea.

Then they were past the housing development and at a garden apartment project. O'Neil pulled in. Carmody drove past, turned a corner and shut off the engine. He got out and ran back to the garden apartment full tilt, staying behind the bushes as much as he could, but still taking the most direct route because if he was fast enough he might still see—

There was no sign of movement on the parking lot. Carmody searched for O'Neil's car and found it. He tried the entrance to the nearest building. Sure enough, the names were on the mail boxes. But no O'Neil. Maybe the bastard was using an assumed name on the mailbox. Carmody would have. Or maybe O'Neil was the assumed name.

Carmody went to the next building and found the name Donald F. O'Neil on the box for apartment 2-E. That was his man. There just hadn't been a parking space next to the right building. Carmody took the stairs to the second floor and found 2-E. He adjudged its location in reference to the building, then went back outside. The lights were on in 2-E's windows. He squatted in the shadows behind the cars and watched. He would wait until the lights in 2-E went out, or until he had to go meet Timmons.

Twenty-two minutes passed. The lights went out. Carmody edged toward the driveway entrance, still in the shadows behind the cars, watching the doorway to O'Neil's building. A man emerged. It looked like O'Neil, but now in work clothes instead of the sport jacket. The man headed for the car O'Neil had driven up in.

Carmody edged to the end of the drive. When the other man turned his back to get into his car, Carmody sprinted across the lighted mouth of the drive and down the street, around the corner to his Ford. Engine on, no headlights, he U-turned slowly to the corner, where he could get a view of O'Neil's car coming out of the drive. There it came. He followed it.

They were on the Meadowbrook again, and then Sunrise Highway headed east. When they came to the American Freightways terminal outside of Freeport, O'Neil headed to the gate. There was no guard on duty. O'Neil was driving toward the large, unlighted parking lot for cars on the left side of the building. The outside lights were all beamed toward the right side, where the trailers were parked. Carmody drove past to a diner, made a U-turn on the diner lot, waited several minutes, then headed back on Sunrise toward the terminal. He pulled into the unlit lot, headlamps off, and parked as far as he could from O'Neil's car. Several other cars pulled in and parked, their drivers going to the terminal building.

When the lot appeared quiet, Carmody got out of the Ford and slipped behind the rows of cars to O'Neil's. He kept careful watch on the gate, and when another car drove in he crouched low till it parked and the driver had gone into the freight terminal. Carmody continued on to O'Neil's car, opened the hood and yanked the ignition wires loose. Then he quietly closed the hood and returned to the Ford.

He waited. It started to rain, a hot, steamy, summer rain. By the time a few men left the terminal and went to the trucks, the windows were fogged and it was hard to see. The trucks, one by one, backed toward the freight dock, hidden from Carmody's view on the other side of the terminal. It would be difficult to try to probe further tonight. Besides, Carmody had already learned a lot, and it was after 3 a.m. There was barely time to make it to White Plains, where Timmons waited with million-dollar information.

2

Stanley Timmons waited at the wheel of his car in the alley behind the A & P, exactly as he had been told. But Timmons had been ten minutes early and now Carmody was 15 minutes late. All the time Timmons felt his adrenaline flowing faster. It had been raining for more than two hours, and though it had stopped the air was still steamy. But Timmons felt obliged to keep the windows up and the doors locked.

Every pair of auto headlights that swung in from the main road and ricocheted off the back of the A & P added to the eeriness. Maybe it was cops. Sooner or later he would come under suspicion, he didn't doubt that. But how would it look, how would he explain, if he was caught now, nosing around the Quincy grounds with an armed gangster. And maybe if he got caught before they pulled the swindle the mob wouldn't forgive him. There would be no way to pay back the $80,000, and maybe they'd kill him for it.

Now another car pulled into the alley facing his and stood for nearly a minute, its headlights on high-beam, nearly blinding Timmons. The headlights faded and he could see a man get out of the other car and walk toward his. A face appeared at his window.

"Hey, Stan, what have you got the goddamned windows rolled up for. It must be 85 out here." Timmons could tell the voice was Carmody's. He unlocked the door and opened it.

"Let's get a move on," Carmody said. "Sorry I'm late."

"What happened to your limo and the chauffeur?" Timmons asked, adopting Carmody's loud whisper.

"I don't use it in this kind of work," Carmody said. "Got to keep a low profile."

"You see any cops around?"

"Nah. Don't you worry now. Besides, even if somebody stops us, you're the treasurer, aren't you? You got a key. They got nothing to arrest us for."

"Yeah, but if I get stopped out here and then something goes wrong with the accounts it makes it pretty goddamned obvious who was responsible for it."

"That's why we parked at the A & P instead of the company lot, Stan. We're gonna do everything we can to protect you."

Carmody had them walking in the shadows, as far from the road as possible.

"I know they'll catch on eventually," Timmons said after awhile. "I don't expect to stay at Quincy much longer."

"That's smart, Stan. Go somewhere and have some fun."

"But there's no sense in their knowing right away. I'd like a chance to make my plans first, get out smoothly."

"Sure. That's why we're being careful. How long you been married, Stan?" Carmody asked.

"Twenty-one years."

"That's a long time for one woman. Lived in the same house all that time?"

"Nine years."

Carmody smiled and shook his head. Suddenly Timmons grabbed his arm. "That's a police car!" Timmons whispered.

"Just relax, Stan," Carmody said, pulling him along. "Just keep walking. We're not doing anything illegal. We're not going to do anything illegal all night. Just don't act suspicious."

The police car drove past, not even slowing down.

"Your kids must be pretty grown up by now," Carmody said.

"We have a daughter, eight."

"Just eight. Well, you'll still be able to see her. Even if you have to move west for awhile. They'll never prove anything on you. The problem's the damn women, you know? You leave for awhile and they start playing around."

Timmons didn't say anything.

"You think your wife's gonna play around if you leave for awhile?" Carmody asked.

"I don't know. I never gave it much thought."

"I think mine stayed clean a damn long time. Till just this year. Even while I was away for a year—I mean, if she did anything, at least she didn't flaunt it in front of the kids, you know? That's the worst part. When another man starts coming around in front of your own kids."

"I never gave it much thought," Timmons repeated. "Guess if I left she might go back to teaching."

The truth is, he decided, he didn't really give a damn what she did or who she lived with. It was over. He was too bored with her to care, and that was a large part of why he was walking along this highway at 4:30 in the morning, sneaking onto the grounds of the Quincy plant with a gun-toting gangster, preparing to cast aside a career and a way of life. For what, a little money? No. To get the hoods off his back? He had put those hoods on his back in the first place. This was the first time he had admitted it to himself: he had known what he was doing all along. He was getting rid of a woman and a job and a community that bored him. But he didn't say any of this to Carmody.

"You know, I was chasing that son of a bitch just tonight," Carmody said. "That's why I was late. I'm always on time, man. I believe in being on time. But that son of a bitch was parked in front of my house. With my wife in there. They weren't up in that bedroom, I know that, or I would have taken that son of a bitch—" Carmody calmed himself and smiled. "Well, hell, Stan, you don't want to hear about all that. You're lucky you got a wife you can trust."

They had reached the edge of the Quincy property, which was bordered by high shrubs. "Now you look through there," Carmody said, "and see if there's anything at all unusual."

Timmons did as he was instructed, and shook his head.

"Any sign of the watchman?" Carmody said.

"No," Timmons whispered, as much from fear as from a conscious effort to keep his voice quiet.

Carmody himself peeked through the shrubs. "Those hallway lights they've got on. They look about like that every night, do they?"

"I don't know."

Carmody looked at him quizzically.

"I'm not usually around here at four a.m.," Timmons explained.

Carmody grinned. "Maybe they'll be enough we won't need the lantern I brought. Your office, where all the check-writing stuff is, which side of the building is that on?"

Timmons hesitated. "The right side. The far side. I think," he said.

"You think good about it now and make sure."

"That's it," Timmons said.

"Okay. It's at an angle away from the highway. Nobody's going to see us unless they come looking. The key you got's for that front door?"

"Yes."

"Okay. The driveway's close. We'll walk straight through these bushes without going out to the highway. Just walk normally but fast, right up to the door. Get your key out first. Come on."

There was no sign that anyone saw them. The halls were lit at about half the daytime wattage and they had

no difficulty finding the financial department on the
fourth floor. Timmons led Carmody straight to the machine. "This is it," he said. "The ABMC-2000. This is
what writes our checks."

Carmody walked around the machine, studying it in
the dim light from the hall. He pulled the large flashlight
from his pocket and examined the machine more closely,
smiling at the challenge. "So this is that damn machine,"
he said, mostly to himself. "I've read about these in office
security magazines, but this is the first time I've ever seen
one."

He turned to Timmons. "They say it's foolproof. That's
the word they always like to use, foolproof. Well, you and
me are gonna bust that mother. Let me see what your
checks look like, Stanley."

Timmons went to the safe and opened it, the outside
door with a combination, the inside one with a key. He
pulled out a bundle of checks and took the top one. Carmody looked it over. "What's this?" he asked, pointing.

"That's the number of the check," Timmons said.
"Over here, this line is for the voucher number."

"So the checks are pre-numbered."

"We've always used pre-numbered checks, straight
from the printer. Saves time, insures no duplication."
Carmody stayed silent. "Is that good or bad?" Timmons
asked.

"Well, Stan, a little of both," Carmody said. He was
still examining the check. "It makes the check look safer
to the guy who's going to cash it, and to the banks that are
going to clear it, and to your bank that's going to pay it.
But it means that when we take a bundle of these things
to run through that machine on our own, anybody who
uses these checks is going to know that a bundle of them
is missing. And somebody could report it. How many
people go into this safe?"

"Oh, I don't know. There's five or six of us," Timmons
said.

"And if one of them wanted to report that some of these

checks were missing, would they have to go to you?"

"Well, not necessarily, because some of the account-ants' secretaries, they might go directly to their boss. And of course young Tom Quincy could go in."

Carmody thought about it. "I guess we'll just have to rely on you to satisfy them if anybody complains. Maybe a story . . ."

"Of course, there's no reason you really have to use these checks," Timmons said.

"You got others?"

"Oh, there's whole packages of them in a cabinet downstairs. A year's supply."

"You got a key to the cabinet, Stan?"

"No."

Carmody grimaced. "If we break in, it could leave traces and people could get alarmed. I guess we'll just have to be careful."

"Oh, you don't have to worry about that," Timmons said. "The cabinet isn't locked."

Carmody began to smile. "You aren't shitting me, Stan? There's a cabinet down there full of packages of pre-numbered checks, official Quincy Corporation checks, and it isn't locked?"

"That's right," Timmons said straight-faced. "We keep lots of things in there that people need. We don't lock it."

Carmody giggled quietly and slapped his fist into his hand. "Jesus Christ," he said. "Jesus Christ. Now who has these vouchers? Who writes them up and how do they get numbered?"

"Well, there's one of the accountants normally in charge of that. And a couple of the girls do a lot of the ac-tual writing. Of course, everything comes to me."

"Lemme see one of the vouchers," Carmody said.

Timmons led Carmody to his office, where he opened the filing cabinet and pulled out a monthly Morgan Guar-anty bank statement and a bundle of vouchers that matched the canceled checks.

"These vouchers are pre-numbered, too," Carmody said.

"Isn't that okay?" Timmons asked.

"It's okay. I'll just have to figure something out."

"What's the problem?"

"Well, Stan, if we're jumping ahead on the sequence of pre-numbered checks because we're getting them from downstairs, then we're also going to have to jump ahead on the voucher numbers or people will notice that the voucher numbers aren't matching the check numbers any more. Now with the checks, it's okay, because it takes a couple of months after they go out before the bank sends them back, and that gives us plenty of time. But the vouchers, see, they stay right here in the office. Now, just who keeps the vouchers?"

"But I don't see why you have to worry about vouchers at all—if all you want to do is run some checks through the machine."

"Stanley, look, every time that machine writes a check, it ticks it off, and the number of checks and the number of vouchers have to come out the same."

"No they don't." Timmons was calm, matter-of-fact, as Carmody grew excited.

"Stanley, I've read all about this machine."

"I don't care what you've read," Timmons said. "All I can tell you is what goes on here. The counter on that check-writing machine is never re-set."

Carmody stared in disbelief.

"We don't use the counter," Timmons repeated. "Nobody pays any attention to it. Enough people use the machine that even if somebody accidentally happened to remember the number on the counter had changed he wouldn't know but what somebody else had run off a bunch of checks."

"So nobody compares the number of checks and the number of vouchers."

"That's right."

"Jesus Christ." Carmody shook his head.

Then Timmons told him that the lock box was kept unlocked.

3

In an hour they had gone thoroughly over the cash accounting system. They ran a practice check through the machine for $999,999.99. Carmody was delighted with the machine's reproduction of the signature of Thomas S. Quincy Jr. He put the check in his pocket for future study, while Timmons voided the stub so it would appear on the records as a routine error. Timmons led Carmody on a tour of the storeroom where the check supply was kept.

Now they were walking back along the highway to where the cars were parked. The sky had only the first hint of greyness off to the east.

"You know," Timmons said, "in all the years I've worked here I never understood how easy it would be to steal money."

"It's only easy if you know what you're doing, Stan. There's more to it than just writing these checks. I got to get them cashed, you know."

"I thought you had a banker all set up, out in Montana or somewhere."

"Oh, I got him all right. I'm just telling you it takes a lot of doing."

Timmons sensed that Carmody was already setting him up for a smaller cut of the money. "How much are you going to take them for?" he asked.

"Well, it looks like your balance stays just about under five million."

"We're raising it to eight."

"Oh?"

"I just got orders this morning from young Tom. Couple of new projects bid out in Long Island, and we're to work the balance up to eight million by the end of August."

"You ought to tell me these things, Stan. No, I guess I should have asked."

"So how much are you going to take and how are you going to divide it?"

Carmody grinned. "There's going to be a nice cut of money in there for you, Stan. Don't you start getting greedy now too fast. Remember the first $80,000 of your share is saving your neck. There'll be a nice cut left over in cash for you, don't you worry."

They walked on and Timmons didn't respond.

"Remember," Carmody continued, "we can't take all the money out of there. We don't want to run the account into the red and put them onto what we're doing before we get everything put away safe. I'm going to leave enough in that account that it will be a couple of months before your friend Quincy finds out the rest is gone. And another thing you got to remember, these guys we're dealing with, they're greedy, too. You got us in with those guys, Stan. They're gonna want a hell of a lot more than your $80,000 out of this, I can tell you that."

Timmons looked alarmed.

"Well, don't you worry," Carmody said. "You and I can have plenty of times in Vegas on what we're going to take down. It'll be better retirement than Social Security for you."

"What's going to happen when they find out the money's been stolen?" Timmons asked.

"Stan, they'll never be able to prove a thing. I am just too goddamned careful."

"That's easy for you to say. They won't know who you are. Me, well, there'll be just a handful of people who could have helped this thing from the inside. And when I leave—"

"Stan, now there's where you're wrong," Carmody said. "There you are just completely wrong, because they are going to know who I am long before they ever suspect who you are. They will be on my trail the first day. But I'm not worried because I can beat them."

"How are they going to know you?"

"Stan, you got to understand the government before you can beat them. I can tell you . . . I can tell you exactly which FBI agent is going to be assigned to this case when Quincy reports it. His name is Frank Scanlon. And as soon as he gets the first hint of what happened, he is going to know that I did it."

Timmons looked at him incredulously.

"He is going to know I did it, but he is not going to be able to prove a thing. And maybe he'll get down to where—I mean, probably he won't, but just maybe he'll get down to where he's certain in his mind that you were the inside man on the deal. He won't be able to touch you, Stan. Because no matter how sure he gets, he won't be able to build a case that the U.S. attorneys would be willing to take to a jury. I am just too goddamned careful, believe me. You know that stock deal we were talking about at lunch the other day? That one in Denver? Hell, Stan, I broke—well, hell, to pull that deal off there were half a dozen federal laws had to be broken. And Scanlon knew it. Hell, he came out to my house and told me he knew. But there was nothing he could do. Not a damn thing. Because I just didn't leave any fucking evidence. And it will be the same way this time, too. You are in good hands, Stan, my boy."

They reached the cars. Carmody put his hand on the executive's shoulder. "Now you just sit tight," he said. "When I get everything set up, I'll be back in touch with you. We'll set up a meeting just like this, this same spot, same time, exactly the way we did tonight. We'll go get a package of checks. I'll have a payee company all set up to make the checks out to. Quincy does a lot of subcontracting to construction outfits—they're all over your cancelled checks, construction outfits—so that's just what

I'm going to set up, a construction company for the checks to be made out to. And we'll run the checks through the machine. I'll have it all worked out. Now— you understand what I'm saying?"

Timmons nodded.

"Now this is very important. When we're ready to roll, we have got to roll fast. Now I want you to keep those bank balances in mind, so when the time comes, you know just how much is going to be in there. And try to get a line on how the company is going to spend money out of that account. I mean I don't want to draw those checks and walk in someplace to cash them and have Morgan Guaranty shoot back that the account's just been drained. Right?"

Timmons nodded again.

"Now, I also want you to keep track of what voucher numbers they're using every day. Because I want the phony voucher numbers we put on those checks to look just like they would if old Tom Quincy had authorized them himself. And the numbers on the checks, too. We have to get a package of checks that isn't too far out of line with what they're using now, but on the other hand I don't want somebody going down to that supply room the week after we write those checks and saying, hey, there's a package of checks missing, I can't find the next set of numbers. We want to know the numbers we're using are like three months ahead."

"I understand," Timmons said. "Don't worry."

"Now"—Carmody reached into his pocket for pencil and paper—"now, I'm going to give you a phone number. This isn't my number, but it's somebody who sees me sometimes and can get me a message. Now when the Fibbies suspect something, they're going to go into everybody's phone records. They may even tap your phone. So don't call this number unless there's a real problem. Unless you absolutely have to."

Timmons nodded again.

"And if you got to call, just say your name is Fred. Fred, got it? But don't call unless you really have to. It'll just be one more thing they can trace."

Carmody opened the car door for Timmons. "Now you take care," he said. He walked slowly toward his own car, fading into the steamy summer night. "You just remember all I told you, and I'll get in touch with you soon. Maybe a few weeks. As soon as I get everything set up. We're going to have us a real sweet deal here if you just remember everything I said."

CHAPTER NINE

1

Actually, the first time I stuck one to Mickey Carmody in my official role as an FBI agent, I didn't even know Carmody was involved. I certainly had no idea that what I was doing would provide an ironic footnote to the Quincy caper. It was last July and I had just returned from vacation when the assistant S.A.C. told me I had better go downtown to see this lawyer who was absolutely livid over a $1,350,000 rubber check.

"What kind of shit is this?" the lawyer asked over and over, goosestepping behind a nine-foot teak desk and stabbing the air with his uncollectable paper treasure. I finally calmed him down enough to get his story and take a look at the check, which appeared to be a duly certified cashier's draft issued by no less an institution than the Gully National Bank of Circle, Montana.

He said he had accepted the check on behalf of a client, in exchange for the client's textile mill in Raleigh, North Carolina. The mill had been turned over to the buyer two weeks ago. Since then the $80,000 in cash reserves had been drained and the accounts receivable had been used to collateralize a $400,000 bank loan. Most of the loan proceeds had been suddenly withdrawn. And the son of a bitch who gave him the check and took the mill seemed to have disappeared. Now the client was stuck with a bankrupt textile mill and a bounced check for $1.35 million.

Not believing that a bank could refuse collection on its own certified cashier's draft, the lawyer had put calls in to Circle, Montana. He was told that the check had been issued only on condition that supporting funds were in turn collected as promised from a bank in the Bahamas. The bank in the Bahamas had declined payment on *its* check. So Gully National was following suit. Futhermore, Gully National had told the lawyer, he should not have assumed the check was guaranteed; it had been marked clearly on its face, "Hold pending collections."

"Now what the hell kind of language is that on a certified cashier's check," the lawyer wanted to know. "Hold pending collections. I never heard of such a thing." Besides which, he said, he hadn't seen any such notation on the check when the son of a bitch had given it to him. Then he looked at the damn thing under a magnifying glass and sure enough, there had been an erasure. The son of a bitch had swindled him, he insisted.

I told him he was probably right and asked if he could remember the son of a bitch's name.

"Well, the name he gave me was J.F. Gomez, but that's probably a phony. He was supposed to be from Puerto Rico, but I can't find a trace of him there."

"Did he call himself *Doctor* Gomez?" I asked. The lawyer looked at me, a bit taken aback. "And did he say he was the heir to a tobacco fortune down there?"

"Yeah," said the lawyer, astonished. "How did you know?"

"Oh, that's Julio," I said with a smile.

"Hoolio?"

"Julio Gomez-Weinberger. *Doctor* Gomez-Weinberger, the footloose podiatrist."

"Gomez-Weinberger?"

"Well, his father was supposedly from Latin America. Obviously he got Spanish blood in him from somewhere. But he was raised in New York by his mother, Dorothy Weinberger. And you know how the Spanish are with hyphenated names from both sides of the family. People just tease him about it that way." The lawyer looked stupefied. "The doctor part is from podiatry school," I went on. "Look, why don't you come back to the office with me and try to identify some pictures so we're sure. Bring the check so we can take a study of that. Do you have any papers—samples of handwriting, anything the guy gave you besides the check?"

2

It was Gomez, all right—the photos and handwriting both nailed him. I took down the client's name and other data.

"If you knew all along this guy was a con man, why didn't you arrest him?" the lawyer demanded.

"People always ask me that after they've been swindled," I said. "Actually, Gomez did have a collar on him in Houston for awhile. That was back in March or April, when this bank deal of his collapsed. It was one of these affairs where you set up a one-room office in the Bahamas and advertise in the international press that you can give people a tax shelter."

"And then the bank folded?"

"Well, those things are kind of planned," I explained. "You take in the money, you arrange to lend it out to some little company that you or your friends have set up in another country, and then you don't repay the loan. So the depositors can't get their money back, the Bahamian authorities close down your bank and you take off."

"And Gomez took off for the U.S. Why didn't you arrest him then?"

"For what? Violation of the Bahamian banking laws? We did keep an eye on him. We knew he was carrying some of these Bahamian bank checks around. But there was nothing we could do until somebody turned him in for trying to use one. We heard he was going to pull a deal in Houston and our office down there got the local police to pick him up at the airport on a vagrancy charge. But when they brought him to the station and had him empty out his pockets he had $325,000 in cash and a $250,000 certificate of deposit on him, so the judge threw out the vagrancy charge and that was the last we saw of Dr. Gomez."

"Well, can you send out some kind of warrant for him now?"

"Sure. We'll do something. But if I know Gomez, he's in Europe now. Or maybe South America. Hell, with all that money, wouldn't you be? And even if we got him, even if he walked into this office right now and said, 'I'm Dr. Gomez, what can I do for you?', I'm not sure we could arrest him. What would the charge be?"

"Grand theft."

"In the first place, that's not a federal crime. And in the second place, all he took was money from the textile mill, which he owned. Your client sold it to him."

"Sold it to him for a worthless check."

"So Gomez will say he thought the check was good. He'll say it's the bank's fault."

"But Gomez tampered with the check," the lawyer said.

"Prove it. The check's not even made out in his name. It's in the name of Metropolitan Development Company."

"But Gomez *owns* Metropolitan Development Company."

"Does that prove he altered the check? Look," I said, "I'm not trying to give you a hard time. That's just the way these guys operate. If you think you're frustrated, remember, I do this for a living. I see hundreds of thousands of dollars stolen all the time and nobody ever goes to jail for it." He stopped arguing.

"We'll open a file on this," I assured him. "I'll notify our office in Raleigh, and they'll go see your man. If the mill really does go into bankruptcy maybe we can get some kind of federal bankruptcy fraud charge that will stick against Gomez. If we ever find Gomez. Just remember that your client turned over his factory on a moment's notice to a complete stranger."

"Gomez said he needed the mill as assets for some kind of financing package he was putting together July 1."

"Sure," I told him. "Gomez is always in a hurry. But your client must have wanted that money awfully bad, too, or thought he was getting an awfully good deal. A little prudence might have avoided this."

"Prudence? How can you erase a hold notice that's written clearly on the face of a check? I thought checks were supposed to be designed so they'd void themselves if there's an erasure."

"You know, that's an interesting story," I said. "Gomez has done this before. See, he doesn't really erase the check. He uses a scalpel, a surgical scalpel. He shaves it, very carefully, under magnification. And do you know where he learned to do that? In podiatrist's school. It's the same technique they use to shave bunions."

I laughed and finally forced a smile out of the lawyer, too. "This guy's really a practicing foot doctor?" the lawyer asked.

"Used to be. He was licensed in California, but they took his license away 10 years ago when he went to jail for a commodities futures fraud."

"So he's got a record."

"Everybody slips up once. He got an early parole."

"Look, what about the banker," the lawyer said. "The guy in Montana. Can't you do something about him? How did he get involved with Gomez? And this business of 'hold pending collections'—is that legal?"

"I doubt we can arrest the banker, either," I said. "See, every con man needs a banker. Sometimes they bribe one. Sometimes the banker has been looking around for a deal, because he's in debt. Sometimes the Mob gets influence over the banker and he's afraid they'll break his neck. But whatever happens, it's hard to prove to a jury that the banker has knowingly gone along with the fraud. Juries just don't understand that if you put 'hold pending collection' on the front of a cashier's draft you have to know you're doing something wrong."

He was still clearly dissatisfied. "Look," I said, "I'll notify our Montana office, and also the Comptroller of the Currency's office. At least we'll embarrass the hell out of your banker by investigating him in front of his outside directors. Maybe he won't do any more of this shit for awhile. If you want to proceed civilly against him, that's your business. I wish you luck."

I don't know whether the lawyer ever did sue the president of old Gully National. I did learn later, however, that when federal agents marched into Circle about the end of July and started gathering up the records of the local bank, it really gave Michael Carmody fits.

CHAPTER TEN

1

"That dumbbell. That shithead," Carmody said and slapped the wall.

Dr. Sybil Manwaring smiled and calmly took another sip of coffee as her husband, who would in a matter of weeks be her ex-husband, threw himself into an armchair.

Dr. Manwaring put the *New England Journal of Medicine* down next to her on the couch and picked up *The New York Times.* "So another million dollar deal goes by the wayside," she said. "You'll find more, Mickey."

"Do you remember Gomez?" he went on. "You gotta remember Gomez. Tall, black hair, mustache." She was shaking her head, still smiling, looking down at the *Times.* Carmody kept trying to remind her. "He looks like one of those European movie stars. We ate at Patsy's on 57th Street. It was just after I got out—"

"Mickey, I can't remember one of those guys from another. There were so many."

"He somehow got this banker, my banker, to issue him a check for a million, three hundred thousand or so, and Gomez doesn't have any money. He says he's getting it from the Bahamas. My banker, he's an honest guy, naturally he puts conditions on the face of the check, you know, so Gomez can't cash it. And Gomez, the son of a bitch, scrapes the conditions off with a razor blade or something—"

"Oh, if this banker's such an honest guy, what's he dealing with you for?" She threw him a glance and a small laugh and turned to the book review page.

"Sybil, this was legitimate. This guy is the president of a large bank out west and we were setting up financing for one of the biggest companies in America. Don't laugh, damn it." He stood up and began pacing again. "This is a major company, on the New York Stock Exchange. If I could tell you the name of it, I guarantee you'd have heard of it. I've got to find a bank."

"If this is such a legitimate deal, why can't you go ahead with the same banker you had? What does this Gomez thing have to do with it?"

"Jesus Christ, this Gomez thing almost caused the bank to fold."

"A major bank—because of a million-dollar check that wasn't even cashed?"

"Well, maybe not fold. But they're gonna get sued over it. They've got government examiners crawling all over them now. Between the government and the board of directors, the guy who was working on this deal for me is so tied up he can't even get a dime to make a phone call."

She dropped the newspaper onto her lap and looked up at him, her voice still controlled. "Oh, Mickey, for God's sake, how dumb do you think I am? We've known each other ten years. You think I'm so stupid I don't know what kind of deals you're into?"

"Hey," he said gently, and walked toward her. He sat on the arm of the couch and put a hand on her shoulder.

"You know I never thought I could pull any wool over your eyes. The only few times I tried I couldn't get away with it. I'm still crazy about you."

Her smile broadened and she brushed his hand away.

"Look," he said, "when I get this deal arranged and I get these commissions, I'm going to set up a trust fund for the kids. You and the kids. I ought to be contributing more and I know it."

"If you want to set up something for the kids, fine, but I'm not asking you or expecting you to contribute anything to this house," she said. Her voice seemed a little choked and Carmody thought he saw a mist in her eyes. Her emotions, he told himself again, were hard to read. "There's nothing in the settlement about your paying anything," she said. "I'm making a good living and we're doing okay."

"But you're not making as much as the other surgeons make. The men. That bothers you. I know it." His voice was deliberately soothing. "And you're not making as much as I do when things are going well. I know you're not happy there at the hospital. You want to move. And you ought to be able to."

His hand had fallen onto her shoulder again, and again she pushed it gently away. "Come on," she said. "We'll be divorced in another few weeks. Look, the kids will be home any minute and if you're going to call your friend Connally I want you to do it before they come. They're getting old enough to understand the kind of thing you guys talk about."

"Oh, Christ, Sybil, I haven't seen Bill Connally since—" He left the sentence dangling, and she finished it.

"Since Green Haven. That's why I don't want you talking to him in front of the children. In fact, call him from the bedroom, in case they come home."

"When did he call?" Carmody asked.

"Yesterday. The day before. He's called three times

and says it's important. Believe me, I wasn't about to ask him the subject matter. Where is old Bill living these days, anyway? Ossining? Attica?"

Carmody got up and gave her a scornful look. "As a matter of fact, the last I heard he was living in Atlanta."

She laughed out loud and fell away from him on the couch.

"God damn it," he said. "There's more places to live in Atlanta than the federal prison. And don't give me any more of that crap about how holy you are and how you never knew what I was doing for a living right along. You knew goddamn well what kind of deals I was in, as much as you wanted to know. You aren't dumb, Sybil. And you sure weren't ashamed to live off of it."

Her look turned cold, but he thought he detected hurt in it. He wanted her to feel as wounded as he felt. He ripped the number off the telephone pad and ran up the stairs to the bedroom. He stopped. He sat on the bed, his hand on the phone. Just sitting there made him think of his wife's body and how it looked lying there, the red nipples pointing up at his eyes. There was a headboard of brass bars, and he recalled as if it were happening now the way she had raised her arms over her head and grasped those bars when they were making love, eyes closed, her face looking almost pained in its ecstasy, as if she was handcuffed there, his willing prisoner. Surely she wasn't doing the same for another man, not this O'Neil. Fucking, maybe, yes, but not holding those brass bars, not with the same look.

He heaved the thoughts out of his mind and dialed the number Connally had left. It was a Nashville area code. Nobody answered.

He put the phone down and ran his hand over the brass bars. Suddenly he was seized with a desire to see what nightgown she had been wearing. He went to the closet and looked on the hook inside the door, where she always hung it. It was white, filmy, not one he knew. And draped over it, on the hook, was a red paisley necktie. Michael Carmody had never owned a red paisley necktie.

He grabbed the tie and ran down the stairs in a rage. "What's this doing here?" he demanded. "What is this?"

"Mickey, for Christ's sake, have you been going through my closet?"

"Your closet? This house is still half in my name, you know. And when did you start wearing neckties?"

She sat back down with the paper, not answering.

"Are you fucking around with that O'Neil guy with our children in here?"

"Mickey—" she put the paper aside. "We're getting a divorce. You've been seeing other women. You've even told me about Barbara. You can't expect me to live like a nun the rest of my life."

"But with our children in here?"

"I have never done anything to disgrace or dishonor you in front of the children. I've never criticized you in front of them. I've even blamed myself—"

"But what about this O'Neil?"

"We're friends. The children know we're close friends. We don't carry on physically in front of them. It doesn't have any reflection on you and they don't see it as having any reflection on you. Mickey, it's not inconceivable that someday Don and I will get married."

"Oh, Jesus Christ. It's not inconceivable. Jesus, you think you're going to marry this guy? He's a truck driver."

"You drove a truck, too, Mickey. Remember?"

"Oh, come on. That wasn't what I—that wasn't what I *did*. I mean, I drove a truck for awhile because I didn't want you and your friends to think I didn't have a job. But that wasn't what I *did*. I always had business. I could always earn more money than you did."

"Maybe Don has a mind for things besides truck driving, too. Did you ever think of that?"

"Come on, Sybil. He drives a four-year-old car. He

lives in a crumby garden apartment stuck in the middle
of some parking lot over in the cheap section of East
Meadow. He drives a night shift—"

"How do you know all this?" She was up off the couch
and for the first time her voice had lost its calm. "How do
you know all this? My God, have you been following him
around?"

"I know a lot of things, Sybil. I'm not stupid either.
You think I'm not going to find out about a man who's
hanging around my children?"

"Mickey, please, please don't do anything to spoil
this."

"You think I want my children to see my wife marrying
a man, a guy trying to take my place as their father, who
can't bring in money any better than to live in that mangy
apartment?"

"Mickey, please don't say anything to Don about
money." She was pleading now. "It would hurt him.
Please, if you care anything about me at all, don't make
him feel worse about the money."

They were quiet a minute as Carmody eased out of his
rage. "That bothers him, huh? That you make more
money?" It was a note of triumph.

"Sure it bothers him. Just like it probably bothered
you."

"Oh, now what does that mean?"

She walked to the window and looked out. "Didn't you
ever consider that maybe the reason you'd do anything
for money is that you knew your wife was in a respected
profession and she'd always be earning a lot of income?
Didn't you ever consider that?"

"Christ, Sybil. That's the most ridiculous thing you've
ever said. I was in Green Haven before I ever met you, remember?"

"Oh, Mickey." She turned to him and came closer. "I
don't want Don to feel that pressure, at least any more

than he has to. Don't make it worse on him, Mickey. Please. I really think I love him. Please try to understand. If you care for me, then help him. Don't make him feel worse."

"That's a laugh. Maybe I ought to set him up in business."

"He doesn't want charity. Or need it. What you ought to give him is some kind of respect. I don't want to go through hell between the two of you every time you want to see the children."

"What I really ought to do is set him up in a good con."

"Don't make jokes."

"Why not? Then we'd all be rich. No pressure. And he'd have done it on his own. After all, the guy must have some sort of brains, or why would a smart girl like you want to marry him, right?"

He was smiling slyly at her, and she saw something in his eyes that she had seen years ago. She burst out laughing. "Oh, Jesus," she said. "You'll never change, will you?"

Just then the door opened quickly and two children rushed in, calling, "Daddy's here! Daddy's here!" and hurled themselves at Mickey Carmody, their arms wide.

2

That evening on the way back to Brooklyn, Carmody stopped at a phone booth on the Sunrise Highway and tried the Nashville number again. This time Bill Connally answered.

"What are you doing in Nashville—they open up a new pen there or something?"

"Cut the crap, Mickey. Listen—"

"What were you doing down in Atlanta, anyway? I mean, how come you keep getting caught?"

"Treasury bills. It was just Treasury bills."

Carmody laughed, and the voice on the line spluttered, "God damn it, I didn't know—how was I supposed to know they were hot?"

"Yeah. Some guy just walked up to you on the street and offered you eight T-bills at ten cents on the dollar. And they're all from the lot Tony Snorkles pulled out of the Chase Manhattan in 1972, which was about the worst blown heist in history."

"I didn't know—"

"Those serial numbers were printed in every newspaper in the country within a week, and you come along two years later—my God, Billy, I wouldn't have wiped my ass with those things. You got to be careful—"

"Listen. I got a deal. You want to hear it or not? I mean you can just kiss off if all you're going to do is—"

"Go ahead, go ahead. What've you got?"

"Is your phone safe?"

"I'm in some goddamned paybooth at some railroad station out on Long Island for Christ's sake. Now what's on your mind?"

"Okay, look. I met this guy in Atlanta, a real cracker. His name's Ellis Bardell. He's like out of a comic strip somewhere. A big prick. In for moonshining."

"Come on. Moonshining?"

"Mickey, you got to understand about Atlanta. This is one crazy prison. You got all these New York con men and some midwestern bank robbers and then you got a dozen or two dozen guys in all the time for moonshining. It's big business down here."

"Jesus. Okay, so what's the deal. We're gonna sell warehouse receipts on bootleg whiskey? Like we did with that cow piss they had stored over in Scotland a few years ago?"

"No. Now listen. He's got these other brothers, see? Everybody down here's got big families. They're all cousins to one another. In fact one of this Ellis Bardell's brothers, Pete, got busted in the same moonshine raid, but they gave him probation. Okay, anyway, so they got this other brother, Abner."

"Abner? Come on, Billy. Not Abner."

"No shit. And this Abner—"

"Where are these guys from, anyway? Dogpatch?"

"Mostly around Crockett County, Tennessee. Little town there called Caliquatta is the county seat. Now listen, this Abner"—Carmody was laughing—"this Abner is one, a deputy sheriff—"

"Oh, Christ, man, you got to be kidding."

"—and two, a director of the Caliquatta National Bank." At the word "bank," Carmody turned serious.

"Now the president of this bank," Connally went on, "he's really into this guy Abner."

"The brother of these moonshiners?"

"Yeah. Listen, you got to understand these people. These moonshiners are bankrolled by this bank. They take out regular loans to buy their sugar and stuff. Now listen, this thing sounds ripe. The president of this bank is seventy-one years old, he's run the thing for practically fifty years and he's gonna retire soon. Now this Ellis told me when I got out to call him, and he'll set up a meeting with this Abner. So I did. We got together in this motel somewhere near Nashville. That's where I am now. I'm still hanging out here. If we can get some paper, Mickey, we can really cash in. We can buy this little bank president. For a percent, he'll take anything. I mean it. I need paper. T-bills, anything you can get that's not too hot."

"Oh holy lordy Mary mother of God," Carmody whispered to himself.

"Can you get ahold of anything?"

Carmody paused and gathered himself together. He didn't want Connally to know how sweet it was. He would have to get Connally to settle for a fee, not a percentage. There were too many percentages to the deal already.

"I think I can get something," Carmody said. "Yeah, definitely. How long you gonna be there?"

"Whenever you can get some stuff."

"Now, Billy, I think I can lay my hands on something. But it may have to be quiet, you know? Like I may have to deal directly with this Abner myself."

"Hey, what are you trying to do, cut me out?"

"Not gonna cut you out, man. You know that. I'm just in partners with these guys up here now, and I think they can supply me something, but the only way they'll do it is on a fee basis. I mean, they'll know what it's worth, they'll know everything about it, and they won't give up a cut."

"What kind of a deal is this?" Connally sounded highly suspicious.

"Listen, Billy. I'm into Ruggiardo now. I can't tell you how it happened. But if I do this, I got to do it through him. Now I can come up with something. Maybe it will get us a few hundred thousand. But it belongs to Ruggiardo's people. All I may be able to get is my fee. Now how could you do with, say, ten—no, say, twenty thousand or so?"

"Mickey, damn it, I found this deal."

"Okay. Maybe we can work it up to twenty-five or so. Remember, it'll be all my risk from now on. You'll be out of it."

"Out of it, my ass. I got the deal. I handle the money."

"Billy, hey, you can—in the first place, you fucked up with Ruggiardo's guys once before. You can't handle their paper. They wouldn't stand for it."

"Well, who's gonna handle it? You?"

"Don't worry about it now. Let me try to line up some paper and I'll figure something."

"Fuck, you'll figure something. You find some paper and I'll cash it. Why are you all of a sudden gonna run the show?"

"Billy, for Christ's sake. You and me are both too well

known, right? The FBI'll figure us right off. I'll find
somebody clean to handle the paper and we won't let
anybody from the bank see you or me. We'll just get our
cut."

"Goddamn it, if—"

"This is my kind of job. There's got to be no identification. I'll make sure somebody clean handles the money.
You and I'll get our cuts."

"I don't like bringing nobody into this. There's too
many people into this money already. I want to know
who."

"I don't know."

"Don't fuck around with me, Mickey."

"Listen, we'll work it out when I find the stuff. Trust
me. You know I'll do it safe. You do it with me, you won't
go back to Atlanta. Now don't you call anybody else,
okay? I'll get back to you real soon. A couple of days.
Now you won't call anybody else, okay?"

"I'll give you a few days. But I got to have at least
twenty-five if this is a winner."

"That's cutting me all to hell, but I'll do it, Billy."

"And that's just for me. You're also going to have to
take care of this Abner. And the bank president. And
they're going to want plenty."

"I'll handle it, Billy. Now you just sit tight."

"Yeah."

"Oh, and one more thing. Can you find out what you
have to do to register a company in Nashville? Do you
have to file legal papers, or can you just register your
trade name somewhere? Oh, and how long does it take to
get a phone listing?"

CHAPTER ELEVEN

All right, I should have pursued it. I shouldn't have passed it off the way I did. But considering the circumstances, and considering exactly what I knew about Mickey Carmody at the time, I don't think I have any reason to be ashamed of how I reacted when Dr. Sybil Manwaring came to see me at the FBI office on East 69th Street in late September. She had called and said it was important. I offered to go up to the hospital, but she preferred to come to my office.

"The divorce came through. Mickey's not my husband any more," she told me.

"I assume that calls for congratulations," I said.

She smiled languidly. "It would if it was really over. But Mickey doesn't want anything to change. He doesn't want to recognize that I'm independent now."

"Well," I said. "I'm sorry."

"Mr. Scanlon, there's a man I've been seeing recently, a man I may even want to marry. And Mickey's threatened to kill him."

"Wow."

"It's happened a couple of times now. The most recent was at my house just last night. It was Don's birthday and I had him over for dinner, and my mother was there, and of course my children—Mickey's children. And he just barged in. He saw Don's car out front—he's always driving by looking for Don's car. Mr. Scanlon, he spies on us. He's followed Don to his house, to his job. . . ."

"What did he say last night?"

"Well, he told Don—well, at first, he said to me, like, what's he doing here? He, meaning Don. See, you've got to understand how Mickey can go into these rages. I know how smooth and charming he can seem, and that's the way he's been when he's talking to you, but he can be like an animal."

"Go on with what happened."

"I told him please not to interfere. It was just a little birthday party. And he said, 'But this is my house.' And I said, 'Mickey, it's not your house,' you know, that the divorce had come through and that I got the house. And all the time he's giving Don these menacing looks, and the children were quite upset by it because they *love* Mickey, and he just doesn't act like this in front of them. And I know that Mickey carries a gun, and Don knows it, and Don knows that Mickey's followed him. Don's scared. He doesn't want to get into a fight with Mickey. He doesn't know what to do."

"Did Mickey say anything to Don?"

"Well, finally, he said something like, 'You better watch the shadows when you go home tonight,' and 'Don't you let Sybil around when you start your car,' and 'Don't you dare take my children in your car 'cause it may be wired,' and so forth. Always stopping just short of 'I'll kill you.' But we knew what he meant. Don knew. Finally he just said to Don, 'I wouldn't like to be your life insurance company right now,' and walked out."

"Did you say anything?"

"Mr. Scanlon, I was crying. I didn't know what to say."

"Why don't you try calling the police? You know, this isn't really a federal matter."

"I've called the police twice now," she said. "Once when it happened before. They said he probably hadn't broken any laws. That he hadn't literally threatened to kill anybody, and why don't we just cool off, you know. These family things happen all the time. Well, they just don't know Mickey."

"What did they say when you called them again?"

"Well, I tried to find the same officer, so he'd know this wasn't the first time it had happened, but I couldn't. They just said there wasn't anything any of them could do. If I wanted to they said I could come down to the municipal building in Baldwin and sign a complaint, and they'd give Mickey a summons and have a court hearing about it."

"I know that's not a very palatable solution, but maybe you should consider it anyway," I said.

"Oh, the only way they could serve a summons on Mickey is when he's there in Baldwin, at the house. You know, in front of the children. That would be an awful scene. And besides, you know Mickey. It wouldn't have any effect on him—unless it just made matters worse. He'd be furious."

"Well, what is it you want *me* to do?"

"Can't you talk to him? Make him understand that this is wrong, and that if anything happens to Don everyone will know who did it?"

"Why can't the local police do that? It's not my job."

"But they won't. They say it's just one of these family squabbles that happen all the time. Mr. Scanlon, you know what Mickey's like. They don't. Please talk to him for me."

I thought a minute. "It won't do any good," I said. "All I can tell him is that you came to see me, and what you said, and he'll just reply that it's none of my business, and it isn't. I know that might sound callous, but let's

face it. I'm an FBI agent. I'm not a Baldwin policeman,
I'm not a psychiatrist, I'm not even Ann Landers."
     She looked down, disappointed. "Okay, Mr. Scanlon.
Thank you," she said in a low voice, and rose to go.
     Suddenly I was staring at myself. You lout, you are be-
ing callous. "Okay, wait a minute," I said. "I'll call him.
I'll try to get to him this afternoon, and I'll keep trying
until I do."
     "Thank you," she said. We were both standing, look-
ing at each other. Carmody had known a poised, good-
looking woman when he saw one, neurosurgeon or not.
     "But you've got to understand that what I told you is
just what will happen," I said. "He'll politely tell me it's
none of my business, and he's absolutely right. Mickey
knows how we work. He knows what he can do and what
we can do. Even if he had actually pulled a knife out last
night and taken a swipe at this man, and you called me,
all I could do is call the Baldwin police and tell them the
same thing you'd tell them."
     "I know," she said. "Thank you."
     "Is he still at that place in Brooklyn?" I started fum-
bling through my card file, and she gave me the number
from memory.
     "You want me to call Don, too?" I said. "Maybe I
could suggest he take a little vacation, get out of town for
awhile. Maybe things would cool off."
     "No," she said. "He's taken his vacation this year. He
was out of town just not long ago for awhile. That doesn't
do any good."
     "Okay," I said. "You haven't heard Mickey talking
about any deals lately, have you?"
     I didn't get an answer and looked up in time to catch
her worried expression. "I guess I asked that at the wrong
time," I said. "It's not a price. You don't have to answer.
I'll call you after I talk to Mickey."
     "That's okay," she said. "If I knew anything, I'd tell
you. It's like always, you know? There's a deal going this

week, another one next week. I try not to pay any attention."

"I understand."

"He has been talking recently about some bank out west," she offered. "Some kind of financing deal involving some bank out west."

"Did he ever say where? Which bank?"

"If he did, I don't recall. I honestly don't."

I got Carmody on the phone an hour later. The conversation went exactly as I had predicted.

CHAPTER TWELVE

1

A warm October sun poured out of a blue sky onto the streets of Caliquatta, Tennessee. It was a pretty town. The trees were taller than the buildings. A light wind blew occasional swirls of dust up from alongside the ragged edge of the tarmac that was called Main Street. Some of the dust settled on the steps of the First National Bank, right across Main from the railroad station.

Inside the bank two overalled farmers chatted with a woman teller while she handled a deposit for one of them. At the other tellers' cage, Danny McGinn, the young assistant cashier, had already returned the passbook and $40 to Will Puterbaugh, but he was trying to convince Puterbaugh to stick around.

"I tell ya, he's gotta be comin' by this afternoon sometime," McGinn said, in low tones so as not to be overheard. "That armored truck come in from Nashville again this morning. Every dang time that means ol' Portaquil comes by the same day. You just watch."

Puterbaugh rubbed a hand around the open collar of his shirt and chuckled. "Well, I'd love to see it," he said. "But I got to get back to the office. Got two people maybe wants life insurance, and then that dang Haigley kid got his arm caught in the combine. I got a hell of a claim over that."

"You just wait. Betcha it won't be five minutes," McGinn said. "Look there, right now."

A stranger walked through the door of the bank dressed in a flashy plaid suit and brightly flowered tie. He wore large steel-rimmed eyeglasses that seemed reflective a lot of the time, yet still permitted an occasional glimpse of narrow, almost oriental eyes. The stranger had bushy hair and a Fu Manchu mustache that drooped around both sides of his mouth. He carried an oversized leather briefcase, really more the size of a suitcase, that sagged from its emptiness. He approached McGinn. Puterbaugh moved aside in awe. The two farmers began to giggle. McGinn flashed a look of annoyance to the woman teller who shushed the farmers. Two clerks on the opposite side of the room from the teller's counter looked up from their work. Everyone's eyes were on the stranger.

"Howdy, Mr. Portaquil," McGinn said. "Back already, huh? You want me to go tell Mr. Peerce?"

The stranger nodded.

McGinn made a move out from around the tellers' counter, then stopped. "Hey," he said to the stranger in friendly fashion, "would you mind tellin' me again where this new interchange is gonna go? Folks keep askin' me and I don't know what to tell 'em." He said it loud enough for Puterbaugh to hear.

"Well, now, that's going to be up to the highway department," the stranger said. His accent was northern, not of a kind with the others in the room.

"But you're gonna build the thing," McGinn said.

"Well, actually, my company's going to build a shopping center by where the interchange is," the stranger replied.

"Well, gol dang, a new shopping center. Right here in Caliquatta?"

The stranger nodded. "Crockett County," he said. "I didn't say it was necessarily going to be in Caliquatta."

"Well, where else in Crockett County would you put it?" McGinn said, obviously puzzled. "They's just mostly chicken farms and stuff out there."

The stranger gave a slight smile. One side of his mustache seemed to droop more than the other. He didn't say anything.

"Well," said McGinn, "I'll go tell Fud you're here," and moved toward the boss's partitioned office in a corner of the room opposite the door and the tellers' counter.

Puterbaugh stood nervously eyeing the stranger from a few feet away. Each gave the other a smile and a nod.

"How long you been in these parts?" Puterbaugh asked, fishing for conversation.

"Oh, a few weeks. I work out of Nashville."

The two farmers had edged toward the door, but were still watching the stranger and holding back their giggles with obvious effort.

"How do you like our town?" Puterbaugh asked.

"Very pretty," the stranger said.

McGinn approached with the aging, craggy-faced bank president behind him. Peerce was dressed in a rumpled navy suit with an open collar shirt and no tie. He extended a hand to the stranger and invited him into the partitioned office. The stranger followed without a word.

As soon as the door closed behind them everyone in the room became more animated. The farmers released their giggles. "Now you watch this," McGinn instructed Puterbaugh, who clearly didn't know what to make of the stranger.

A moment later Peerce came out with a figure written

on a piece of paper and handed it to McGinn. Then Peerce went back to the partitioned office.

"Six hundred forty-two thousand five hundred twenty-seven dollars and ninety-eight cents," McGinn read off. "That's about the average load, maybe a little heavier than most. A few days ago he only got four hundred and thirty thousand or so."

"He gonna be able to get all that in that satchel?" Puterbaugh asked.

"Oh, he carries a bag in there for any overflow."

"Just writes out a check for it."

"Yep. Signed Hezekiah X. Portaquil, president of the Portaquil Construction Company."

Puterbaugh laughed. "I sure never heard of no Portaquil Construction Company," he said.

"Me neither till a couple weeks ago. Got an address right on Jackson Street in Nashville, though. Says so on the little card he gave me," McGinn replied. Then he turned to the woman teller. "Come on, Edna," he said. Edna turned her name sign around to indicate that her window was closed. She followed McGinn into the vault.

Twenty minutes later they emerged. No one had moved. Edna stood guard at the entrance to the vault. McGinn went to the door of Peerce's office and knocked. "It's all counted," he said.

Peerce and the stranger left the office and went into the vault. After another ten minutes or so, they came out. The stranger was lugging the suitcase, obviously full now, with his right hand, and slung over his left shoulder was a bulging white cloth bag. The weight of it seemed to cut into his shoulder. Without turning toward Peerce or exchanging words, he headed for the door. McGinn caught his eye and they nodded at each other. Everyone's eyes followed the stranger out the door and saw him turn right, along Main Street.

The stranger turned right again at the first corner, then left at the next, and found the waiting car. He put the suitcase and bag in the trunk and got in the front seat beside another man. The car drove away.

2

For the third and presumably the last time, Stanley Timmons sat in the deuce and a quarter parked behind the A & P at four in the morning, waiting for Mickey Carmody. This time he huddled in an overcoat against an early October chill. Four weeks had passed since he and Carmody had met previously, gone to the supply room, pulled a package of checks, run 50 of them through the check-writing machine in the accounting department and scurried off. Carmody had taken the rest of the package of checks and promised to burn them.

For three weeks Timmons had heard nothing. There was not a word said at the office, not an eyebrow raised to indicate that anything had been noticed amiss. Finally Timmons could stand it no more. He had called the number Carmody had given him. A woman answered. Her voice was soft, with a hint of south or midwest in it—not at all the snappy, business woman's voice he associated with Barbara, and certainly not Judy's voice, which he would have recognized. He had asked for Mickey, and the voice, slightly surprised, had told him that Mickey was out of town on business. Could she take a number? Tell him, Timmons said, remembering his instructions, that Fred called.

The next night Timmons had received a phone call from an anxious Carmody. "What happened?" Carmody had demanded. "Nothing—nothing's happening. That's why I called," Timmons replied. Now Carmody was annoyed. "God damn it, Stan. Couldn't you have held off a few days longer? Did you at least call from a pay booth?"

"No," Timmons had answered. "But I used my sister's phone. It's unlisted."

"The cops don't need a listing. All they need is a bill-ing name to go to the telephone company with. Christ, your sister doesn't live with you, does she?"

"No, no," Timmons had responded.

"Well, it's done now, never mind. They're probably not going to dig out your sister's toll records. Just use your head from now on."

"I'm sorry, Mickey."

"Forget it. Even if they find the call, they're still a long way from making a case. Now, look, you remember what you told me came on the seventh of the month?"

"Yes."

"Well, the seventh is Friday. Nobody's going to look at them that day, are they?"

"Not if I put them in the file."

"Well, then, you put them in the file. And Sunday night you meet me again behind the A & P, okay? Just like before. Four o'clock Monday morning."

"What are you going to do?" Timmons asked.

"Those records have to be gotten out of there, and in a way that won't make them suspicious of you. That will give us more time."

"I don't understand."

"Now, Stan, you just trust me. Just be there."

Timmons had agreed, and now there he sat. At seven minutes after four, Carmody's Ford pulled up just as it had twice before. The greetings, everything, seemed normal.

"The bank statement come?" Carmody asked.

"Yes."

"With the checks?"

"Yes."

"And you filed them?"

"Right."

"Okay." Carmody brought Timmons to the trunk of the Ford and opened it. There were two suitcases, and Carmody gave Timmons one of them. It was unexpectedly heavy, almost pulling Timmons to the ground.

"Good God, what have you got in here?" Timmons whispered.

"You'll see. Now let's get going. We want to be sure we've got plenty of time for this one."

They walked to the Quincy building even further back in the shadows than usual, saying nothing, each man straining with his load. When they reached the bushes, Carmody said, "Now, Stan, you go ahead and unlock the door. When you see it's safe, signal me like this. If I see the highway's clear, I'll get to the door with both suitcases. You be ready to swing it open for me. Let's do this fast. If anything goes wrong, I've got a way out for us, but it won't be fun, so let's do it right. Now you head for that door like always."

Timmons took off and was halfway up the steps before he realized that he had forgotten to take out his key. At the door he had to fumble under the overcoat to find it in his pants pocket. He felt shadows moving all around him, but glanced to the highway and saw nothing moving. Finally he was inside, and motioned for Carmody.

The heavy burden of the two suitcases slowed Carmody's normal scamper across the lawn. Suddenly, Timmons, watching nervously, saw the on and off glow of a rotating red light from over the crest of a small hill. The light was approaching. Carmody evidently saw it, too, and headed for a large stone replica of the Quincy corporate logo that stood in the center of the lawn. Struggling, Carmody just managed to duck behind it as the vehicle appeared over the crest of the hill. It was a police tow truck. Both men watched until it passed. Then Carmody resumed his ragged run across the lawn.

Timmons was panting by the time Carmody had joined him inside, but Carmody seemed unshaken, and led the way to the accounting department. There, on the floor, he displayed his wares to the astonished Timmons. Each suitcase held a large plastic container filled with a clear liquid, some candles, a package of large balloons and a funnel. Carmody emptied the stuff onto the floor.

"Now, first," he said, "you show me the cabinet where those checks are."

Timmons brought him to the cabinet, opened it, and located the brown envelope.

"Nobody's seen these but you?" Carmody asked.

"My secretary opened the package. Maybe she made sure they looked roughly in order. She couldn't have seen anything wrong or she would have told me."

Carmody, leafing through the envelope, already had found the checks he was looking for. Grinning, he examined them. Timmons edged around behind him to see over his shoulder, but Carmody covered the checks.

"It's better you don't know what's on here, Stan. That way the government can't pressure you with it." Timmons looked about to argue. "By the way," Carmody went on, reaching into his coat pocket, "I forgot about these. These are yours."

Carmody tossed three piles of bills on Timmons's desk. Each was wrapped in a rubber band and contained a stack of smaller packages wrapped in paper bands as if they had just come from a bank. One stack contained $50s, another $20s and the third $10s.

"There's a lot of money in there," Carmody said. "Now you put it in your pocket and count it when you get home. And remember, all your gambling debts have been taken care of, and that took a hell of a lot more than $80,000. And there's going to be some more packages of bills like these for you when we get through with this deal. Now you put those away in your pocket—"

Timmons hesitated, obviously suspicious, wanting to count the money. "We're short of time," Carmody said flatly. Timmons did as he was told.

Carmody took the checks he had selected from the envelope, plus a fistful of other checks and the bank statement itself, and tossed them into one of the open suitcases. He tossed the rest of the checks like confetti onto the floor. Then he went back to the cabinet and pulled out half a dozen other files at random and tossed them into the suitcase, and pulled out more files and began strewing them around the floor.

"What the hell are you doing to my files?" Timmons demanded.

Carmody laughed. "You won't need them much longer anyway, Stan. Now, look, we got to take these checks out of here, but they can't be the only things missing, right? We are going to stage us a real vandalism raid. Now here's where you get to mess up everybody else's files, too. Anybody in this department you don't like? Anybody you want to fuck up? Here's your chance. Now you take the empty suitcase and I'll take this one, and we are going down every office and cubicle down this hall. We take some files out and put them in the suitcase so they'll be missing, and other files we take out and dump on the floor, so it looks like we had a real good time at it, okay? Now let's get going."

Timmons watched, dumbfounded, as Carmody went into an accountant's office and gleefully began rifling the files. "Come on, Stan," Carmody called in a hoarse whisper. "Gimme a little help on some of these other offices. If there's any cabinets locked, just let me know. I got a screwdriver here I can pry them open."

Slowly, Timmons began. In less than half an hour, the offices, the hallway and the central open area that housed the checkwriting machine and the clerks' desks, all were badly littered. "Now," Carmody said, "tell me the truth. Could you look at this mess and tell which one of these offices we were really aiming at?"

For the first time, Timmons found himself laughing in the spirit of the prank. "Looks pretty general," he conceded.

"Okay, now for the next step," Carmody said. Timmons watched, fascinated, as Carmody took one of the balloons and the funnel, then unscrewed the top of one

of the plastic jugs and began filling the balloon with liquid.

"What's that?" Timmons asked.

"Gasoline."

"Gasoline! Are you crazy? What are you going to do?"

"Relax, Stan. We're just going to set a few firebombs
around here to really confuse them." He tied the end of
the balloon tight and carefully set it to rest on the floor.
Then he took a book of matches from his coat pocket and
a candle from the pile he had made on the floor, wedged
the bottom of the candle into the book of matches at the
coated end, and balanced the gadget carefully on the balloon.

Timmons looked curiously at the wrapper that had
been around the candles. It seemed to have Hebrew let-
tering on it. "What kind of candles are these?" he asked.

"They're what the Jews call Chanukah candles, Stan.
Best goddamn stuff for firebombs there is. Used to use
birthday candles, but they burn down too fucking fast.
No time to get away."

Carmody stood up to admire his handiwork. "There,"
he said. "Ain't she beautiful? Now about four or five
more and we light 'em and take off."

"My God," Timmons said. "You could blow up the
goddamned place."

Carmody laughed. He pointed at the ceiling. "See that
little metal gadget sticking out right there?" Timmons
looked. "That's part of the sprinkler alarm," Carmody
went on. "Every one of our little bombs is going to be
within range of one of those things, and as soon as they
go off, this whole place is going to get a bath, on top of
everything else."

Timmons looked at the ceiling and then nervously
back at the balloon.

"Don't worry, Stan," Carmody grinned. "The last
thing in the world I'd want to do is burn this fucking
company down before they get all our checks paid."

Timmons watched in awe as Carmody set up five more balloon bombs.

"Now, one more thing," Carmody said. He picked up another, smaller plastic container and a brush. He unscrewed the top of the container, approached a wall of the hallway and began painting.

Timmons seemed almost beyond further surprise now, as he watched the words "PIG BASTARDS" appear in crimson on the blue wall.

"You know," Carmody said as he worked, "it's a shame these guys are named Quincy. If they were named Goldberg or something we could write 'Jew bastards' and draw swastikas and stuff. It's much more effective."

He finished and again stepped back to admire it. "Well," he said, "this will have to do. Now, Stan, you take those two suitcases with the files we're taking out, and go stand by the stairwell. You get ready to run, cause I'm going to light these candles and then we don't really want to hang around here very much longer."

Timmons nodded and obeyed. The next thing he knew, Carmody was emerging from the accounting department in a trot, whispering, "Go, go," and they were running down the stairs and around the first floor hall.

"Now give me the suitcases," Carmody said, "and you get out the keys and lock the door. They'll spend about a week trying to figure out how anybody got in here."

A minute later they were through the bushes and walking back in the shadows to the A & P lot. When they had partially caught their breaths, Carmody grinned. "Quite a party, huh, Stan?"

"All this just to gain a little more time?" Timmons asked.

"Time's important," Carmody said. "Besides, it could be a lot of time. Without these checks and the bank statement, nobody is really going to know there's anything wrong until the company starts spending money that isn't in the bank any more. Then the checks are going to start bouncing, but that won't happen until these construction projects on Long Island get underway. You can take care of a couple of monthly bank statements between now and then, can't you, Stan?"

"I don't think it's going to be so long," Timmons said. "We started giving subcontracts for the Continental Brands plant a few days ago. There's going to be money going out of that account from now on."

Carmody turned grim. "How much have you written so far?"

"About $800,000. But in a couple of weeks it will start building fast. If the weather stays good, we could have to shell out $5 million in the next month or so."

"Let's hope for an early snow," Carmody said.

PART TWO:

THE SEARCH

CHAPTER THIRTEEN

1

On Wednesday afternoon, October 26, while I was hanging around the office conveniently in between cases and cleaning up files, the Quincy people finally called the FBI. The executives at Quincy had spent several days arguing first with lower and then with higher level functionaries at Morgan Guaranty. Finally they had become convinced that their company had been swindled out of approximately $4.5 million.

Just before going home that night, I was assigned to the case, and the first thing next morning Bent Morrison and I drove out to White Plains. I have seen corporate officials in pandemonium over a measley few hundred thousand dollars. Considering that this was the biggest single corporation fraud loss I had ever heard of, top level management—specifically a father and son named Quincy—had remained amazingly rational. It was especially amazing because I was later to learn that the Quincy family still held 50% of the company's stock. To a large degree, it was really their money that had been stolen, not just the entrusted funds of a legion of faceless shareholders.

About the only person who seemed to have forfeited his emotional control was the corpulent public relations man, who kept babbling about how unbelievable it all seemed. But eventually he led us to the top floor suite where the Quincys were waiting with their lawyer.

Thomas Quincy Senior obviously had been a handsome man not too many years ago, but was beginning to show the sagging shoulders, wrinkled skin and muscular tremors of age. I heard he had been seriously ill the previous spring. His son seemed at the peak of life. The public relations man introduced us all and began to explain the situation, but before he got a few words out Quincy Senior silenced him with a wave of the hand.

"I want my son Thomas to explain this," the older Quincy said. "He has responsibility over the financial department and is familiar with everything that goes on there. Or at least we thought so until this week." That impressed me. If the old guy was still calm enough to joke, maybe we could piece the facts together coherently the first time around. Sometimes it takes two or three interviews just to understand a victim's story.

"On Monday morning at about eleven o'clock," the son began, "our assistant treasurer, a man named Stanley Timmons, came into my office. He said he had just received a call from Morgan Guaranty Trust Company, our principal bankers, and they told him that our accounts were overdrawn by approximately $350,000. Mr. Timmons told them that was impossible, but they insisted it was the case. So Mr. Timmons of course decided he had better inform me.

"Now, until this summer, we had kept balances in the Morgan account averaging $5 million. They required this as part of our credit agreement with them. But this summer we signed up two new and very large projects on

Long Island, and that led us to raise the balance to $8 million in August. The largest of these projects got underway this month, and so far we've spent more than $3 million on subcontracts and supplies. In addition, the account was charged with normal administrative expenditures of about $550,000. So obviously this should have left us a comfortable balance of about four and a half million.

"My first thought after being told the money wasn't there was to see our latest statement from Morgan, the one for September, so we could get an up-to-date accounting. But then Mr. Timmons and I remembered that our September statement was one of the items missing after a massive vandalism in this building a few weekends ago."

"Now that you mention it," I said, "I think I read about that in the *Times.*"

"It was a firebombing," young Quincy said.

"We assumed it was the work of some radical organization," his father explained. "We thought it might have something to do with a hotel project we're building in Puerto Rico. A lot of the records from that job were among the ones destroyed. You know, these Puerto Rican liberation groups have been so active lately."

Young Quincy started to go on with his story, but I was curious about the firebombing and wanted to hear more. "Did you keep the Puerto Rican stuff and your monthly bank statement in the same place?" I asked.

"No," young Quincy said. "As a matter of fact, they were in files at opposite ends of the accounting department. The destruction was pretty general."

"Who did you report it to?"

"Well, of course, the White Plains police department investigated. And Cumberland Mutual, our insurance company." Young Quincy saw me writing a note on that. "You think there's some connection?" he asked.

"Can't ever tell," I said. "Go on."

"Well, the bank keeps microfilm records of all those checks, and a duplicate bank statement. And I decided we'd better take a look at them. So Monday afternoon I called and asked for a compilation."

"Of course," old Mr. Quincy smiled, "at this time we thought Morgan was crazy, and they thought we were crazy."

"Tuesday afternoon," young Quincy said, "they called back. They had found 16 out-of-sequence checks. Well, our checks are all prenumbered at the printer's, and these 16 checks were more than 3000 checks ahead of the other checks we were using in September. We wouldn't have gotten to these checks for several months yet. So we asked to see copies immediately. And they said they would have a messenger up in the morning. Well, they called back a little later and said that they had decided to go through our checks for October and had found nine more of these out-of-sequence checks, from the same series of numbers as the others.

"So Mr. Timmons and I went downstairs to the storeroom where we keep the checks we haven't used yet, and started looking for the out-of-sequence numbers. And sure enough, the package of checks containing those numbers was missing.

"The next morning, yesterday, the messenger came." Quincy reached into an envelope on the desk, pulled out a stack of papers and handed them to me. "These," he said, "are photocopies of the out-of-sequence checks, made from the bank's microfilm. Each sheet is one check, front and back. The 25 checks total $4,449,875.94."

Looking through them, I could see they were for varying amounts of money, even down to odd pennies, and bore varying dates throughout September and early October. But it wasn't hard for me and Bent—who was looking over my shoulder—to see what they had in common. Every one of them was made out to the Portaquil Construction Company. Every one of them had been endorsed by Hezekiah X. Portaquil, president. Every one of them had been submitted for deposit to the Portaquil Construction Company account at the First National Bank of Caliquatta, had been cleared by the Tennessee Bank in Nashville, and had been submitted for payment from the Quincy account at Morgan Guaranty. And every one of them had been paid. I didn't even have to ask the next question; young Mr. Quincy was already giving the answer.

"Needless to say, Mr. Scanlon, the Quincy Corporation has had construction projects in Tennessee. But no one here has ever heard of the Portaquil Construction Company or so far as we have been able to determine has ever had any business with them. We can't find a trace of any such company except on these checks."

"Mr. Quincy—" I kept sorting through the checks, trying to decide which of my many questions to start with— "your handwriting on all these checks seems to be identical, more identical than the ordinary signature would be when repeated. Is there any chance—"

"I forgot to explain," he said. "It doesn't show too clearly on these photocopies, but all our checks are signed by machine."

"How many of these machines do you have?"

"Just one," he said.

"Let's see it."

2

I'm embarrassed to say it was the first time I had ever seen the ABMC-2000, one of the most interesting recent devices designed to allow a company to substitute machine processes for manhours without sacrificing security. Supposedly, the machine even improves security. I should have had training in this kind of stuff.

But as young Quincy, with the aid of one of his accountants, demonstrated the machine to me and ran some sample checks through it, I could see that there was no real security at all. Quincy didn't limit by lock and key all access to the checks that had gone through the machine the way ABMC had intended. And on top of that, they didn't even count the checks that passed through the signature device, the way ABMC had also intended. As the ABMC-2000 was set up at Quincy, it was a machine for printing money. In fact, someone had just proven that.

Then I learned how wide the access to this mint really was. While they were showing us the machine, somebody asked if we wanted coffee. One of the secretaries was going downstairs to bring up a tray. Sure, we said. A little while later, after the ABMC-2000 demonstration was finished, I asked young Quincy if we could see where the missing checks had been kept.

"You should have asked before the girl went down for coffee," he said. "We use the same storeroom for the coffee cups and things."

"Why do you bother locking up your coffee cups?" I asked.

"Oh, the storeroom isn't locked," he said. "I guess that was one of our problems."

"But why wouldn't you lock the storeroom where you keep your prenumbered checks?"

Young Quincy smiled and shrugged. "I guess because somebody might want a cup of coffee. Until now, nobody ever stole any checks. Anyway, we decided yesterday to put a lock on that door and find somewhere else to keep the coffee cups."

Just then the secretary returned with a cardboard tray containing 15 or 20 cups of coffee plus containers of milk and sugar. The tray was in her hands and under one arm was tucked a small package wrapped in brown paper. She gave the package to one of the accountants, who opened it. It was checks.

I told Quincy I wanted copies of the out-of-sequence

checks he had shown me, and he had them made. I also
wanted a list of people who had access to the keys to the
check-writing machine, but that seemed to present a
problem. While young Quincy at first assured me that
only four persons including himself had access to both
keys, the accountant we talked to insisted that at least six
people did. He also said that the master key was often left
lying on Timmons's secretary's desk, and that Timmons's
secretary was accustomed to other secretaries taking the
key for their bosses to use. So a really comprehensive list
of persons with access to the check-writing machine
couldn't exclude anyone in the financial department.
Terrific, I thought.

"Okay," I said, "do you suppose you could get me pictures of everybody in this department, identified by
name, job title, length of service here and any other perti-
nant information you have handy?"

Young Quincy addressed the P-R man, whose name
was Perry Lingham: "Perry, get that for Mr. Scanlon
right away." Lingham looked a bit alarmed, but said,
"Yes, sir," and fled.

"What do you propose to do with the pictures?" the
elder Quincy asked me.

"Show them around," I said. "To people who hang out
with the guys who might have thought this up. To see if
any of your people have been around any of my swin-
dlers recently."

"You think you know the people who might be responsible for this?"

I looked briefly at Bent. "Mr. Quincy," I said, "this
took a lot of planning. They went all the way to Tennessee to cash these checks, and maybe even staged a firebombing to give themselves more time. There are maybe
eight or ten guys in the United States who dream up deals
like this. Only one of those guys has worked Westchester
County. And as a matter of fact, maybe he's the only one

who could not only dream up this deal but actually pull it off so well. I think I know exactly who's behind it. His name is Mickey Carmody."

"But if you know somebody like that, why isn't he in jail?"

I smiled. "People always ask me that after they've been swindled," I said. "Bent and I did put him in jail back in 1970. They paroled him in nine months. I tried to put him in jail again just a year or two ago for a stock swindle that brought in a million or so, but—"

Bent gave me a look that said shut up. I did.

"Well, why don't you go bring him in now?" Quincy wanted to know.

"Because we've got no proof—yet. He's not going to confess it."

Quincy nodded. "You know," he said, "we're going to have to report this to our shareholders unless you can get the S.E.C. to let us keep it quiet for the sake of the investigation. The newspapers are almost sure to pick it up."

"Well," I smiled, "I think newspaper publicity helps in the long run. Hell, you get this all over the front pages and all sorts of informants and leads are liable to turn up."

Bent was giving me that look again. "Mr. Scanlon used to be a newspaper reporter," he explained to Quincy nervously. "The bureau discourages publicity for reasons of fair trial, among others. But you do what you have to do with the S.E.C. We can't exempt you from the securities laws. We just promise you there won't be any publicity or leaks about this coming from us."

I liked Bent, but he could be an awful stuffed shirt at times, especially considering that we got to know each other because he had been willing to swap information with a newspaper reporter. Quincy just nodded.

Lingham came in with a stack of personnel folders. "The only photos and records I can produce right away are the ones in the personnel folders themselves," he said. "If you can wait a few days I'll get copies made."

The elder Quincy looked at me. "Do you need them right away?"

"It would sure help," I said.

"Then let Perry go through them and remove any inappropriate material, and he'll have them ready for you in an hour or two."

"Terrific," I said. Lingham started to carry them away. "Could I just look through those very quickly right now?" I asked.

I counted 18 folders, each with a picture, and enough information to tell when the employee came to work, where he lived and what his marital status was. There were reference letters and other papers inside that Lingham was welcome to remove. But there was something missing.

"Mr. Quincy," I said, "are you insured against theft?"

"You mean, is this loss covered? Well, we think the first $2 million will be. But that's the limit on our policy. Apparently they got away with a lot more than that."

"All the same," I said, "do you think I could get pictures of you and your son also?"

Mr. Quincy looked alarmed, but turned to Lingham and nodded. "By all means," he said.

3

There's no telling how long the Quincy caper might have stayed secret if it hadn't been for the exceptionally enterprising reporter that *The Wall Street Journal* assigns to its real estate and construction beat. The reporter, Karen Rothmyer, found the swindle in the fine print of Quincy's October public disclosure filings. Less than three weeks after the swindle had been reported to the FBI, Rothmyer's story was picked up by newspapers and television stations all over the country.

CHAPTER FOURTEEN

It was getting on half past one of an uncommonly warm fall afternoon, and Ellis Bardell had just sat himself down to a lunch of bacon, lettuce and tomato on white bread, plus three pieces of roasted chicken, au gratin potatoes, baked beans and a quart bottle of Coca-Cola, when the German shepherd started barking in the front yard.

Bardell's customary frown deepened. He threw the first half of the bacon, lettuce and tomato back on the plate and went to the living room. Peeking around the edge of the venetian blind from behind his black recliner chair, his hand resting on the shotgun that stood in the corner, he saw the car of George Hewlitt, president of the Caliquatta State Bank. The doorbell rang. The shepherd was straining toward the porch at the end of his taut chain, growling.

"Joaquil!" Bardell called, in a tone that could scarcely be distinguished from the dog's. A slender Spanish woman of about 35 appeared from the dining room. "You go out back," Bardell said, "and go around the house. Tell him I'm eating. He wants to wait, you go back around the house, come in again and let him in the front door. He can wait on the sofa there till I'm done."

Joaquil was used to strange orders and did as she was told. Bardell went back to his lunch. In a few minutes he heard the front door open and heard Hewlitt's heavy figure traverse the squeaky hardwood floor to the couch. Bardell didn't look up until he had finished lunch. Then he walked into the living room in his slow, gorilla-like manner, ignoring Hewlitt until he had settled himself into the recliner, taken a package of Beech Nut from a nearby shelf and toyed with the wrapper for a minute. Finally, without looking up, he said, "You want to see me, George?"

"Well, I was just driving by . . ." Hewlitt laughed nervously, but got no response. "You seen the *Nashville Banner* the past couple days?"

Bardell reached into the package of Beech Nut and slowly began separating off a portion. "Don't know. What about it?"

"Well, you seen the *Caliquatta Dispatch* this morning?"

Bardell didn't react at all.

"Well, I guess it's just as nice I didn't take you up on that little deal you were proposing up by Stoney Lake a few weeks ago, huh? I mean, I guess old Fud Peerce just bought himself a peck of trouble, don't you reckon?"

"Don't know what kind of trouble you're talking about," Bardell said. "Whatever it is, it's got nothin' to do with me." He put the portion of tobacco in his mouth and let out a loud throat-clearing sound.

"Well, I mean it looks like Fud just took in quite a bit of hot checks. They say four and a half million dollars worth." Hewlitt laughed nervously again. "That's just about more than old Fud's total deposits." Bardell wouldn't respond.

"I mean," Hewlitt went on, "just because your brother

Abner's a director over there, and how he saved old Fud's ass back in sixty-three on that drunk driving charge, I mean, I don't suppose that's got anything to do with it. That maybe you offered Fud the same deal you offered me."

"I don't know what deal you're talking about," Bardell said. Suddenly he was staring Hewlitt down.

"I mean that little deal about the checks you wanted me to cash at the bank? That out-of-state customer who was going to be doing big business here in Crockett County, and had all this money coming in from some outfit up north? And he needed a banker to cash his checks for awhile? Heh-heh. And I was going to get a $50,000 commission, kind of, on the side, kind of my personal fee for the deal?"

Bardell just stared at him coldly.

"And," Hewlitt went on, "I told you it sounded illegal, like the kind of thing they were bound to catch you on? And I told you you better stay away from that deal, not have anything to do with them people. Well, I guess it's just a good thing I told you that. I just hope you took my advice, Ellis. Cause pretty soon now there's going to be FBI and all sorts of people from Washington down here asking questions. Shoot, that kind of money, they could be insurance investigators—I mean, they might even be offering a reward to find out who took all that money."

"Now listen, George." Bardell was leaning forward. He spat a swill of tobacco juice into a tin. "Now I don't remember any such conversation as you're talking about, and you goddamned well better not remember any such a conversation yourself."

"Well, Ellis, all I mean is, it's a lucky thing you've got me. I mean, you know I don't go around talking to no FBI people, that's for damn sure. Heh-heh. Why, we've done enough business together, you and me—it's just a good thing you were talking to somebody you can trust. Now who was that Hezekiah X. Portaquil fellow, anyway? The one that cashed all them checks. Damn, where'd you ever find him?"

Bardell reached behind the chair and pulled out the shotgun. He slowly laid it across his lap. He reached to the shelf and pulled down a can of polish and a cloth. He slowly unscrewed the top of the can and began polishing the weapon. "I mean," he said deliberately, "we never did have any such a conversation and I don't know what you're talking about. And you don't go mentioning no such nonsense to nobody, you hear? Now if that's all you came to see me about, you can git now. I got me a guy coming over this afternoon to pick up some chickens. I got to go out and see how them boys I got are getting them ready."

"Well, now, Ellis, there just is something else. You remember Billy Moon, don't you?" The banker got nothing more than a stare from Bardell and went on. "I know you remember Billy Moon. You Bardells sold a lot of good whiskey to old Billy all these years." Hewlitt waited again for a response and got none. "Well, I been hearing a lot of things about what old Billy's up to now. They say he's not only got those shothouses in Nashville, he's spread all the way to Chattanooga and down across the line to Huntsville. Couple of those local boys got sent up and they say old Billy's taking over. That's what I hear. Lot of nigger towns down there, you betcha. Old Billy's gonna need him some whiskey, right? I hear five thousand cases for a starter."

Bardell sat like a muscular Buddha, fingers beginning again to rub the shotgun barrel with the polishing cloth, saying nothing.

"And I bet you he's gonna come to Caliquatta for some of that whiskey. I just bet you he will. Because, you know, old Ed Norbel is one of my customers down at the bank. I been financing old Ed for 18 years now. And you know Ed's all of a sudden started building himself up quite an inventory of sugar up in Nashville. Quite an inventory—like the old days. Folks around Crockett County gonna be eating an awful lot of pies to use up all that sugar. Heh-heh. Gonna be making an awful lot of sugar syrup."

Still Bardell didn't react.

Hewlitt turned more serious. "Come on, Ellis. I know you Bardells been banking mostly with Fud for four or five years now. I know goddamned well the only reason you came to me with that check deal was that somebody told you they could of handled more money with two banks than just one. But Fud's in trouble now. They gonna be FBI and people from the comptroller's office and everybody else down here on him. Now you gonna need another banker for some of this stuff and I want that business. That foreclosure on you was five years ago and you got no reason to be pissed off about that. Them revenue boys busted up your still and took all that sugar and all I had was them chickens. I had to take 'em, Ellis. I had that collateral on paper, them chickens, and Fud would have done the same thing. You know he would have."

Bardell stopped polishing the gun. "Any deals with Billy Moon," he said, "you got to talk to Pete about that. You got to talk with my brother. I don't have nothing to do with that."

"Now, Ellis, I know Pete may do the operations, but you got the collateral. I know you been giving Fud a hunk of this farm and them chickens, same as you used to give me. Now, that's what makes it a good deal, Ellis. Not like them checks where they can take 'em right back to the bank and stick you with 'em. I can give you a good, clean, collateral loan on this, Ellis."

"I said you talk to Pete."

"But, Ellis, what Pete does with the money don't concern me. I mean, we're all better off with me not knowing. What I need's your signature on that collateral."

"Whatever you work out with Pete, I'll sign the paper."

Hewlitt waited for more, but Bardell was quiet again.

"Now am I supposed to go to Pete right up this afternoon?" the banker asked. "Tell him you said so, to do it?
Are you gonna call him?"

"Goddamn it, George, now I said I'd sign and I've said
all I'm goin' to say. Now you want to see Pete, fine. You
don't, I don't care what you do."

Hewlitt began to smile again, relieved.

Bardell slowly swung the shotgun around on his lap so
the barrels were pointing at Hewlitt. "Now, George," he
said, "what I'm telling you is that that conversation you
say you remember up at Stoney Lake, that never happened. It never happened, you hear? And you don't go remembering any more, or telling people things that never
happened."

"Now, Ellis—"

"Now you pack up in that rig of yours and git. I ain't
gonna tell you again, George."

CHAPTER FIFTEEN

The first thing I wanted to do when we got back to the office from Quincy headquarters in White Plains was to go down to Caliquatta, Tennessee, and find out as much as I could about how those checks had been cashed and who the hell this fellow Portaquil was. Bent told me I wouldn't stand a chance of obtaining authorization to do this, and when I pushed it, he turned out to be right. The special agent-in-charge told me exactly what Bent had told me—that's what the FBI has an office in Nashville for. Bent and I were to prepare reports of all we knew and forward them to Nashville, which would handle the Caliquatta end of the investigation.

Now, I have no doubts that there are some good FBI people in Nashville, and the fuck-ups I will be relating concerning this investigation aren't due to incompetence by the office down there, or to my being particularly smarter than anybody else. It's just that a lot of times a committee doesn't function as well as the best man on that committee could function alone. Criminal investigations frequently turn around on nuances that don't get transmitted in reports. The morsel of nervousness in a subject's voice may tell you much more than does a written transcript of what the subject said, let alone someone's brief summary of what the subject said. Bent and I on the one hand and the team in Nashville on the other would be operating without benefit of such nuances. The damned bureaucracy, not any particular incompetence by the FBI men in Nashville, was reponsible for what happened, as far as I'm concerned. But we'll get to that.

Bent and I got a memo ready—as the ex-journalist, I did the writing—and were told that two agents named Flowers and Cartright would handle the Caliquatta end. We got them copies of the checks, of the pictures of Quincy employes (in the most unlikely event that the inside man also helped on the outside) and other relevant material.

Bent went to work compiling detailed backgrounds on the eight or ten most likely Quincy insiders. He was treating the investigation as if we were starting from scratch, and that was entirely proper. If I had been special agent-in-charge, or S.A.C., that's exactly what I would have had one of my best agents doing. But for my own part in the chase, I just assumed that Mickey Carmody pulled the Quincy job, that he got an inside man at Quincy to help him the same way he got his bank examiner friend to help him on those Westchester jobs five years ago, that he found the banker in Tennessee through some contact or other, that he just planned and executed the whole thing. I considered it much more than a mere hunch—and, after all, if I was wrong I could always jump in with Bent.

I began to check Carmody's close acquaintances, starting with Dr. Manwaring and Walter Fakazzi. I wasn't afraid that Carmody would find out he was being investigated; if he knew anything about the Quincy job at all, even if he hadn't been responsible for it, he would be damn well aware that he was the prime suspect. These initial inquiries drew a complete blank. Of course, this didn't necessarily mean I was tracking the wrong man. Perhaps it just meant that I hadn't found a source with the proper knowledge or incentive to talk.

So I decided to try a wider circle of acquaintances. To cull the list as much as possible, I began to check who of Mickey's acquaintances were in trouble at the moment. When you're trying to get something out of a crook, leverage helps. I would like to point out that this was one more instance of the bureau's benefiting from those voluminous files I kept, the ones everybody said were cluttering up the office and merely duplicating the work of a well-paid records staff. I had a folder—one of the ones the S.A.C. kept telling me to get rid of—full of people who might know what Carmody was up to. There was still a lot of legwork to do, and I took liberal amounts of time aside to make sure I was thoroughly familiar with everything that had been reported by our Nashville office. But in a couple of weeks I scored big.

There was a New York schlock stock operator named George Bender whom I remembered from the swindle out in Denver that I had wanted to put Mickey away on. When I called my friend at the S.E.C. to find out if Bender was back in the securities business and where I might find him, my friend laughed and told me to call the S.E.C.'s Miami office.

So I tried Miami and bingo. There was an outfit called Earth Systems Research Inc. Although its full-color literature gave you the impression that the company was relandscaping half of Montana and two thirds of Wyoming, in fact, Earth Systems had been evicted a few months ago from a one-room rented office in Fort Lauderdale for failing to pay the utility bills. Bender had been peddling the stock all summer. Not only had the S.E.C. obtained injunctions against Bender and a half dozen others, but the Justice Department had subpoenaed them before a grand jury and seemed about to indict them.

I located the federal prosecutor in Miami who was handling the case and told him I needed cooperation from Bender on the Quincy investigation. This was just two or three days after the caper had landed on the front pages, so the prosecutor was interested immediately. He told me that Bender knew he was about to be indicted, and that in view of his history of stock frauds Bender was well aware the government was going to seek time on him, not just a plea bargain for a suspended sentence.

I said I didn't want to give Bender up on the Earth Systems case, but asked if I could just tell him that I had been in touch with his prosecutor and that his cooperation now would be duly reported and appreciated. The prosecutor authorized me to use his name if necessary.

The S.E.C. had suspended Bender's license to sell stock again, and I found him selling insurance in Paramus, New Jersey. "Better this than used cars," he said. I wasn't so sure.

We talked cat-and-mouse about Carmody for a little while. He really hadn't seen Mickey since summer. Mickey hadn't been involved in the Earth Systems deal, they had just talked about it. At that, I stopped him cold.

"Can't talk about Earth Systems," I said. "I'd have to read you your rights, the whole routine. That's between you and Miami. Let's just talk about Mickey."

"Why don't you have to read me my rights to talk about the Quincy deal?"

"How'd you know I wanted to talk about the Quincy deal?" I said.

"An easy guess. It's in all the papers."

"Yeah. But what makes you connect it with Mickey?"

"You obviously think he had something to do with it," Bender said. "Look, don't I get a lawyer here?"

"You can have one if you want. Only I don't intend to use anything you say against you. I want to use it against Mickey. You got nothing to be afraid of."

"I got to be afraid of Mickey. He's still walking around with that .38, you know. Look, I'm not saying I know anything anyway."

"What we talk about, Mickey isn't going to find out. If you got anything to testify to, they can worry about that at the trial." Bender seemed to be thinking it over. "Look," I said, "if the time ever comes, you can take the fifth or whatever. I'm looking for leads. There's no record of this interview. You're confidential. That's guaranteed."

"Can you get me a deal in Miami?"

"I just talked to Miami. They want your ass in jail. No way around it."

"Then why should I talk to you?"

"One year's better than ten." I saw fear flash across Bender's face.

"Did they say ten? They can't get ten on mail fraud."

"But they can if they add conspiracy. Look, George, they didn't tell me anything except that they're interested in you helping me. If I say you helped, they'll consider it and they'll make sure the judge finds out about it before he sentences you. You want to hear it from them, call them." I motioned to the phone. "You can use my credit card."

He picked up the phone, looking suspiciously at me the whole time, and called his prosecutor. "You know an FBI agent named Scanlon here?" he asked.

I sat there in the chair by his desk with my fingers crossed. The guy in Miami could ruin the whole deal. All he had to do was try to cover his ass by bringing in Bender's lawyer and it could monkeywrench me for weeks. But maybe Bender wasn't up to paying a lawyer before he had even been indicted.

Whatever the explanation, there is one assistant U. S. attorney in Miami who could get a favor off me anytime. Bender just grunted, hung up the phone, and with his hand still on the receiver, announced to me, "Mickey had lunch with some executive from Quincy about the middle of last summer. I was with them. We were at Jim Downey's on Eighth Avenue in New York. Okay? Does that help? I wouldn't be able to remember the guy's name if my life depended on it. They didn't talk anything about any kind of deal, at least not while I was listening. Now, if you got what you need, then leave, and don't forget to tell Miami. And for Christ's sake, don't let Mickey find out I talked to you."

I reached into my briefcase and pulled out the pictures. I tossed them on the desk. "If you don't remember a name," I said, "maybe you can pick one of these."

"Jesus Christ, you want a lot, don't you," he said.

"I guess you're right," I told him.

He went through five or six pictures, then stopped. "That's him, okay." He handed the picture back to me. Stanley R. Timmons. Assistant treasurer. With the company 23 years. Nice suburban address in Merrill Heights. Wife. Four kids. Community leader. Treasurer of the town for the past 12 years.

"You sure?" I asked.

"You don't want to believe me, don't believe me," he said. "That's the guy. Stanley something-or-other. Now, goddamn it, this didn't come from me, right?"

"I absolutely guarantee that this is a confidential interview," I said. "Who else was at this lunch?"

"Just Mickey, me and this fellow. Oh, and Barbara Grover, that's Mickey's girl. Well, there was this other chick dropped by, too. Mickey's always got chicks around, you know. But Barbara was the one he took in the limousine with him."

"Where do I find this Barbara?"

"Christ, I don't know. They talked about one time she lived up in Westchester, but I don't think so any more. Seems to me she was near the shore somewhere. Maybe New Jersey."

"What did you talk about?"

"Now you're getting on toward fifth amendment time. I'm not supposed to talk about Earth Systems in front of you, remember?"

"But nothing about Quincy."

"It may have come up what this guy Stanley did. I don't know. But there was nothing about any scheme. I figured something was probably in the works, or what was Mickey doing with this guy, you know? But I didn't ask. Just when I saw this business about Quincy in all the papers, I figured it out. Had to be Mickey. But, look, you figured the same thing without even knowing about the lunch, right?"

"Was Fakazzi around?"

"Fakazzi was driving the limo. He was never around while there was any conversation." I made a mental note that Fakazzi had been lying to me a few weeks before, and that I needed something on him to make him talk.

"And outside of Earth Systems and what this guy Stanley did for Quincy Corporation, you don't remember anything that was said?"

"That's right."

"Nothing about what this guy might have owed to Mickey in the way of favors, or how they got together?"

"Nope. Just that Mickey sent this young chick with the guy when they left. But they were talking about just driving him back to his office. I don't remember."

"Did you get an address or phone number for any of these people?"

"Nah. Don't think so."

"How did you get in touch with Mickey?"

"Oh, well, Mickey had this other number he was using. Not the place in Brooklyn. You know, he always thought that might be tapped. This other number."

"What was it?"

"I'd have to look. Besides, he's probably not using it any more. You know, those guys always change around the phones they're using."

"Look for it. It's important."

"Come on. I can't stand for anybody to find out where this came from. You wind up knowing too much, it's going to be obvious where you got it."

"We're completely off the record. But I need that phone number. I'll tell Miami I needed it."

He dug out a scrap from his pocket diary. "JK-5–7118," he read off. "Area code 212, New York. Now, for God's sake, remember you didn't get it from me."

I had a lot to do when I got back to the office. First, I kept my word and called Miami. Then I gave a full report to Bent. Then, as he and I agreed, I called the public relations man at Quincy and told him I had better have a meeting fast with one of the Quincys, or maybe both of them. I refused to tell the P-R man anything, despite his insistence that I do so. I put a query out on Barbara Grover—anything we could find out about her.

And I called the phone company. JK-5–7118 was registered in the name of Sara Rushington at 800 West End Avenue.

CHAPTER SIXTEEN

1

Sara Rushington's naked body lay spread across the bed like a buffet breakfast set in fine white English china. The liquid blue eyes; the special smile that seemed to show more tongue than teeth; the shoulders, like lightly-freckled porcelain; the pink nipples pointing up to catch the daylight reflecting off the cut-glass ceiling fixture; the curly brown bush, its peculiar line of reddish hairs projecting upward from the top of the triangle almost to the navel; the lips of the vagina open to show a protrusion of pink; the graceful legs tapering smoothly across the slightly wrinkled sheet and ending in painted toenails.

It was a sight Mickey Carmody often delighted in. But there were occasions, such as this one, first thing in the morning, when he hoped to avoid it. He was needed elsewhere today.

He continued into the bedroom, beads of shower water still on his body. As he passed the bed she reached out a hand and held him fast by the buttocks. Rising on an elbow, she engulfed his soft penis with her mouth and began to suck it long.

"Hey," he said, trying to chuckle it off as a joke. "You should have got me up earlier for that. I thought you had your fill last night."

"Please, again this morning, Mickey. One more time. Go in between my legs again." She managed to talk without ever removing her lips completely from the head of his organ, and when she was done speaking she immediately took it all back inside her.

"It's after nine already," he said, trying to be tender as well as factual. "I told you I have to be all the way out in New Jersey this morning. It's a big deal."

Again she pulled back from around his penis but kept her lips on the tip of it. "I'm flying today," she said. "This'll have to hold me for a week. Besides, it'll take a while for Walter to get the car over."

"He's on the way now."

For the first time she drew completely back, and his cock dropped heavily. "You called him already, while I was in the bathroom, didn't you?"

He nodded.

She fell back on the bed, disappointment on her face. He turned and pulled on his shorts and pants, then got a pair of sox from his special drawer.

She rose and walked on her knees to the end of the bed, where he was sitting. "I didn't mean to be angry with you," she said. "You were wonderful to me last night." She massaged his back. He turned, took hold of her shoulders and kissed her. Then he turned away again and resumed dressing. She returned her hands to his back.

"Mickey," she said. "I love you."

He turned and took her shoulders again, more affectionately this time. "Sara," he said. "I appreciate that. I really, really do. But you know I move around a lot. So do you. It just doesn't do any good—"

"Oh, I know—I know it's probably not going to come to anything. All my friends tell me that." She put her arms around his neck. "Didn't you ever want to say something so bad that it felt like you'd just burst open if you didn't say it?" She kissed his neck. "I really do love you."

She was smiling and he smiled back, put his arms around her and kissed her. Then he turned again and put on his undershirt.

"Thank you for my early Christmas present," she said.

He just smiled.

"It's the most beautiful ring I've ever owned." She studied her finger. "I don't think I've ever even seen a real emerald this close up. Maybe in a jewelry store, but not on somebody's finger. I never ever thought I'd have one."

"I'll offer again to have it adjusted."

"No. I'm not giving it back. I can have it adjusted myself. I'll wear it with tape for awhile. Like the girls used to do in high school when a boy gave you his ring."

Carmody stood to fasten his trousers.

"I wish I knew more about your work," she said. "If you can buy things like this you must be doing something very important."

"Oh, it's complicated," he said. "Just real estate. Money deals. You know I don't like to talk about business when I'm away from it. Maybe someday." He adjusted his sportcoat over his turtleneck, glancing briefly in the mirror, then walked to the window. "There's the limo outside. Looks like Walter's here already."

He looked back at her. She was still on the bed, stark naked. "Aren't you getting up?" he asked.

"I'll get up later," she said. The voice came out a whisper. There were tears in her eyes. He came over to her.

"I'll be all right," she said. "I just won't get to see you for awhile. Till after Christmas." They hugged. "Will you call me Christmas? At the Canterbury Hotel in San Francisco?"

"Sure." He smiled and kissed her.

"Why don't you come out, too? You used to have business in San Francisco. You went out three or four times—"

"No. It's just not a good time now. Look, I used to have business a lot of places. Now I've got business here. I'll call you. I promise."

Her eyes held his for a moment, frightened. "I won't be trouble for you," she told him. "I mean what I said about loving you. I just had to tell you. I know it's probably not going to come to anything. I don't expect things from you. I just wanted to say it."

He smiled and kissed her again. "It already has come to something, Sara. We've had wonderful times together. You mean a whole lot to me. Let's not worry about it."

They shared one more kiss. Then he looked down with a bit of a scowl. There was a small pink spot on either side of his jacket.

She laughed, embarrassed. "It's just blush powder," she said. "I put it on my nipples so I'd look nice for you. It comes right off." She brushed him and proved herself correct.

2

The last traces of snow had melted. The sun was out and the temperature was in the forties. Michael Carmody felt relaxed and good, stretched out in the passenger seat of the limousine as it cruised down the New Jersey Turnpike held carefully to sixty miles an hour.

Walter Fakazzi felt neither good nor relaxed. "A guy named Willie Shutters is after me," he said. "He called once. Then he came by the house last night when I wasn't there."

"Who the fuck's Willie Shutters?" Carmody asked abstractly. His eyes were closed.

"Willie muscles for Mr. Richards. His real name's Willie Ariolo."

"Maybe I've heard of him. What's he want?"

"They want the money, Mick," Fakazzi said, irritated. "This guy Shutters kills people."

"They're getting their money."

"About ten thousand a week, Mickey. It's not enough. They been reading in the paper about four and a half million. That was in the paper nearly a month ago, and it's been a hell of a lot longer than that since you took it down."

"For Christ's sake." Carmody's eyes were still closed. "What do they want me to do? Drive up to Richards's house with a trailer and dump it on his tomato patch? A lot of that dough's in small bills, man. They want me to go down to Chase Manhattan and get them a cashier's check?"

"Just sit down with Richards. Talk to him. Explain it."

"There's nothing to explain, Wally. He knows what the Internal Revenue Service is. You can't go around just passing that kind of money under the government's nose. Jesus."

"Then just tell him where it is so he can keep an eye on it. Maybe increase the payments. I mean, I don't know what he wants. See what he says. These guys have a way of handling money. They're supposed to got money men who can take it out of the country, or what they call wash it."

Carmody's eyes opened and he sat forward, suddenly animated. "That's me," he said. "I'm the money men. All those guys you read about who handle the Mafia's money? Well, I'm it, Walter. Richards came to me because he needed me to do just what I'm doing. He hasn't got anybody that can handle this money any better than me. Or he wouldn't have come to me."

Fakazzi was quiet as the car approached the toll booth. Inside his coat pocket was $10,000 in fifty dollar bills and another thousand in twenties that Carmody had just given him, still wrapped as they came from the bank. But he couldn't break the package in front of the toll collector, and he couldn't find ninety cents in his pocket. Carmody saw him searching and waved a single at him, grinning. Fakazzi took it, paid, and drove down the ramp onto the Garden State Parkway South.

"Mickey," he said, "Richards would kill us over this money. And he'd start with me because he knows me. He's got nothing but my word that all I'm getting from you is ten thousand a week to turn over to him. He thinks he's getting stole from and it doesn't matter whether it's you, me or both of us. He's gonna do something about it and that's what he's sending Willie Shutters around to tell me."

Carmody laughed and stretched out in the seat again, his hands folded behind his blond head. "You got to handle Richards. They're your people."

"Oh, man. He don't even know about the extra thousand a week I'm taking down from you. Ten percent for Walter. Boy, he might be pissed at that."

"You earned it, Wally. You're a good man. As for me, the farther I stay from Richards now, the better. For him, too. Hey—you haven't been holding back on them, have you? I mean, really?"

"Huh?"

"Say, keeping six and only giving them five?"

"Oh, fucking shit!" The car jerked and Carmody lurched forward, barely keeping his head from hitting the windshield.

"What the fuck you doing, Walter?" he shouted. "You want to get us stopped on the road like this? With money and guns?"

The car resumed speed.

"You gotta be crazy," Fakazzi said. "Sweet Jesus, you got to be crazy."

"It was a goddamn joke, Wally. Forget it. If I didn't trust you, would I give you all that money every week?"

Fakazzi was shaking his head. "You just don't get the

picture, do you?" he said. "They could kill me in two seconds. And then they could find you. They could find you no matter where you went. And if they couldn't find you they'd find Sybil and the kids. They could find Sara through that phone number."

"They're not gonna do nothing, Wally. I got four million dollars. Half of it's theirs. I know where it is. They can't kill the goose. They're getting ten thousand a week from me. Maybe when the heat's down I can make it more."

"Shit, you don't know what heat is. Will you just see him? Just once? Let me set something up."

"Wally, every morning when I look out the window there's a car parked somewhere on the street with a guy in it. Every morning it's a different car and a different guy. You think the Fibbies don't know who pulled the Quincy job? They could be tailing us right now. The one thing I am not going to go near is the big money. And Richards doesn't want me near him, either. If you got to tell him something, tell him that."

"You ever consider that maybe it's not a Fibbie in that car? You ever consider it might be one of Richards's?"

3

The limo purred down the strand of Route 35 that stretches south of Point Pleasant between the Atlantic and Barnegat Bay. If they were being followed, it was from quite a distance. The peninsula seemed deserted except for an occasional figure entering or leaving a house. Few people enjoy the shore in the dead of winter. Mickey Carmody was one of the few.

Not far from Mantoloking they branched along a side street in the direction of the ocean, turned right again and stopped in front of a rambling wooden "cottage," with six wooden columns rising from the base of the stone porch to the roof, two and a half stories above. On either side of the house you could see the white sand beach and the ocean directly behind it.

"Beautiful, ain't she?" Carmody said with a proud smile. "I love these old-fashioned colonials."

Fakazzi said nothing. He slouched down behind the wheel with a copy of the *Daily News*. Carmody left the car and went up the walk. As soon as he reached the porch he was met and embraced by a tall, dark-haired woman.

"Hi, Barbara," he said, and kissed her.

"I missed you, baby," she said.

"You know I had to be out of town awhile. I got back as soon as I could. Show me what you've done with our house."

Arms around each other's waists, they went inside.

The surroundings were familiar but sparkled as Mickey had never seen them before. The sun streamed in through washed windows and reflected off the chandelier that hung from the second story ceiling over the expansive center hall. The hardwood floors were polished, the rugs vacuumed, the sparse but elegant furniture fluffed and cleaned. He surveyed it and smiled approvingly. "Beautiful. Just beautiful," he said.

"For $2,500 a month it ought to be."

"I mean what you did. Fixing it up. Just beautiful. Here." He drew his arm from around her waist and reached into his coat pocket. "Twenty-five hundred. That's not so much," he said, pulling out four or five packages of bills still wrapped in bank paper. He handed her a package of fifties. "Here's $2,500. So you won't have to worry at the end of the month. And here's a thousand more—you don't want to go hungry."

Gracefully, her hand swallowed it up. "I hate to take this," she said. "It makes me think you're not planning to be around for long."

"But I can twist your arm," he said.

She had gone to the table where her purse was sitting.

Not saying anything, she dropped the bundle of bills inside and closed it. Then she turned and saw him grinning.

She returned the smile. "You know I'd a whole lot rather have you here than the money."

"Then give it back," he teased.

"No kidding, Mick." She walked toward him and put her arms around his neck. "You are going to be here for a while now, aren't you?"

"At least till after Christmas. Except, you know, I've told you Christmas Eve is always a big deal with my family. I got to be with my kids then."

"But you'll be home with me afterwards."

"Yeah."

"And we're still going to Las Vegas."

"I said we'd go in January and we will." He kissed her.

"You have to marry me, you know," she said. "Otherwise I can testify against you."

"You got nothing to testify against me about."

"You think I can't guess where all that money came from?"

"It came from business deals. That's all," he said. He smiled. She laughed out loud.

"Just trading a lot of nickel-dime stocks," she said. She hugged him.

"That's right."

"Have it your way. But you still better marry me." Her hands dropped below his waist.

"Don't you want to walk on the beach first?" he asked. He was still worried about pacing himself. He had gone twice last night. She might want to go twice now, and three performances in twenty-four hours was all he could really count on. After that, like the oilmen, he needed a depletion allowance. But he might not be able to get one from Barbara.

"It's too cold for the beach," she said. "Let's fuck first."

CHAPTER SEVENTEEN

Sara Rushington turned out to be an airline stewardess. By the time I tried to get her, she had just taken off for a trip west that would last past Christmas. I knew how Mickey manipulated women; Rushington might not have any idea that her phone had been used to plot a bank job. So I decided I wouldn't frighten her by disrupting her trip. I could sit down with her more productively when she came back. Still, I arranged with the airline for someone to call me the first time she failed to show up anywhere on schedule.

Eleven Barbara Grovers had been arrested in the past fifteen years. Eight of them were white. Four of those matched the general age and description of the woman Bender had told us about. Two of those had lived around New York, but neither of them in Westchester or the Jersey shore area. One was a massage parlor receptionist who had been trading coke. The other was a shoplifter. I doubted either one was our gal, and besides, they both had left their last known addresses more than a year ago with no forwarding place.

Bent and I got a court authorization for a wiretap on Stanley Timmons's home, made sure it was installed, then drove up to Quincy headquarters. Despite the likelihood from the first that there had been inside help, old Tom Quincy seemed shocked and appalled that one of his employees had been lunching with our suspect Carmody. "What do we know about this man?" Quincy Sr. kept asking.

Young Tom seemed scarcely able to believe the news about Timmons either. "He's been with us twenty-four years . . . good family man . . . model citizen. . . ."

"He's always been a quiet fellow," Lingham, the P-R man, interjected. Did you ever notice that when some guy has just shot forty strangers with a tommy gun the TV interviewer always goes to the killer's neighbor for a character analysis, and the neighbor always says, "He was a quiet fellow . . ."?

Timmons certainly was quiet when we interviewed him—which happened away from the Quincys despite their requests to be present. I wanted to hit Timmons hard with the fact that we had the goods on him. Maybe we could get a quick breakdown and confession. I think it almost worked. He didn't seem frightened at the Miranda warning—he must have figured we were talking to a lot of the employees there. But then I quickly told him we knew he had set up the check scheme with Carmody. I told him they had been seen having lunch together at Jim Downey's. It was as if Timmons had been wearing a wax face and we had lit a candle to it. There was no way after that he could have denied everything. But somehow he came up with a successful tack.

"Boy. . . . How did . . . ," he began nervously, still groping. "I met a fellow named Carmody at Downey's once. There were a lot of people at the table. What makes you think he had something to do with the checks?"

"Come on," I said. "Mickey Carmody's the best goddamn check swindler there is. He's been at it for years.

We want his ass bad. If you can give it to us the Justice Department will arrange something for you. First offenders almost never go to prison if they cooperate."

"Carmody," he repeated. "You mean a blond fellow. Kind of tall?"

"Oh, look, Mr. Timmons. It's obvious what happened. We want Carmody. The Quincys want their money back. We know you didn't get much. Carmody never gives up a fair cut. How much did he give you?" I paused repeatedly for him to take the bait, but he wouldn't. "Twenty-five thousand? Fifty? A hundred? Aren't you a little pissed off that the cut was so small after you read he took four and a half million?"

"You—you know, if you persist in this, I'm going to have to take your advice and get a lawyer. I honestly don't know anything about this."

"You're perfectly entitled to call a lawyer," Bent said. "There's a phone right there on the desk. He'll probably tell you the same thing we're telling you—that it's in your interest to come clean now."

"Look, I met this guy Carmody at a lunch table one day. I had no idea he was a bad guy, if that's what he was. They introduced him to me as a—as a matter of fact, I think they said he was a doctor, although then I think somebody at the table said that was just a joke, he isn't really a doctor."

"How did this luncheon come about?" I asked.

"I was just down there checking on this construction project we have back of the Port Authority. I had hoped to have lunch with the subcontractor, but as I recall that didn't work out. We made it another day."

"You ate lunch with this subcontractor at Downey's?"

"Absolutely. I can give you his name."

"Was that before or after you ate with Carmody?"

"I guess it must have been after. Maybe it was before, and we were going to have lunch again. This was last summer. Maybe we finally settled it on the telephone."

"You got this guy's name?" Bent said. Timmons looked in his file, wrote something on a memo pad and gave the page to Bent.

"How did you wind up with Carmody?" I asked.

"I don't know. Just a bunch of people. You know how things are at Downey's bar. Ever been there? I mean, this is just a meeting place. Carmody's an awfully gregarious fellow. And there were these girls there, very good-looking young women."

"Who else was at the table? You remember any names?"

"Not really. There was a couple of girls, as I say. I think there was a stockbroker of some kind—I could never remember his name. People kept coming over all the time, and this Mickey fellow would go over to other people's tables. This was a very informal affair, not at all like you're making it out."

"Did you ever see him again?"

Timmons hesitated. "Well, I think I may have talked to him."

"Where?"

"On the street. On the street—I guess in New York somewhere."

"Where?"

"Maybe the same neighborhood. I don't know. This all happened six or eight months ago. Look, this is getting silly. How the hell do you know who I eat lunch with anyway?"

He had gone on the offensive. That was a bad sign. "Mr. Timmons," I said, "maybe you really ought to talk to a lawyer. Tell him what really happened. Tell him we want Carmody and that the U. S. Attorney's office would probably make a deal to get him. Tell him we know you don't have much of the money and that if you can help lead us to the rest of it, well, the Quincys seem to me like very forgiving people. You think it over, and we'll be back in touch."

"There's nothing to think over," he said as we left.

We told the Quincys that Timmons had denied any role in the theft and had contended he met Carmody by coincidence. The old man replied that in view of the circumstances, they would have to let Timmons go, much as they were concerned for his family, much as it grieved them to stain the company's image, much as it would throw a damper on the upcoming office Christmas party.

I told them we couldn't recommend firing anybody, that such matters were up to the Quincys. Personally, I thought firing Timmons would be the greatest conversation-sparker in Quincy Christmas party history, but I didn't say so. Bent and I just left and spent the next couple of days alternating shifts listening to the Timmons wiretap.

All those ritualistic libertarians who think the wiretap laws are too permissive would sure be put at ease to know what really happens. Of course the White House plumbers and CIA spooks may operate differently, and even the bureau may when it works on foreign embassies. But I can tell you that on criminal investigations like the Quincy case, wiretaps are a pain in the ass.

It would be perfect to just put a voice-activated tape recorder onto the line and go on about your business, then listen to the tape at the end of the day. But the courts say you have to monitor the line in person. That's because of what they call minimization: you aren't supposed to tape a conversation after you learn it's not about the crime. In other words, as soon as we would find out that Timmons's kid was calling up his girlfriend, we had to quick shut off the recorder and stop listening until the line went dead again. If we even went out to take a leak or buy a sandwich, we couldn't leave the recorder on. One improper conversation on tape, and a whole case can be thrown out of court. So we lived off sandwiches from home. No way to monkey with the tape, either—they have to be transcribed at once and sealed until opened in court.

And, as we would have predicted, Timmons never

tried to get in touch with Carmody or any one else incriminating, at least not on his home phone. We disconnected the thing after two days.

It was beginning to look as if the Quincy investigation would sit in neutral over Christmas. At the same time, I felt unusual pressure to make progress. The assistant agent-in-charge kept mentioning Quincy's insurance company, Cumberland Mutual, and finally asked me to talk with an officer of the company—even though I had debriefed the company's security people of their paltry knowledge right at the start. Then the same thing happened with Boston Life, Morgan Guaranty's insurer. I became convinced that money was the issue.

That much fuss is seldom made over bringing a criminal to justice. Somewhere out there was four and a half million dollars and Quincy, Morgan and their insurance companies wanted it desperately. It seemed as if the FBI was just sending me out to babysit with these executives to take the heat off. Perhaps the bureau shared my higher consideration for law and order, but nobody ever told me that. I resented being made to feel that my constituency as an FBI agent was made up of multimillionaire corporations—corporations that clearly would have given Mickey Carmody and Hezekiah Portaquil (whoever the hell *he* was) their freedom in a minute, plus a 10% reward, to recoup the missing cash. (To be fair, the Quincys, father and son, alone among the executives I talked to, did express concern about the eventual prosecution of the criminals and seemed to recognize that the case involved a public interest beyond their own financial equilibrium.)

Philosophical priorities were only part of the problem. Anybody who's familiar with big-time swindling knows that as a practical matter, the law is much more likely to lay its hands on the larcenist than on the loot. Rarely is money found. The crooks always say they spent it all. Personally, I think it's just well hidden. A lot of it eventually slips into the pockets of international bankers (they aren't all Swiss) who agree to keep vigil over it while the crook serves his time. By the right "investments," the banker can divert the money to his own interests. A lot of loot is probably buried, quite literally, like pirates' treasure.

Given the pressure I was getting to find the money, it became all the more ridiculous that I was forced to rely on reports from our office in Tennessee for critical information about the fraud. Our people had got nowhere in determining who Portaquil was, or why the president of the bank had agreed to cash these checks. Their messages gave me more questions than answers.

The bank employees in Caliquatta couldn't identify pictures of Carmody, Fakazzi or Timmons. Besides, they were very clear tht Portaquil had been of medium height and build. Fakazzi was noticeably shorter and stockier, and Carmody was six-one. More striking, the bank employees said that Portaquil was a phony from ten yards off. He talked and dressed like a New Yorker. He had a glued-on mustache, Fu Manchu style, and some people thought his bushy hair was a wig. He claimed to be up from Georgia to do some construction around Caliquatta. One day it was a shopping center. The next day it was an interchange, though it wasn't clear how that could be, since there weren't any multi-lane highways going through the area.

Nobody had seen the offices of his alleged construction company, or called the Better Business Bureau or Dun & Bradstreet to see whether it existed. They just took his business card. That was on orders of the bank president, Fud Peerce. Peerce had owned the bank forty years and everybody there took his orders as a matter of course. Later, our office found out that the construction company's address in Nashville was a vacant lot.

Yet every couple of days Portaquil would walk into the bank, endorse a couple of checks, get the money in mixed bills never larger than hundreds, and carry it out in a cloth bag or sometimes a briefcase. Hardly ordinary behavior. A few bank employees admitted they had been a little suspicious. But Peerce said Portaquil was all right, and that was enough. Peerce said the checks were good. And in fact they *were* good. After they cleared the biggest bank in Nashville, and Morgan Guaranty as well, Peerce wasn't going to turn them down in Caliquatta. Never mind that they made Portaquil the largest customer in the history of the Caliquatta bank. And that his construction company front turned out to be a phony and easily could have been proven so.

What kind of car did Portaquil drive? Was there an accomplice waiting for him? Apparently nobody knew. The stranger just walked out the door, turned right on Main Street and vanished. Once, a teller followed him out and thought she saw him get into a car a block or two away, but couldn't supply more detail. I longed to question her myself—to question everyone in the bank, especially Peerce, whose hollow explanations made me all the more upset that I couldn't see for myself how much he squirmed when he talked.

For awhile I thought I had argued the point so well to the A.S.A.C. (our term for the assistant special agent-in-charge), that they were going to let me go down there. But the system was stronger than my argument and I was told to keep working from New York.

Anyway, I wasn't in the best of moods that Christmas season. On top of everything else I had just been shit on all over by a lovely girl the month before. My friends were leaving town and the only social invitation I had was to visit my aunt and uncle out in Sweet Springs, Missouri. I declined.

Then the phone rang and it was Mickey Carmody. He said he wanted to meet me right away on the beach at Coney Island, right in front of the Aquarium. I glanced out the window. There were snow flurries. Who the hell would go to the beach at Coney Island in a snowstorm in December? Then I realized that was probably why he picked it. I quickly agreed and headed for the D train.

From a quarter mile away I could see a black speck, a lonely figure on the beach. As I walked toward it, the figure grew ever more obviously Mickey. He was standing at the crest of the sand, about halfway between the boardwalk and the ocean, wearing a shearling coat, the collar turned up with his blond hair blowing above it, his hands in his pockets. He actually looked warm. It must have been about twenty-five degrees, and the wind off the Atlantic was cutting right through my label-less storm coat that the guy on Nassau Street had assured me was a genuine London Fog.

Mickey waved, showing me a gloved hand. I waved back. When I was up next to him he just motioned with his head and we began walking west toward the thin black skeleton of the Cyclone hanging phantom-like in the fog. For awhile neither of us said anything. I thought of commenting on the cold, but by God, it didn't seem to bother him and I wasn't going to let on that it bothered me, either. If he couldn't hear my teeth chattering, though, he was deaf. I hadn't gone to work prepared for this.

"What's happening with the Quincy deal?" he said finally.

"You'll have to be more specific, Mickey."

"Have you got any evidence you think pins it on me? Besides your gut?"

"Not a fair question."

"You got any plans for a grand jury now?"

"If I tell you yes, you go to Europe?"

"You tell me no and I just spend the holidays with my family and I don't worry about it."

"You can spend the holidays. Nothing's going to happen, far as I can see right now."

"What about the tail?"

I looked at him, waiting for evidence that he wasn't just fishing.

"Come on," he said. "There's cars with a guy in 'em parked out front of my apartment. There was a Volkswagen hugging my ass all the way down here. He's probably perched up there on the other side of the boardwalk with binoculars on us right now, wishing he could hear what we're saying."

"If there's somebody up there now, he's not one of mine. I can tell you that. As far as occasional tails, if it was up to me we'd have somebody watching you twenty-four hours a day the rest of your life. We just don't have that kind of manpower. I'll take what I can get as long as I can get it."

"How 'round-the-clock are you?"

"Can't tell you, Mickey. That would spoil the whole purpose of it, wouldn't it?"

"Okay." He was smiling. "So I'm gonna have a peaceful Christmas but not a private one."

"You could look at it that way. Lemme ask you a question this time. What'd you do with the money?"

He grinned broadly. "Whoever handled that job sure did it right, didn't he?"

"Who was Portaquil?"

"Description said he was dark, about five ten or eleven. Couldn'a been me. Besides, I was right here in town some of the days he was cashing those checks. I can prove it."

"I didn't say it was you. I said who was it."

Mickey didn't say anything, just walked on, grinning.

"You carrying a gun?" I asked.

"Me? I'm talking to a federal officer." He unbuttoned and opened his coat—a courageous act in that weather that I never would have requested. There were no bulges under his turtleneck. "I'm counting on you to protect me," he smiled.

"How's Sybil?"

"You ought to know. You talked to her. Doing fine. But I don't want her to be hassled by this. Certainly not over Christmas. You know, my kids are there, too."

"I know. She hasn't complained so far."

"Maybe not to you. I get it different. What about you? You got any people for the holidays?"

I shook my head. "It's an off year. There were some relatives invited me out to the midwest, but it's too far."

"We got to get you a woman, Frank. There'd be a lot of women be nuts over you. You got interesting work. Tall, not bad looking. There's lots of babes not so hot on money. You ought to let me check it out for you. But your boss probably wouldn't go for that, would he?"

"'Fraid not, Mickey. Wouldn't mind it if you willed me your address book, though. 'Cept you'll probably be going a long time after I will."

"Glad you think so," he said, and stopped on the sand. He stuck a hand out. "I won't take off the glove. You won't have to either," he said. "You take care, now, and have a merry Christmas."

We shook hands and walked in opposite directions. Maybe thirty yards down the beach I turned to look back and he did the same thing. We waved at each other and I didn't look back again.

CHAPTER EIGHTEEN

1

"You're coming right over? What do you mean you're coming right over? Who is this? Is this you, Mickey?"

Fakazzi held the phone briefly away from his ear as if testing it, then pressed it close again.

His wife stood a few feet away, hands on hips. "Mickey!" she barked. "Walter, what does that creep want?"

Fakazzi waved her off. "It's Christmas Eve," he was saying. "Are you crazy? Mickey?" He held the phone away from his ear again. It was dead. He hung it up.

"So what was that all about?" she said. "Are you getting out of here or aren't you?"

Fakazzi still seemed puzzled and upset by the call. "It was Mickey," he said. "He says he's coming in a half hour to pick me up. We got something important to do."

"A half hour's too long, far as I'm concerned."

"From Baldwin?" Fakazzi said. "I don't see how he can make it that fast."

"Not too long for him—too long for you, damn it. If

you took the subway you could be out of here now. I got half a mind to make you wait outside."

"Come on, Elena. It's Christmas Eve."

"That's what I heard you say to him. It's Christmas Eve. Time for you to go out robbin' somebody again with your no-good friend who got you into prison in the first place."

"That ain't right for you to talk like that. Mickey's takin' good care of us. Includin' you and the kids. Where do you think the money for these toys come from?"

"They came from Santa Claus as far as Paul and Gina know. Not from their no-good bum of a father. At least Mickey's good looking. And I'll bet he has a thing that stands up straight between his legs."

"Elena, come on. It's Christmas Eve." He was reaching out for her, trying to be tender.

"It's Christmas Eve. You said that three times. Well, this ain't no manger, Wally. The kids are in bed. You seen 'em. Now I want you out of here."

"You gonna be alone Christmas Eve?"

"Alone? Who said I was gonna be alone?"

A look of pain came across his face. Elena seemed to be gloating.

"Oh, God, Elena. You got that guy coming over here tonight?"

"None of your fucking business," she said.

"Don't talk like that."

"What! Ain't your woman supposed to talk like you do? Well, I ain't your woman no more anyway."

"That guy's not going to be here in the morning with the kids before I get here. . . ." He said it more as a question than as a statement.

"He'll do what I want him to do. Like I said, it's none of your fucking business."

"Elena, look, be reasonable. A man's gotta have some pride."

"You aren't runnin' my life anymore, Wally. I had

enough grief from you. Now go wait for your creepy friend outside."

"But it's fifteen degrees out there."

"I don't care if hell's freezing over. I don't want to see your face no more. You can wait on the porch with the outside door closed. It won't be so cold there."

"Elena, look—"

"Don't look me nothin'. I mean it, get out."

"Okay, look, I'll go on the porch. But I mean it about not having him here when I come tomorrow morning. I want you to promise me."

"I ain't promising you nothing. I don't got to."

"Elena, it's Christmas. I'm tryin' to be nice to you."

"Well, if that's what you mean—" She walked across the room, picked up a new animal-skin purse from the white gift box it was sitting in and hurled it at him. It bounced off his chest. "You can take it back, for all I care. If you think you can buy me—"

"For Christ's sake, I'm not trying to buy you. I was trying—"

"But you better not stop the money comin', or you're gonna wind up back in jail, that's where. I'll see to that."

"Okay, I'm going." He left the purse lying on the floor. "But I really mean it about tomorrow morning, Elena. I really mean it."

"Take the purse. Take the purse," she hollered as he left.

He waited on the porch and felt like crying.

2

The Ford jerked into gear almost as soon as Fakazzi's bottom hit the seat. They had gone thirty feet before he could get the door slammed.

"Jesus Christ, Mickey! Take it easy!" he said.

Carmody stared grimly at the street ahead of them and didn't reply. There were halos around the streetlights.

Fakazzi watched the rows of parked cars stream past them on either side. "So where the fuck are we goin'?" he asked. There was no answer. "What's this about?" More silence. "You know it's Christmas Eve? I thought you were counting so much on being with your kids tonight. Did Sybil throw you out?"

"Shut up. I know what day it is," Carmody finally answered. "'Dja bring a gun?"

Fakazzi's jaw dropped. "For God's sake, it's Christmas—"

"Will you stop saying that? I know what day it is. What are you, a fucking calendar? You gotta keep tellin' me it's Christmas Eve?" Carmody reached under the seat with his right hand, keeping his left on the wheel, and in a few seconds pulled out a snub-nosed revolver. "Here," he said, handing it to Fakazzi at knee level. "Keep it low. As soon as you get the feel of it, put it back under the seat."

Fakazzi let the gun rest in his hand, as if weighing it. "Mickey, where are we goin' we're gonna need guns?"

There was a pause. "Guess," Carmody said.

"What?"

"You know where we're going. Figure it out."

They were headed southeast now on the Van Wyck Expressway, toward Sunrise Highway and Long Island.

"Oh, shit, no," Fakazzi said. "Not that. Are you crazy?"

Carmody didn't answer.

"What are we gonna do?" Fakazzi asked. "We're not gonna kill him, are we?"

"Just scare him."

"Oh, Mickey, Jesus, you don't go. . . . I thought you had everything worked out. I thought— What happened, something with your kids tonight or something? Mickey, I'm getting screwed around by my wife on Christmas Eve, too, but you don't go—"

"Shut up," Carmody said.

Fakazzi held the gun and stared at him. Carmody

reached into his inside coat pocket and pulled out a large packet of wrapped bills. "Here," Carmody said. "Some more for you." It was so dark Fakazzi couldn't even see the denominations. But it felt hefty. He looked down and tried to see—the gun in one hand, the money in the other. But it was too dark. He slipped the money into his pocket and began to feel the gun.

"Mickey, have you been to Richards yet about the money?"

"I don't want to talk about that now."

"You haven't, have you? You haven't done anything about it."

"I said I don't want to talk about that now."

"Oh, shit, shit, shit, shit, shit," Fakazzi whispered to himself. He continued to feel the gun. "Oh, shit, shit, shit, shit, shit."

Fakazzi looked up when he sensed they were in Baldwin. He saw them leave the main highway, turn onto Milburn Avenue and slow past Carmody's house.

"He's gone. His car's gone," Carmody said. "Good."

The Ford speeded up. They were back onto the Sunrise, then the Meadowbrook. Then they were in East Meadow, driving through a housing development, and then slowly past a garden apartment project.

"What time is it?" Carmody asked.

Fakazzi held up his watch and waited until they were under a streetlight. "Quarter after twelve."

"Shit, that's early. Wait—it's Christmas Eve. It's not too early. It's just right. Everybody's either in bed or at church."

"Mickey, for God's sake, this is crazy. Don't fuck everything up just because—"

"Shut up. I don't want to talk about it," Carmody said. He turned the car around and parked it so it would be headed back toward the highway.

They got out, and, keeping as close as possible to the shadows, entered the parking lot. Carmody found the car he was looking for and smiled. Then he motioned Fakaz-zi toward a building. They went upstairs to the second floor.

"Stand here by the light switch," Carmody whispered. "Turn it out if anybody comes."

Carmody went to a door a few feet away. He pulled a jimmy from under his coat and quickly, expertly, quietly, went to work on the door. It took him only about ten seconds. The door started to swing open, then jerked back on its chain. Carmody took out his cutters. The chain wouldn't snap. He put the jimmy back in his coat and tried the cutters with two hands. The chain broke. "Remember where the stairs are," he whispered to Fakazzi. "Now douse the lights."

3

O'Neil was in his pajamas, in bed, when he heard the noise. First just the light scraping of the jimmy, then the snapping. Then he saw through the bedroom doorway the two shadowy figures outlined in the moonlight coming from the living room window. The gun was on the floor under the bed. He reached for it. He was terrified. He propped the pillow up on one end of the bed and slid to the other. Maybe, if they shot, they would shoot at the pillow. The two figures entered the room single file. There wasn't a word said. O'Neil fired—and was surprised at the loudness of the clap.

There was a scream from one of the shadows and a return of fire. O'Neil heard something hit the wall behind him. He fired at the other shadow and heard a cry, then saw it turn to flee. He lunged forward and saw two more flashes of light, heard the claps, and felt searing pain in his right thigh and hip. He staggered, then regained his balance, and chased after the other shadow. It was limping, just as he was.

O'Neil tripped over a body on the floor in the doorway.

He thought he felt it move. He fired straight down at what appeared to be the man's head. There wasn't a cry, not anything. He stepped over the man toward the fleeing figure and raised his gun to fire. Then he felt an awful, unbearable pain all up and down his right side and felt himself falling forward, then, mercifully, blacking out.

CHAPTER NINETEEN

1

Well, I sure can't complain it was a dull Christmas.

I was shaken out of bed at 5:15 a.m. by Officer Policz of the East Meadow precinct of the Nassau County Police Department. There had been a shooting. They had a guy named Donald F. O'Neil in Nassau County Medical Center in East Meadow with a couple of bullets in him. He wasn't supplying much information, just babbling that he was afraid somebody was still out to get him. At first, the name O'Neil didn't ring a bell. Then Policz told me this "good-looking young blond babe" had shown up claiming to be a doctor. She was hovering around O'Neil, repeating that somebody was still trying to kill him, keeping the cops and reporters away, stoking the hospital staff into action.

"She really is a doctor," I said. "I know her."

"That's a shame," Policz said. "I was getting ready to arrest the broad. She and this O'Neil character finally gave me your name and said you was the cop maybe they could trust, you know?"

"I may know what happened. I'll get out there."

Then Policz told me I better stop in the morgue first. There was a body maybe I could identify. The "blond babe" wouldn't leave O'Neil long enough to do it herself.

I went to the bathroom, urinated out the previous night's scotch, brushed my teeth, dressed in something less than my Christmas best and started down for the car. Then I realized I had to go back, call Policz's headquarters and find out where the hell all those places were.

It was almost 6:30 by the time I got to the morgue. I saw more than I cared to of the body and headed for the hospital. A cop met me at the door and walky-talkied up to Policz, who was waiting in O'Neil's room. The surgeons had finally pried O'Neil away from the cops and reporters long enough to dig the bullets out of his leg and hip. He was out of the anesthesia but still considerably more subdued than when they had brought him in.

The elevator was so slow I ran up the two flights of stairs. Dr. Manwaring was by O'Neil's side, holding his hand. There were the usual tubes running into him. Policz was pacing by the door. We shook hands and he pointed out Dr. Manwaring. She and I locked eyes and nodded, but she stayed seated by the bed, both her hands around O'Neil's. O'Neil started to talk, excitedly, but obviously restrained by great pain. "You gotta . . . you gotta . . . ," he started.

"Quiet, Don," Dr. Manwaring said. "You shouldn't try to talk now."

"Ma'am," Policz broke in, "we may have a potential killer loose and he's the only guy who knows what happened."

I waived the officer quiet. "Let me talk to her," I said.

"Mr. Scanlon," she began with considerable passion, "we're afraid. Don's terrified. Mickey and some other man tried to kill him. If Mickey got away he'll try again. You've got to protect us."

"Who's Mickey?" Policz said.

"Mickey's dead," I told Dr. Manwaring.

I'm pretty good at judging facial reactions, and I thought I saw relief rather than grief in hers. But, then, all things considered, that seemed a pretty logical response.

After it had been quiet for a minute, I asked, "Who was the other man in the room? Do either of you know?"

Dr. Manwaring shook her head.

O'Neil, who was watching, said, "But I think I hit him. I think I did."

"The blood samples may tell us," I said. "They're doing tests on them now."

"Are you sure it was Mickey?" Dr. Manwaring said finally.

"I saw the body."

She leaned, or really almost collapsed, across the bed.

"I'm sorry it had to happen this way," I said.

She shook her head and waved me off with her hand.

"Did anything happen tonight to start this?"

"The same kind of thing I told you about before," she said. "Just, he came over, and Don was there for Christmas Eve, and Mickey resented it. That's all. The same thing. But nobody would ever do anything about it."

"Did he make any threats?"

"I don't remember."

"No," O'Neil interrupted. It obviously took considerable effort for him to speak. "He didn't say anything like a threat this time. Just left. But you could tell from his look. I mean, he had already said all there was to say."

"Doctor," I said, "I know this is a bad time for you. There are still some things I have to ask about. You want me to call later, after you've had some sleep?"

"You go ahead. It's all right."

"I just want to know if he had mentioned what he was working on."

She shook her head.

"Had he said anything at all about any deals he had going the past few months?"

"Mickey was always talking about deals. There was nothing special."

"Had he said anything about any trips he was taking?"

"He was always taking trips, going to airports."

"Do you know anyplace he went in the past few months?"

"Not in particular."

"Do you know who he was hanging around with recently? Any new friends? Was he still close to Fakazzi?"

"I don't know. I tried not to know."

I sighed. "Did he ever mention a guy named Portaquil, or somebody who was using the name Portaquil?"

"No. Not that I remember. I really can't be sure."

I looked at O'Neil, who was clearly in pain. He shook his head.

"What about women?" I said. "Did he ever say anything about a Sara Rushington?"

Dr. Manwaring turned away from me, toward O'Neil. "We were divorced," she said. "We didn't talk that much. At least, I tried not to. I know he was seeing other women. I don't know who they were. I don't remember any Sara."

"What about a Barbara Grover?"

"I think there was a Barbara he mentioned. I don't know anything about her."

"Do you know where she lived?"

"If he told me, I don't remember. I wiped the idea out of my mind. I tried not to listen. I really don't know anything about her."

I looked at O'Neil again and he shook his head.

"I'm sorry things have been so rough," I said. "They

tell me the leg wounds are going to heal okay. Maybe we'll talk later when you're both feeling better."

They didn't appear particularly anxious. I didn't blame them. I turned to Policz. "Where's your homicide man?" I asked. "He and I better have a talk."

2

If a doctor treated the bullet wounds on the man who fled O'Neil's apartment, then he didn't report it. Fakazzi, my own best guess as to who the mystery man was, couldn't be found. I did locate his ex-wife, who said she had last seen him when he left with Carmody late Christmas Eve. That pretty well confirmed my guess, so I told the Nassau County police. The shooting wasn't in federal jurisdiction. What was in federal jurisdiction was the Quincy caper, which Mrs. Fakazzi pleaded total ignorance of. I tended to believe her, leaving me stuck.

Three days after Christmas, however, I got word on Grover and Rushington. I went to Rushington's first. Her airline had said she flew in the night before, so I gave her till 10 o'clock to sleep before I showed up at her apartment.

As I've said, I like to pop in on people without warning, to note their reactions. But at the doorman's urging I called up from the lobby. When I announced myself as an FBI agent there was such a long silence I was afraid for a minute she had fainted.

The door opened on a very attractive young woman with fine brown hair just long enough to break at the shoulder, large liquid blue eyes and a slender but beautifully proportioned figure neatly wrapped in a white sweater and slacks outfit. When I saw the obvious bafflement on that pretty face I would have bet a week's pay that she genuinely had no idea why I was there. Sara virtually radiated innocence.

"What does the FBI want with *me*?" she asked.

I gave her a relaxed smile and my credentials and asked if I could come in.

"Sure," she said, stepping aside. "Will you have some coffee? I was just fixing some for myself. I really just woke up. I got in on a late flight last night—I'm a stewardess and I've been away for more than a week—sit down."

"Glad to," I said, settling myself at the end of the fuzzy white sofa. "Black with sugar." She was anxious, but seemed totally trusting.

"Well"—she was pouring coffee in the kitchen, looking at me over the countertop room divider—"are you going to tell me why you're here?"

I waited till she had set the pot down. "It's about Mickey Carmody," I said.

She looked up, goggle-eyed. "Is something wrong? Is Mickey in some kind of trouble?"

I had hoped that she already knew from the papers. Not only didn't she know, but everything about her reaction told me she very much cared. "Sara . . . I mean, Miss Rushington . . ." I almost never latch on to first names on FBI business, but there was something compelling here.

"That's all right. You can call me Sara. Just tell me what happened." She had come into the living room, leaving the coffee on the counter.

"Maybe you'd better sit down." She did, her mouth and eyes open in expectation. "Mickey Carmody died," I said. "Christmas Eve."

"Died?" She looked as if somebody had slugged her. "What happened?"

"He was shot to death."

"My God. Was somebody trying to rob him?"

"No."

Her words had been coming out as air with hardly any voice behind them. Now she put her hands to her cheeks.

I noticed long, graceful fingers and pretty red nail polish. Her voice grew slightly stronger, about the the level of a little girl's. "He was supposed to call me Christmas in San Francisco. I got worried when he didn't. But I didn't think. . . ."

"How much did you know about Mickey?"

"I—" Her voice seemed to fade again. There were tears in her eyes.

"Here, can I get you something?"

"I'll be all right."

I went to the counter and brought her the coffee with the milk in it. She thanked me.

"You want me to come back a better time?"

"No. I want to know what happened."

"Did Mickey ever talk to you about his business?"

"Sure. But not a whole lot. I know he put deals together for people. Businessmen and things. Like the time I met him, he was flying out to Denver to help a man buy a bank."

"Do you remember the man's name—or the name of the bank?"

"Oh, lord, I wouldn't remember details like that. I probably never even knew. But he was doing very well." Sara had settled down now, her voice pretty and midwestern.

"Did you ever meet any of his business associates?"

"Oh, probably. I met some people. He always knew a lot of people, was running into them. I just knew them by their first names. I certainly never sat in on any business discussions."

"He used your phone, didn't he?"

"Sure. You should have seen some of the bills. He always paid me, though. He wanted to give me double if I would have taken it."

"Why did he say he needed to use your phone?"

"It was just convenient. He wasn't renting an office in the city 'cause he spent so much time traveling. And he lived out in Brooklyn. I'm not home half the time anyway. Look, how do you know these things? What is going on?" Her face, intent, moved to within a foot or two of mine.

"Mickey Carmody was a gangster," I said. "An extraordinary one, but still a gangster."

Again she seemed in shock, and drew away from me. "You mean he was shot by gangsters? I can't believe that."

"He wasn't shot by gangsters. He was shot by a man he was trying to shoot himself. His ex-wife's boy friend."

"Wife! Mickey was never married."

I began to feel sick. I was laying a sledgehammer to something very fragile. Sara reminded me of the heroine of a Bob Dylan song who "takes just like a woman . . . but she breaks just like a little girl." I was convinced there was nothing I was likely to learn from her that was worth the damage. I got up to leave. "I'm sorry I had to do this to you," I said, and headed for the door.

She ran after me. "Wait." She put a hand on my shoulder until I stopped and turned around. "You have to tell me. What's this all about?"

I reached in my pocket and pulled out the two stories from the *Times*. The first was an item about the shooting of an East Meadow truck driver by two unidentified men, one of whom was killed and the other of whom escaped. The next day there was an item identifying the dead man as Mickey Carmody and giving his prison record. She sank back against the wall as she read them.

After a long while she looked up. "How can you think you know someone so well and then you don't?"

"Mickey fooled a lot of people," I said. "That was his business."

"Are you sure it's him? Do you have a picture?"

"It's him. If you really aren't sure, I'll drive you over to my office. We have pictures there." She looked down again. "It's him," I said again. She nodded.

"If you already know who killed him, then what are you doing asking all these questions?"

"We think that shortly before he died Mickey pulled one of the biggest swindles in history. There's four and a half million dollars missing, and a couple of accomplices still loose."

"Four and a half *million*? Mickey had *that* much?"

"Stole that much. From the Quincy Corporation."

"The one in the newspapers? With the checks?"

I nodded.

She sank back against the wall again. "You keep telling me these things, one right after the other. I just can't—if he stole all that money, how come it wasn't in the newspaper clipping you showed me?"

"It's never come out. We've never proved it."

"Then how are you so sure it was Mickey?"

"I'm sure. For one thing, he practically told me so himself just before Christmas. He picked a place out at Coney Island where we'd be alone and he knew I could never use anything he said against him. I also know that he had been meeting an executive from the Quincy financial department before the theft, the man who probably helped set it up. And when you get right down to it, Mickey is just the only guy who could have done this. The only one with that kind of mind."

Sara walked over to the sofa as if to sit down, then evidently changed her mind and went to the counter that opened onto the kitchen and leaned on it. She looked lost. "So you know he had a key to this apartment?" she said. "I've never given a key to anyone else before—not anyone. He never stole anything from me. He was always so generous. And now you're telling me I didn't know him at all. Was he just using me?"

"If he spent time with you, it must have been because he liked you."

"How did you find out he knew me?"

"Your phone number. He used it a lot."

"Then he was just—just using me."

"That's not necessarily true. There were a lot of phones he could have used. You told me yourself you offered it because it was convenient. He had a lot of women. If he spent time with you it was because he liked you."

"A lot of women?" She turned her back. "You know, I can't even show you the other numbers he called—he took the bills."

I smiled. "We have copies of your bills. I know who he called."

She turned back to me. "How do you get copies of my phone bills?"

"From the phone company. I'm sorry if the idea's offensive, but we have to do it. If they didn't give them to us we'd go to court and get them."

She began to smile for the first time since I had hit her with the news. "You not only know more about Mickey than I do, you probably know all about me, too."

"Very little," I said. In truth, I knew she was born in Effingham, Illinois, was twenty-six years old, 5'7", 120 pounds, graduated Effingham High School with honors and did some modeling. That much had come from her airline personnel department.

"Who did he call from my phone?"

"Quite a few people. A banker down in Tennessee, name of Peerce, for instance."

"Is that important?"

"Could be. He runs the bank that cashed the checks. Um, just for the record, you, uh, didn't call a guy named Peerce in Caliquatta, Tennessee, did you?"

She smiled and shook her head.

"Any idea where Mickey might have put the four and a half million?"

"Lord, no. I never dreamed—I mean, he always had a good deal of money, more than most people carry in their wallet. He would always buy anything he wanted, or anything he thought I wanted. But four and a half *million*—I just can't believe it."

"Did he talk at all about his business, or where he kept his money, or any investments he had? Try to remember any little thing."

"I'll try to remember, but—I just never had a clue to any of this. I feel like such an idiot."

"Did he ever mention the name Hezekiah Portaquil?"

She smiled. "Who?"

"Hezekiah Portaquil. Did he ever talk about a Barbara Grover—ever hear that name?"

"No. Who is she?"

"Just—somebody Mickey knew. Uh, well, if you can remember anything that might help, things he told you that might make more sense now that you know about his business. . . ."

"Did he know this Barbara Grover from business or from—socially?"

"Well, from business. . . ."

"I want to know these things." She had walked away and now was close again, pleading. "You've made me feel like such an idiot. At least let me know who this man was. Please, don't just tell me a little bit and then ask a bunch of questions and then walk away. That's not fair."

"Well, the bureau doesn't like to talk about pending investigations," I said. She looked terribly disappointed. "Oh, hell," I said. "That's not the reason. Look, I don't get sadistic pleasure out of telling you these things. I had to come ask you these questions. But now I'll accept it that you don't know—" She was just looking at me with those pretty eyes. "Look, you were taken advantage of by a con man. If you can just forget you ever heard of Mickey Carmody you'll save yourself a lot of pain. Okay?"

"But"—the eyes were tearing—"haven't you ever cared about something to the point where you can't just forget it? I'll worry about this the rest of my life if you don't tell

me what's going on. If I couldn't know who he was while
he was alive, at least tell me now. There are still people I
have to talk to who knew him. Friends of *mine*."

"Okay, okay."

"Who was this Barbara Grover person?"

"Barbara and Mickey—Mickey had, well, he knew a lot
of women. I told you, he must have really liked you to
spend so much time with you. But Barbara and Mickey
lived together a lot."

"What? Was she his wife?"

"No. His wife divorced him a few months ago. They
had been separated since just after Mickey got out of prison a few years ago, although Mickey still—he resented
the separation and he saw her a lot. They have a couple of
kids."

"He had children. Are they boys or girls?"

"He had one of each. They're cute, I've seen them."

"How old are they?"

"One's about six or seven, the other maybe nine or ten.
I'm no good at ages. What do you want to bother yourself
with that for?"

"Did his wife know about this Barbara? Or about me?"

"She knew he attracted women."

"And she didn't mind."

"Mickey gave Sybil a lot of grief. She also went quite a
while without knowing how bad a guy he really was. By
that time—look, you just ought to be grateful you didn't
have the problems he gave her."

"Where did he live with this Barbara? I've been in his
apartment in Brooklyn and there weren't other women
there."

"When you were there, I guess she was gone. Right
now they've got a house down on the Jersey Shore. They
rented it this fall. They were living in it. I just found out
about it this morning from a real estate broker down there
who claims they owe her January rent. She couldn't find
them, and then somebody told her they had read about

him being killed. So she called the police and got led to me. As a matter of fact I'm supposed to be headed down there right now. I've got to take a look at the house and talk to this real estate woman."

"Can I go with you?"

"Oh, now wait a minute. I've told you more than I'm supposed to as it is. This is still an FBI investigation, you know."

"But I want to see where he lived. Besides, it will save you time. You can tell me about Mickey on the way down. Do you have a car?"

"Yes."

"Then it's okay, isn't it? Please?"

"It may be night before I get back."

"All I planned to do today was be available for Mickey."

"Shit. Get your coat."

The truth is, I agreed to it less out of compassion than because she was turning me on. I hadn't been out with a woman in several weeks. Okay, she was a lost lamb. But I've always found innocence attractive, and Sara had the kind of expressive face that the more you looked at it, the prettier it got.

As we were heading for the elevator, she said, "You know, you swear a lot. I guess all FBI agents do."

"Not really," I said. "I'll try to watch it."

"Oh, I don't mind. It's just bad for you. You know, that's one thing about Mickey. He was so considerate of being a gentleman all the time. He never swore much at all."

I winced.

"At least, not around me," she added.

CHAPTER TWENTY

1

Walter Fakazzi reached under his coat to feel the cloth he had wrapped tightly around the middle of his body. It was still dry—no fresh bleeding. And the wound seemed to be hurting less this time than last, although maybe he had just gotten used to the pain. He looked sorrowfully at the darkened Food Fair. If he had gone out this afternoon, he could have shopped there and saved himself two blocks' walking each way. But he might have been seen. The Pathmark was open all night, and safety was paramount.

He had been two weeks now, holed up alone in the tiny room just a few blocks from Journal Square, where he had staggered off the PATH train. The cops would never find him here, not unless he collapsed on the street from loss of blood, and he wouldn't do that. Even the threat of Willie Shutters seemed more remote. The paisano were mostly gone from the neighborhood. It was predominantly Latin now, which Fakazzi liked.

Still, there was danger in every shadow. Every taxi that passed, the driver might be working for Richards. The guys hanging around doorways, even the Spanish guy he paid rent to, they might be collecting numbers or somehow be on the payroll. The whole idea of staying in Jersey City was probably foolish. The smart thing would be to get a Greyhound out of here, maybe see what the midwest was like, or the south, while there was still the thirteen thousand left from what Mickey had given him. But he wasn't well enough yet. The damn gut wound would have to heal itself—maybe it would in a few more weeks. Meantime he would have to hope nobody knew where he was.

The collapsable food cart he pulled behind him hit a jag in the sidewalk and sent a streak of pain across his midsection. He stopped and reached under his coat again. Maybe a little moist over the wound, not bad. In the light of the Pathmark door he examined himself to make sure there wasn't any blood showing. Then he went in, headed for the canned goods section and filled his cart as quickly as possible with food that would keep without refrigeration and cook on the hotplate. Crap from Chef Boyardee, corned beef, baked beans, sardines, tuna. Then to the health and beauty aisle: bandage, adhesive, antiseptic. Cans of soda. Last, the treats: a quart of fresh milk he would drink tonight and three fresh apples in a little grey tray with a plastic wrap top.

There were a couple of people ahead of him in the checkout line. He pulled the scarf more around his face so he couldn't be recognized. Then he decided he might look suspicious with the scarf up, and he pulled it down a little. He felt himself growing weak, but he determined to hang on. He fumbled putting the cans on the counter and a couple of them nearly dropped. He caught them on the edge of the counter. He never could have picked them up off the floor. He had put a couple of twenties in his coat pocket and now he withdrew them and flipped them on the counter by the food. The checkout woman was grey and fat and never looked at him. He dumped the bags into the cart and scooped up his change.

Back out on the street he felt his stomach again. Definitely bleeding. The money this time he had carefully wrapped in plastic. It would be all right. But a couple thousand already had been stained with blood the night of the shooting. He wondered if he ever would be able to spend it. In more pain now, he pulled the cart through the darkness toward his rooming house.

2

The financial district emptied out at night and became a cold, quiet hell in angular stone architecture. That's why they had told Connally to wait there. Worse yet, it had been raining. Connally hoped it wouldn't rain again, not before they came. He was standing alongside the chill marble wall of the Chase Manhattan Bank building across Battery Park from the Staten Island ferry entrance. There was no shelter where they had told him to wait.

Over and over he told himself that they had no reason to kill him. He had been cheated by Carmody as certainly as they had been. He would show up as told, as if he had nothing to fear. If necessary, he would even agree to give back some of the money, though he had been cut short to begin with. For now, he had the money stored where it wouldn't be found.

The car appeared on time out of the blackness, a blue LTD. The front door opened for him. The driver never looked his way. In the back seat he could see a man in a grey overcoat. "I'm Danny," the man said. "Get in."

Connally did, and the car pulled away with a jerk, made a few turns down darkened streets and pulled to the curb opposite a dock. There was not another car or person in sight.

"You're a lucky man," Danny said. "It could have been Willie Shutters here 'stead of me."

"I told you over the phone," Connally said. "I got next to nothin' out of this. If Carmody fucked you guys, he fucked me worse."

"Yeah. This is two deals you been in where the mister got burned," Danny said.

"I didn't know Mickey was gonna score this big. I set the whole thing up and I get next to nothin', a few thousand. You think if I had known what he had up I would have cut him in almost free? The only reason I did, he told me he was working for you guys. He said all the money was going to Richards. That's why I let him in."

"Well, you don't know much you're supposed to know. If it was up to me I say Willie should have had you. The mister says you got a way to make up to him for it, though. He'll give you a chance."

"What does he want?"

"He wants you to find the money."

"Me? I thought you had this Willie character looking for it."

"Well, just say he figures two heads is better than one. You knew Carmody. You know who his friends are, the way they acted and all that."

"Yeah, but I ain't no detective."

"You are now. You get twenty percent of what you find. If you try to take any more, you ain't gonna live so long. You know? You do a good job and you maybe redeem yourself in the eyes of the boss. He don't think so much of you now. You need a clean gun?"

"What does he want me to do?"

"Anything you got to do to get the money. There's more than four million bucks out there. Don't worry what happens to people. Here. If some son of a bitch has it coming, and if that's what it takes . . ."

"What are you giving me? I never done anything like that before."

"Take it. It can't be traced. Just don't think it's gonna help you if Willie comes. Willie always gets the first shot."

"But I don't even know you."

"That's good for all of us. Here's one more thing that might help."

"What's this?"

"It's a list of all the people he called from the number he was using last fall. Also the broad the phone was listed under. You ever heard of her?"

"It's dark. I can't even read this. Mickey was married. I think he was getting divorced. How do you get this stuff?"

"From the phone company. The mister has a niece or something works in there. We get what we want, you just figure it that way, Bill. Right now, we want the money."

"Yeah. You and me both."

"You think Fakazzi knows?"

"How the fuck do I know what Fakazzi knows? I'd like to get my hands on him."

"You and somebody else I know. Just let's hope you get to him first so there's still enough of him left to lead us to the dough."

"I don't think Mickey'd tell Fakazzi a goddamned thing. Not where the money is. I don't think he'd tell anybody. He probably took it to the grave."

"Then maybe that's where we'll have to send you to find it. Joe, get the car going. Where can we drop you, Bill?"

"Shit. If I find anything out, how do I get in touch with you?"

"Yeah, that's one more thing. There's a coffee shop called Herky's on Twenty-Sixth Street, just off Seventh Avenue. Guy behind the counter there named Alphonse. You want to see somebody, just tell him. He'll fix it up."

CHAPTER TWENTY-ONE

1

I told Sara the whole story, or as much as I knew of it, on the drive down to the shore. And she told me some things about herself. She had lived her first 19 years on an Illinois farm attending Catholic schools, and still went to church at least once a week. After Mickey would stay in the apartment with her she felt obliged to go in the next morning and confess it. Jesus, what an earful that priest must have had.

She had come to New York on the Greyhound for a modeling career. Eventually she needed the airline job to keep herself dressed well enough to get the occasional modeling work that became available. It all sounded like the plot for a comic strip, but everything about the way she told it made it believable. At any rate, I could understand how Carmody had overwhelmed her.

Once across the Raritan River I stopped at a phone and called the real estate agent. She met us at the house. She was a blond, plump, gone-to-waste woman, probably married to some guy who rode the Jersey Central every morning to an office job in Manhattan. "This sure hit me by surprise," she said, after we had all three shaken hands at the curb. "I guess, looking back on it, there were only two possibilities from the beginning—either he was a rich, young playboy with a big inheritance, or else he was a gangster. But he was always the perfect gentleman. They took me out to dinner in their flashy limousine with the driver, paid for everything. They were the last people I ever expected to walk out on the rent."

Sara was looking at the house in awe: the big white pillars, the ocean visible around either side of it, lapping up to the sandy beach that was, in effect, Mickey's back yard. I knew she was trying to adjust to the fact that he had had this and never brought her there—in fact, had shared it with another woman.

"Do you want to go in?" the agent said.

I nodded, and we moved up the walk. Sara was still eyeballing the scene like Dorothy catching her first glimpse of Oz.

Inside, the house was just as impressive: hardwood floors, stone fireplace, curving stairway. "It came partly furnished," the agent explained. "But Barbara did a lot to fix it up. She made those curtains, and the hangings over there. I expected when the year's rental was up they were going to buy the place. They just seemed like the last people in the world—but I guess they weren't."

I asked if she had inspected the house.

"I walked through it. Doesn't look like they damaged anything."

"Could they have left anything behind?"

"There's some clothes up there, and, like, these drapes. I'd say she probably packed in a hurry. What are you looking for?"

"Any clue to where she was going."

"You're welcome to look."

We headed up the stairs. She was right about the

place—it looked like somebody had packed quickly. But the papers I could find gave no clue to Barbara Grover's plans. I made a mental note to check her phone records to see if she had called an airline or travel company for reservations. And I asked if there was anyplace in the house where somebody might think to hide money. That set the real estate agent back on her heels. "You think maybe he hid some of his cash here? He used to carry around a lot of cash."

"You never know," I said. "Any little secret places around here? Hollow walls? Trap doors?"

"You know, when we look over a place to see if we can sell it," she said, "we just don't ask about trap doors and hollow walls. I can tell you one thing—he better not have buried it in the yard unless he wanted it wet and salty."

I gave the house a once-over to check for any obviously just-pried-loose floorboards or wall panels. I couldn't find any, though I grant that if Mickey had done the job carefully, as he usually did his work, I probably wouldn't have found any.

I called headquarters to report. Bent wasn't in, but I got an assistant agent-in-charge. I could hardly believe his reaction. First, he was pissed as hell that I had gone down there myself instead of having turned the matter over to the Newark office, whose territory it was. I told him the Newark office didn't know a goddamn thing about the case and that I wanted to talk to the real estate agent personally. He said this was a big case and that the locals would want to be in on any recovery of money, and were so entitled. Had I told anybody where I was going? I said I hadn't, which was a lie, but I didn't want to get Bent in trouble. The A.S.A.C. got the number of the phone from me and told me to wait there.

Ten minutes later he was back on the line. Newark wanted to send a wrecking crew out to tear the place apart looking for the money and he had concurred. I told him I thought we'd be better off looking for Barbara

Grover than tearing down a $200,000 house, especially when it was probable that if the money ever had been in that house it had left before or at the same time Barbara Grover did. After all, the place had only been rented. But he said the crew from Newark was on its way and I had best watch my step.

"Excuse me," I said to the real estate lady when we were done. "I have some bad news for you." I told her what it was. She could hardly believe it either.

"But can they do that?" she wanted to know.

"They'll need a court order. But they can get that in an awful hurry. All somebody has to do is sign an affidavit about the Quincy deal and that the money hasn't been found and that Carmody just died and the house has been abandoned."

"But the house hasn't been abandoned. We're here right now."

"But Mickey isn't, and that's all the judge will need to know."

"I'd better call the owner," she said.

I went to tell Sara. My instructions were not to leave the house. I had warned her we might have to stay all day, but I hadn't really expected to. She didn't seem at all annoyed, though—in fact, I think the prospect of action stimulated her. "I hope they don't find any money because I don't want Mickey to have stolen it," she said. "But if he did, I hope they find it. I sure don't want that woman to have it. Barbara. You know, just looking at this house—I hope they do tear it down. That sounds like an awful thing to say, I know, but I hope they do. If he was really living here with that woman. Just the fact that he didn't even tell me. . . ."

She was speaking in a little girl's voice again, and there were tears in her eyes. I reached a hand very gently to her shoulder and she kind of lowered her face against it and wiped a few tears on the back of my wrist. Then she turned and fished a Kleenex from her purse. Maybe it was nothing, but I felt there had been a brief exchange of affection between us, and it was pleasant—the first time in a long while for me.

"I'm sorry. I guess I'm being awfully silly," she said.

"Well, I think Mickey stole the money all right. But I don't think they're going to find it here," I said.

"Then why are they going to wreck it?"

I had to laugh. "That's a reasonable question, all right. Someday maybe I'll tell you about the FBI." But not now. It was going to be hard to explain her presence there in the first place and I didn't want to add to my offenses. "Say, you haven't had anything to eat all day, have you?"

"Neither have you."

"Maybe there's some stuff left in the refrigerator. I'll ask the real estate lady." I had just gone a few steps when I heard Sara's voice. "Frank." It was the first time she had called me that. "That is your name, isn't it?" she said. I nodded. "I'd rather not eat their food," she said. "I know that sounds silly, but I'd just rather not. There was a McDonald's back up the road a mile or two."

"I'm not supposed to leave here," I said.

"Why don't I take the car? I'll bring back some sandwiches."

I froze.

She laughed. "Are you afraid to let me take your car? I have a license."

I lifted the keys from my pocket and extended them. "I'm not afraid," I said. "But if you don't bring this bureau car back fast, they're not only going to fire me, they're going to be telling jokes about me to anybody who will listen for the next ten years."

She thought that was really funny. "You want cheese on yours?"

"Yes," I said. "And a vanilla milkshake."

I held out a ten dollar bill.

"Don't be silly," she said, waltzing toward the door. "I'm not that poor."

"And for God's sake stay off the radio," I shouted after her.

2

Bent was the first one on the scene, and immediately wanted to know what Sara was doing there. He put the question to me, but she answered: "I knew Mickey," she said, "I wanted to come."

Bent looked at me skeptically, then back at her. "Would you excuse us a minute?" he said.

He got me into a corner. "Look, James Bond," he said, "she's a good-looking trick, all right, but—"

"Bent, she's a scared kid. This thing really broke her up. She had no idea Mickey had this place, or had any other women."

"Sure," he said. "Frank, I don't care what you do or who you bring along. But you've got to understand there are some things I couldn't bail you out of. Just bringing a potential suspect here—"

"Oh, God, she's not a suspect!"

"A potential suspect. Just bringing her here would be considered a dumb investigative technique. And if you're thinking what I'm thinking about that girl, it would be considered highly unethical and they'd can you in a minute."

"She knew Mickey for months. Sure she's naive about criminal stuff, but just because of that he might have told her something she'll remember later that could open the whole case for us. Besides, she's a sweet kid and I didn't want to leave her after I had upset her so much. You know, she didn't even know Mickey was dead?"

"Okay, you rationalize it any way you want to. I don't give a fuck. I'm just suggesting you don't wave her in front of the guys from Newark and the A.S.A.C. from East 69th Street. They'll all be coming any time. I sug-

gest you have her wait in the car and park it a block
away."

"It's the dead of winter."

"It's up in the forties. The sun's out. She won't freeze.
Besides, Mickey probably bought her a fur coat. I'm serious, Frank. Something like that could cost you your job."

He was right about the weather. I told Sara the situation as diplomatically as I could, and she took it fairly
well.

She was disappointed, she told me later, that we didn't
have one of those big balls swinging down from a crane,
shredding the place with one or two blows. Actually, it
was bad enough as it was—just teams of guys ripping up
hardwood floors, stripping walls, drilling into ceilings.
Some guys even started to dig until they discovered that
the real estate lady was right about the water level. The
real estate lady was upset to say the least, but there wasn't
much she could do about it. She had been unable to locate the owner by telephone, a blessing for all of us. She
wouldn't tell us who the owner was, even though we insisted we could find out anyway. I felt a little easier a
week later when I found out the house was owned by Ro-
ger Rhinestone, the rock and roll star. If the government's
idea of restoring the building to its original state was not
the same as Mr. Rhinestone's, I felt sure he could handle
the extra expenditure, especially since he obviously had
decided he didn't want to live there any more anyway.

What disturbed me more was the ridiculous expenditure by the bureau—when I hadn't even been able to fina-
gle a trip to Tennessee that I thought might open up the
investigation. When the A.S.A.C. got tired of supervising
the wrecking crew debacle, I started a three-way conversation with him and Bent. If we were this desperate for
results, and this free with money, I argued, why the hell
couldn't I get on a plane south in the logical hope that
viewing both halves of the case would enable me to get a

better idea of what happened? Bent backed me up to the extent of saying that the cables from Nashville showed no indication that our office there had gone beyond the most preliminary findings.

The A.S.A.C. seemed to be yielding, but postponed a decision till morning. For all I know, permission for jurisdictional crossings had to come from Washington.

The wrecking crew was still patching up that poor house when the official brain trust finally conceded that it was futile for us to stick around any longer. It was already dark, the temperature had long since dropped out of the forties and I was afraid Sara would be half frozen. I was wrong. She still had my keys and had kept the car warm as toast, even made a couple of trips to the McDonald's for coffee.

A lousy day at the Jersey shore can always be salvaged with a dinner at Evelyn's in Belmar, the best goddamn seafood restaurant there is. Sara, Illinois girl, had never eaten steamers before. We shared a bucket of them before starting in on the lobster and king crab. She talked excitedly about the thrill of seeing real FBI men in action. I just couldn't make her understand what a fiasco she had witnessed.

When we got to her apartment door I was prepared to let her go with a handshake and hope for some encouragement to see her again when the Quincy investigation was over. But suddenly, there in the hall, she had thrown her arms around my neck and was pressing her body to mine. She didn't kiss me then, just buried her face in my shoulder. So I wrapped my arms around her and we held each other in our winter coats. Eventually, I heard that little girl's voice say, "Thank you. You were so kind to me today. It could have been just awful."

"Sure," I said. "I left you sitting out in the car all day in freezing weather."

She lifted her face toward me and was laughing. "That was all right," she said. "You had to do your work. I meant taking me down there when I was probably in the way, and buying me dinner. I would have been so lonely today if you hadn't done that. Will you come in and have some coffee?"

"Sure," I said, though I really didn't want coffee.

"It's this morning's coffee," she said as we were taking our coats off. "Oh, I can make a fresh pot."

"Don't bother doing that."

"Would you rather have tea?"

"I almost never drink tea."

"Well, let me think what else I can offer you."

That was the last thing either of us said until an unusual exchange in the doorway to the bedroom. We had been kissing and squeezing each other, and my hands had slipped under her sweater and undone her bra, and had unzipped her slacks at the side and begun fondling her bottom, when she grabbed me tight around the neck again and said, "Oh, I want to so much. But it's wrong, I know it is." It was the first time I had heard anything like that since college.

"It's not wrong if you want to," I said, hardly believing that the words were coming out of my mouth after all those years.

"I hardly know you. And it would be a sin even if I did know you."

"Well, I am the FBI."

She gave a little laugh. "And you've been so good to me. I just. . ." It was as if she had to rationalize what she was going to do. Then she said, "Could we just lie down awhile and not take all our clothes off? You know."

It really was like college. She was 26 years old. I suppose I should have been turned off, but the truth is, I was touched, or charmed, or whatever you want to call it—intrigued. "If you want," I said.

I wound up masturbating her with her panties still on. She didn't touch me sexually at all before we drifted off to sleep. But then, in the middle of the night, I felt her hand inside my zipper, and my pants were coming off, and then her mouth was on me. I started to raise her so we could make love, but she resisted and kept at her work. When she had done, and licked it clean, she brought her head up to my shoulder.

"You were so generous, so unselfish with me," she said. "I wanted to do something for you."

I wondered if the Catholics taught you that only fucking was sinful. But by then our clothes were off, and I knew that before the night was over there was no way she could escape my going inside her.

And to crown it all, I walked into the office the next morning and found out I had authorization to go to Nashville for as long as I needed.

CHAPTER TWENTY-TWO

Fud Peerce climbed down off the chair. He had been peeking over the top of the office partition. Now the visitor in the business suit had left. Peerce went to the window behind his desk and peeked around the venetian blind. He saw the visitor get into the Ford with the rent-a-car plates and drive away. Peerce went straight to the telephone and dialed.

"Abner?" he shouted into the phone. "Aw, goddamn it, never mind." He hung up and dialed again.

"Ellis, Ellis, this is Fud," he announced rapidly as soon as the other man had got on the line. "I tried to get Abner and he ain't there. What the hell's goin' on?"

"What're you talkin' about?" Ellis Bardell's voice was much slower, and carried a current of annoyance.

"The goddamned FBI's back here. Some fella all the way from New York. He been out to see you yet?"

"Nope."

"Well, he just walked out of here right now. I thought

you guys told me this was over. Everything was taken care of."

"Wha'd he want?"

"I don't know, Ellis. Just the same shit all over again, only all the way from New York. I don't like the smell of it."

There was a pause. Peerce envisioned Bardell spitting out some tobacco juice. "Well, wha'd he ast you?" the voice said.

"Just the same goddamn stuff. About who this guy Portaquil was and how'd I meet him."

"An' wha'd you say?"

"Same as before. I never changed nothin'. Told him the fella just walked in off the street, gonna be a big builder around here. But this guy went on longer than the other ones. Kept talking about all kinds of crazy things. Do I know a Sara something or other, and if I knew Mickey whatever it is."

"He was askin' about Mickey?"

"Who is this Mickey, anyway, Ellis?"

"Never mind that. You didn't give him my name, did you?"

"'Course not. He didn't even mention you. But he did ask about Connally."

"Well, maybe you better call Connally then."

"He's up in New York somewhere now, ain't he?"

"Hang on. I'll get the damn thing. I got it here somewhere. Yeah, New Jersey. Area 201, the number's KL-5-0819. Yeah, you give him a call. But don't say nothin' to nobody else."

"But what's this guy doin' down from New York?"

"It don't mean they know nothin'. They may do that all the time."

"'Cept they know about Connally. He's the guy you said brought this Portaquil character down here. Him and this guy Mickey. If they know about Connally, they gotta know about you. 'Cause you're the only connection, right? How they find about him, anyway?"

"Prob'ly 'cause of what I told you about this Mickey. Now don't worry about nothin'."

"What about Mickey?"

"That he got shot, you asshole. They had one of them gang wars up there or somethin', so they go around talkin' to everybody knew Mickey. Connally don't tell 'em nothin', you don't tell 'em nothin'. Nothin' happens."

"But how does he know to ask me about Connally? He's got to know Connally helped set up Portaquil."

"Fud, you got fifty thousand out of that and you're causin' me more than fifty thousand worth of trouble. Now get lost."

"Well, I ain't gonna get lost, Ellis. That ain't the only bone I got to pick with you."

"Well, it's about all I got time to hear."

"You got time to hear about what a customer of mine saw goin' up one of them hills off Sawmill Ridge Road last night, back of Pete's property?"

Ellis's voice changed. "What the hell you talkin' about?"

"You know goddamn well what I'm talkin' about. Who's bankrollin' all that stuff?"

"Nobody ain't seen nothin'."

"Fourth dirt road off the right of Sawmill Ridge Road, after you cross the highway. Couple of trucks loaded down with sugar, and some old boys, just last night. Now what are you tryin' to tell me, there ain't some distillin' goin' on up there? And you boys ain't part of it?"

"Whatever it is ain't none of your fucking business. 'Sides, you know that kind of stuff ain't my affair."

"Now don't give me that shit about Pete, Ellis. You and Abner do the bankin'. He's on the board of directors here."

"Yeah, and you ain't the only banker in Crockett County, either, Fud. An' a man don't always got to shop at his brother's store. Now you shut your yap and mind your own business. Who is this guy says he saw them things?"

"Oh, just a customer," Peerce said cutely.

"Well, when I got a deal for you, you'll hear about it, Peerce. Now you just keep your yap shut on stuff don't concern you." The line clicked off suddenly and Peerce knew that Bardell had banged the receiver down in anger.

Peerce felt pleased with himself at having hit a nerve with Bardell. The son of a bitch would worry about that still now, maybe have to post extra guards. Then Peerce's mind returned to the FBI agent and that brought a frown back to his face. He dialed the number for Connally in New Jersey. There was an answer.

"Connally?"

"Yeah."

Peerce wondered about a man who was home at 11 a.m. on a workday. "This is D. C. Peerce, down at the First National Bank in Caliquatta, Tennessee."

"Yeah, yeah. What's up?" Connally sounded as if he had just been awakened.

"There's an FBI man snooping around down here from New York. We thought the FBI had finished with this thing a month ago. I just talked to Ellis about it and he thought I ought to call you."

"Yeah?"

"The guy was in here this morning asking about you, about whether I knew you. I didn't tell him a goddamn thing, of course. But how is he asking me about you unless he has some idea you're the one brought that Portaquil character down. And he knew all about your friend Mickey, too. And he kept wanting to know about how much money I made off the deal, like into my personal accounts at the bank. Like he must suspect about them giving me the fifty thousand."

"Wait a minute, wait a minute. This FBI guy was in your office this morning?"

"Yes, that's what I just told you."

"And he's from New York. Is it Scanlon?"

"Yeah, that's his name. You know him?"

"Jesus Christ, where are you calling from?"

"My office."

"Oh, you stupid son of a bitch. And you just talked to Bardell from in there?"

"Now, hold on—"

"Didn't you ever stop to think that Scanlon probably put a tap on that phone before he went in to see you? Because he knew the first thing you'd do would be to pick it up when he left? That's the oldest trick in the book. You stupid shithead!"

For the second time in a row, Fud Peerce was hung up on with an anger strong enough to transmit itself by wire.

CHAPTER TWENTY-THREE

1

"We got him. Hoo, shit, did we get that son of a bitch on tape, and you ought to hear him!"

I could hear Henry Fitchett shouting excitedly before I even got the door open to the second story room we had borrowed across the street from the bank. I had just come from Fud Peerce's office and had driven around the block as a diversionary tactic before returning to Fitchett, who by that time seemed ready to jump out of his skin.

Henry was a young cop from Dornaville, about 12 miles from Caliquatta, who had been assigned to help me with the wiretap I wanted to throw on Fud Peerce before I went to see him. The guys in Nashville told me Henry had spent a week or two at some kind of L.E.A.A. school for local police, which made him about my best bet in Crockett County.

"First thing he did was call Ellis Bardell," Henry said, waving a tape at me. "Then he called this guy Connally up in New Jersey. It's all on here, boy. They said the whole works. Whoo-ee, man, Frank, you sure know what you're doin'."

"I just hope the judge feels the same way, Henry. You got the machine turned off already?"

"I didn't figure there was much sense keepin' it on. Last thing this fella Connally said was tellin' Peerce how you probably had his phone tapped, to shut up, you know. Boy, he knows you, Frank. I mean this fella Connally, he really knows you. You must be famous up there."

"They haven't got that much else to worry about," I said.

"Anyway, I don't see how much more we could get old Fud to say that ain't already on here," Henry went on. "We could keep that recorder goin' all week an' I don't know what. They talked about him gettin' money, fifty thousand cash greenbacks, for cashin' them checks. An' how Abner and Ellis brung in this fella Portaquil, an' how Connally introduced 'em. Hell, ol' Fud even told where the Bardells have got a new moonshine thing goin' up off a Old Sawmill Road. Wait till we tell Elan Warfield about that. Son of a bitch, if he won't croak!"

"What's that? Who's Warfield?" I asked.

"Oh, ol' Elan's the ATF man around here. You know, Alcohol, Tobacco, Firearms. The revenue service. Boy, he's the guy put Ol' Ellis away the last time. You betcha he'd like to get Abner and Pete in the can, too."

"But that's another crime, Henry. You know what I told you about minimization. That's damned important to judges."

"But they went into this whiskey thing right from Portaquil. It wasn't no separate conversation. Just like you said, there's times you can't switch it off because two crimes is really part of the same conversation."

"It still worries me."

"You just worry too much, Frank. That's your whole trouble. You don't mind me sayin' so. Them judges down here's different from the ones up north. Anyway, like you said, it's all one conversation. It was one of them times you can't minimize nothin'."

"Have you heard the tape yet?"

"Hell, it ain't even unwound yet."

"Well, let's give it a listen."

Henry Fitchett put the tape back onto the machine. His fingers were shaking so nervously I thought it would take him forever to thread it. For some reason my expectations weren't high, which was a good thing as it turned out.

The tape started off swell. I heard Peerce call Abner and a guy say Abner wasn't there. Then I heard another number being dialed. I heard the phone ring, I heard a hello, I heard Peerce's voice, still quite recognizable, saying, "Ellis, Ellis, this is Fud. What the hell's goin' on?" And I heard a voice answer "What're you talkin' about?" Then I heard a loud buzz. A goddamn monotone hum. And that's all there was from that point on.

Fitchett was beside himself. He started twisting dials, but all he could do was make the hum louder or softer. I had him stop the machine to see if maybe it had gone on "record" by accident. But the "playback" head was the only one against the tape, and the buzz was all you could hear.

Fitchett began apologizing profusely.

"Well, that's the way it goes sometimes," I said, trying to calm him down. I really would have preferred to kill him, but since I wasn't going to do that it was better not to have him so upset.

"I don't know what could have gone wrong," he said.

"Did you put the radio transmitter in the switchbox all right?"

"Sure, last night. Just like it said in the manual. Just like you told me. Hell, the transmitter had to be wired up all right, Frank, or I wouldn't've heard the conversation."

"That's true," I agreed. "And the machine was working yesterday. We checked it all out."

"Hell, I heard it all, Frank. They said everything. Fud got fifty thousand dollars cash for doing those checks. They said it twice. They talked about Mickey, that Carmody fellow, only they just called him Mickey. They said Connally brought Portaquil down south."

I just nodded and bit my lip, and it was quiet for awhile.

Finally, Fitchett said, in the softest voice I had ever heard him use, "You know what could have happened?"

"No, Henry. Tell me."

"Well, when I heard him calling Ellis right away, and all, I did turn the recording level dial up just a little bit so it would come in loud and clear, you know."

"I guess you turned it up a little bit too much."

"I've had the recording level up on that machine before and it never gave me that kind of feedback."

"Maybe you were never running it through the radio receiver before," I suggested.

"I guess not. I'm sorry, Frank."

"It was my fault," I said. "We should have just got a direct line from outside the building and then we wouldn't have had to send the signal through the radio receiver at all. Just a simple direct line, the first thing they teach you, that was all I had to get. And you would have been listening to exactly what was going into the tape recorder, and you would have known."

"But we talked about that last night, Frank. You said we shouldn't do that 'cause for a direct line we would have had to go through the phone company, and this is such a small town somebody might have told Fud and the other guys what we were doing. That would have blown our security. You said so yourself."

"Yeah," I said. "I kept our security just perfect. All we don't have is a tape."

"I'm really sorry, Frank."

"I know. Well, look, maybe we can still salvage something out of this. Get out your pen and your note paper and write down everything you can remember of those conversations. Every word you can remember, just as they said it, while it's still fresh in your mind. We'll get it notarized today, and it can at least help corroborate your testimony."

"Testimony? Would a judge let me go up there and just say what I heard? Like testify?"

"Sure."

"No kidding."

"Well, it wouldn't be as good as a tape, I'll allow that. The defense attorneys'll have a field day making jokes about that tape going bad before anybody says boo. But your word's a damn sight better than nothing. We'll need something else—some corroboration—but it's a start. Maybe just having it will be enough to get somebody to turn state's evidence."

Fitchett seemed strangely silent. "Maybe old Fud will see your affidavit and plead out," I said.

"But either way, he'd find out I was the one telling on him, wouldn't he?" Fitchett finally said.

"Huh?"

"I mean, without a tape, it'd be just my word, and he'd know that, right?"

"You're a policeman, Henry. That's what you're here for, is to present evidence at trials so we can send crooks to jail."

"Boy, I just don't know, Frank."

"What do you mean you don't know? You're not afraid of Peerce, are you?"

"Well, you got to understand. This is a small place. He could take my daddy's farm away from him. And ol' Fud'd be just the kind of guy who'd do that, too."

"Wait a minute. How can Peerce take your father's farm?"

"Well, Fud's mortgaged my family for years. He's got all our livestock, the land, our house. My daddy has to go to Fud every spring. He has for years."

"Your daddy."

"Sure."

"Why didn't you tell me before?"

"Gee, I didn't think it was that important, Frank. I mean, just making the tape and all, that's what I thought we were going to do. I mean that's fine, you know, old Fud had it coming. But just me getting up and putting my word on the line to send him to jail—I'd have to ask my daddy before I could do a thing like that."

2

I stopped at a pay phone, called Bent and told him what had just happened. He started to commiserate, but I told him that at least we could be confident of our facts now, even if we weren't able to offer them in court. I had no doubt that Fitchett had been telling me the truth.

I told Bent that Bill Connally was in northern New Jersey and ought to be found. Fitchett hadn't written down the number—he thought we had it on tape. It would be on Peerce's phone toll records, but they wouldn't be available for a few days and by then Connally, who knew the call to him had been tapped, might have moved. Still, I thought we ought to try to find him. And if anybody was going to get a deal, we ought to offer it to Connally, even if it had to be immunity. We had no usable evidence on him anyway, and I especially wanted to hang Peerce and Timmons and find out who Portaquil was. Connally was one of maybe only two people still alive who knew Portaquil's identity, the other being Portaquil himself. And Connally was more likely than Peerce or Timmons to know where the rest of the money was, although I frankly doubted that any of them knew.

Bent told me he found my comments about Timmons especially interesting, since Timmons had evidently left town. A week ago he had bought a white Continental Mark IV and neither he nor the Mark IV had been seen in five days. His wife said she didn't have a clue to his whereabouts. On top of that, Bent told me that background investigation showed Timmons liked to gamble, frequented race tracks, may have gone to crap games around New York and had been to Las Vegas a couple of times.

Well, I said, that was nice. As for me, I was going to see Ellis Bardell. Bardell didn't necessarily know about the wiretap. He might still be surprisable and maybe he knew who Portaquil was.

Bardell lived about five miles out of town in a one story brick ranch house about 50 yards off the two-lane blacktop. He lived alone except for a Mexican servant, a menacing German shepherd dog, some equally menacing guns and hundreds, probably thousands, of chickens. For that matter, menacing is the most appropriate word I can think of to describe Bardell himself. I was kept waiting for ten interminable minutes on his front porch with the dog straining on a chain just a few inches away. My hand wandered nervously in the vicinity of my own gun for the first time I could remember outside of target practice. Finally, the Mexican maid let me in. Bardell was sitting in a corner, polishing a shotgun that lay across his lap. He did not get up or even look up.

"What do you want," he growled, emphasizing the "you."

I walked over and flipped open my identification. "My name's Frank Scanlon, I'm an FBI agent, I'm from New York," I said. He still didn't look up. "May I sit down?"

"Suit yourself," he said. "But you better not be plannin' to stay long."

I sat on a sofa a few feet away and opened the latch on the briefcase I was carrying. "Mr. Bardell, I have a tape recorder in here. May I turn it on?" No use taping him secretly—I already knew the truth, and if I was going to get anything usable in court he would have to have his Miranda warnings and the rest of it.

"Fuck, no," he said. "You put that goddamned thing away."

"Mr. Bardell, we already have you on tape once."

"You what?" He looked up that time.

"Did Fud Peerce call you on the telephone this morning?"

"What the fuck are you talkin' about?"

"We know what happened. We know about Mickey and Connally and how they brought Portaquil down here and how you brought Portaquil into Peerce's bank, and about the $50,000 kickback to Peerce—"

"What the fuck are you talkin' about?" he repeated, now straining forward from his chair the way the dog had been straining at the leash.

"You're a conspirator in a multi-million-dollar fraud, Mr. Bardell. If you would give me a statement, either here, or come into our office in Nashville with me, and tell us some of the things we don't know, maybe we could arrange for you not to have to go to trial with the others."

He stood up, a towering figure. He held the shotgun pointed sideways by the barrel with one hand, and gestured at the door with the other. "Now you git outa here right now, and I mean now," he said.

"Look," I said, "if you're trying to threaten me with that gun you better think about it, because I'm a federal officer."

He bit off my words before I could get them all out. "I don't care who the fuck you are, you got no right to be here or bring a tape recorder in here or tell me this shit. If you got charges, you take 'em to the grand jury. I know that much, mister. Now you git that suitcase of yours back into that rig and you git from here. I don't want to see you comin' round here again without no warrant, you hear?"

3

I was really glad that when I got back to the motel Sara was waiting for me. I guess I better explain how that happened. As soon as I found out I would be going south I called her and asked her to dinner that night. We were just digging into that wonderful green fettucini at Il Monello, and I told her I would be leaving town for awhile the next morning. She pressed for details, and since I had told her so much about the case already, I told her more. She said she wanted to come along, that she had a week's time off and nothing to do with it now that Mickey was gone, that it would be nice to get away from the winter weather, that she would stay out of my way and that in Tennessee I'd be glad for company. I told her that agents didn't even take their wives on trips like this, and besides, I couldn't afford her and certainly couldn't put her on the expense account. She said she flew practically free, got discounts on lodging and had been saving plenty of money. I told her she'd be stuck at the motel all the time. She said we could find one with a pool. I said it sometimes snows in Tennessee in January. She said we'd find one with a heated pool. I told her she was absolutely gorgeous and I loved her black dress.

Somewhere between Nashville and Caliquatta we did find a motel with a heated pool, although the weather was sunny and the temperature hit 70. Sara slipped out of the pool wet, wearing a blue bikini that was perfect for her shape and coloring, and kissed me, her breasts leaving two matched wet marks on my shirt. Then she noticed I was in a down mood and asked me what had gone wrong. When we got inside, I told her.

"Can't you just *make* the policeman testify?" she asked. "I didn't think a person was allowed to just refuse."

"Sure, you can make a witness testify. But you can't make him be convincing. Try to build a whole case around what that kid heard and there are a hundred things he could say or not remember on the stand that would just kill us."

"I'm sorry," she said.

"Fucking kid and his tape recorder."

"Don't talk like that, Frank."

"Okay." I sat down on the edge of the bed and she knelt behind me and massaged my back.

"I'm getting you all wet," she laughed.

I turned to look at her and she looked down, still embarrassed like a little kid. "Then I guess we'd better take our clothes off," I said.

While we were lying there in bed I decided I was going to have to look up Elan Warfield, the revenue agent Fitchett told me about. By this time I didn't really give a shit about the fruits of the poisoned tree, or whatever the hell lawyers call it when you get something off a wiretap that didn't go according to Hoyle. If I couldn't indict the Bardells for the Quincy fraud, I at least wanted to cause them a little bit of trouble. Besides, maybe Warfield would have some ideas about how to make a case against the Bardells on the checks.

I got him by phone from bedside. He had the southerner's quick closeness and enthusiasm—"Why, shore, Frank, come right on down," he beamed, practically loud enough not to need a phone. "We'll do anything we can for ya, and maybe we can show ya a thing or two."

I told Sara I was going to the courthouse and suggested she might want to come along and walk around town, though I warned her Caliquatta wasn't exactly like midtown Manhattan. She said it was probably a lot like Effingham, Illinois, so we both got dressed and hopped in the car.

When Elan took one look at her he was having nothing to do with her walking around town. He insisted she come right into the office with us.

"So they're sendin' New Yorkers all the way down here to find ol' Portaquil, huh?" he said, motioning us to chairs. We had lots to choose from. It was a big room, full of gunmetal grey government issue office furniture, and we were the only ones in it. "Boy, that guy got off with some wad, didn't he?" Elan went on. "Four and a half million. You gonna tell me ol' Fud Peerce didn't know they was somethin' funny about that guy?"

"I'm not gonna tell you that," I said.

"No, man. You take my word for it, ol' Fud, he musta known just what was goin' on the whole time and prob'ly got a piece of it. You know, I seen them armored trucks drivin' down here from Nashville just unloadin' tons a money at Fud's bank. Happened three or four times in just a couple a weeks. Why, you never seen nothin' like that—maybe they come once a month normally, and that's a lot. You see all them armored trucks, you know right away somethin's wrong. They must a been truckin' all them tens and twenties and fifties in for that guy Portaquil."

"That's what it was, all right," I agreed.

Elan was looking at Sara. She was smiling and seemed enchanted by his down-home accent.

"You got to wonder how he made off with so much cash," Elan said.

"Folks at the bank tell me he just carried it off," I said. "Sometimes in a suitcase, sometimes in a cloth bag slung over one shoulder."

Elan looked back at me. "You know, I seen that guy, and I knew right off they was somethin' wrong. You know, his mustache, it wasn' real. Fu Manchu, or whatever they call it. Hell, I went over there one day, you could see it, the thing looked like it was comin' off his face on one side, you know? I mean, it wasn't even glued on real well."

"That's what the people over at the bank said."

"So you think you may have a case on Fud? That'd be somethin' around here."

"I know damn well he was in on it. We tapped his phone and heard him say it."

"Phone taps! Jeez, you guys are really into this thing, aren't you?"

"Well, the main reason I'm here is something else we

heard on the wiretap. About booze. And I'm telling you exactly where I got the information, because it could really give you trouble if you try to make a moonshining case out of this. The tap was authorized by the judge up in Nashville strictly on probable cause Fud might know something about the Portaquil job. The other stuff was just thrown in. I didn't even hear it myself. A cop I was working with heard it. He says it was just part of the conversation and he couldn't have avoided listening."

Elan was smiling. "You don't have to make excuses. I don't give a damn about all them fancy rules anyway. You just tell me what ol' Fud said about whiskey."

So I told him, including the exact location of the still the Bardells were supposedly operating, just as Fitchett had related it.

"Sho nuff," Elan said. "Guess I'll have to go up there tonight. Want to come along?"

How do you refuse an offer like that?

"Wonder what ol' Fud was so upset about," Elan mused. "You know, the Bardells been buyin' their sugar and stuff with his money for quite a few years now. I wonder if they gone to some other banker on this deal."

"Are you telling me Peerce invests in illegal stills?"

"His bank does, damn right. Has to. Moonshine's the biggest business around here. Been so for about two hundred years. You cain't make any money by stayin' out of it, that's for sure. Unless you're Hezekiah X. Portaquil."

"But how can you put on your books that you're—"

"Well, son, you don't put that on your books, that it's a still. You put on there that you're loaning it out on any old thing, like land, maybe. Or what the Bardells always do is put up Ellis's chickens. You see all them chickens when you was up there? They been collateral for an awful lot of sugar in their time."

"How do you know?"

"Well, there's two things you got to watch in this business. One of them's sugar gettin' bought or stockpiled or brought into town anywhere, and the other's bank loans to the Bardells, though they're the hardest to find out about. But every time that sugar shows up, you can betcha there's a mortgage goin' on them chickens. Hell, a few years back we busted up one hell of a big still up in them mountains and George Hewlitt's bank foreclosed Ellis on his chickens." Elan began laughing. "Hell, Ellis like to—"

Suddenly Elan snapped forward in his chair and slapped a desk. "Doggone, I'll bet that's it. I'll bet ol' George Hewlitt's loanin' money to Ellis again and that's what's turnin' ol' Fud's belly. Bet you anything. 'Cept I wonder why."

"Maybe they're afraid of all the examiners down at Peerce's bank," I offered.

"Could be. Ain't like Ellis to be afraid of somethin' like that, though. Besides, them examiners didn't find nothin' everybody didn't already know nohow. Maybe we just ought to go ast ol' George. Tomorrow we will, after we bust up that still tonight. Doggone. Sugar back in town and ol' George Hewlitt lendin' the money."

Then Sara, who had been quietly enjoying the conversation, asked a very perceptive question: "If you keep watch on the sugar," she said, "how come they could set up this new still and you didn't know about it?" I had wondered the same thing and not asked for fear of offending our host. Sara could ask it and not offend anybody.

"Well," Elan began, slumping back in his chair, "it's kind of funny. We just been spendin' our time on other things now. Guns and gambling, mostly. Most of our people been transferred back to Nashville, or Memphis or Atlanta. That's why you see all these empty desks. See, things have been awful slow in the moonshine business since the summer of '73. That's when the sugar prices started jumpin'. Went up about three times what they had been. Used to be you could get you a gallon of lightning right there at the still for six dollars. Sugar went up, they wanted fifteen. Hell, you can just about buy government whiskey for that."

"Government whiskey?" I asked.

"Taxed stuff. You know, like J. W. Dant."

"Well, why didn't they raise the price of J. W. Dant?"

"Don't need sugar. They cook that stuff real slow and even like. The sugars come right out of the natural grain."

"Why don't they do that up here?"

"You want to know the reason? You're lookin' at him, pardner. They got to go up in the hills to cook that stuff, and ain't no matter how high up they get in them hills, they ain't no way in the world they're gonna stay up there three weeks without me findin' 'em. And that's how long it takes to cook out a mash from its own sugar. Three weeks. So they got to buy the sugar and haul it up there. On a truck, if they's a road. Sometimes guys'll carry two or three hundred pounds of that stuff on their backs up one of them mountains, and then come right on back for another two or three hundred pounds. The price of that sugar went up, a lot of folks couldn't pay it. You got to understand, that was the major industry around here for about two hundred years. Best way for a farmer to get rid of his corn was to ship it out as whiskey. Hell, they ain't a family in Crockett County hasn't had somebody in the moonshine business. My grandmother had a still on her property. She wouldn't touch no liquor from the day she was born, preached it was sin, but they was a still out back on that farm. I used to watch it. So'd she, when she was younger."

Sara and I looked at each other. "We don't do it in Effingham," she swore.

Elan let himself lapse into dialogue less literate than he obviously was capable of, and his mouth sometimes turned up at the corners. It was clear he wasn't blind to the humor in what he was saying. But he didn't want us blind to the seriousness of it, either.

"Hell, the sugar crisis has probably hit the banking business, too," he said. "Maybe that's why ol' Fud went into cashing stolen checks. Well, anyway, why don't you be up here 'round nine o'clock, Frank, and we'll go take a look. Sara, you better figure to stay home on this one, back at your motel." He pronounced it MOE-tell.

She turned to me. "Are you sure you ought to go, Frank?" She looked at Elan. "Is it dangerous?"

"Nawww, nawww," he said with a wave of the hand. "I been goin' out on them patrols fifteen years now. Just sometimes gets a little bumpity for a lady. Frank and me gonna have a good time, bust up a still, mess on the Bardells, maybe get 'em to crack this Portaquil thing. You just wait, Frank. We're gonna solve that whole case for you."

CHAPTER TWENTY-FOUR

Ellis Bardell drove the battered, ten-year-old Cadillac roughly over the rock-strewn path. The man in the front seat beside him was as bulky and swarthy as Ellis himself. "How the hell'd ol' Fud find out about it?" the man asked.

"Hell, Pete, I don't know," Ellis said. "Some son of a bitch is talking to him. Coulda been somebody just passing by. Maybe it's one of our still boys into him for a loan. I don't know."

Ellis called to the man directly behind him in the back seat, a tall, dark man of about thirty-five with an imbecile's face and a missing front tooth. "Hey, you didn't go talkin' to no bankers, did you, shithead?" Pete and the fourth man in the car laughed.

The man with the missing front tooth didn't laugh. "Nobody call me shithead," he said.

Ellis Bardell's right arm swung around behind him with speed unusual for such a hulking man, and the edge of his hand sharply found the cheek of the man with the missing front tooth. The man's eyes flared in anger and his hand started up by instinct, but he caught the fierce stares of the other two men in the car and restrained himself.

"I call you what I goddamn please," Ellis said. "Now you concentrate on guardin' this place tonight. We got a whole carload of ol' boys just as dumb as you are comin' up to help. Any revenue or anybody else come tonight, they gonna get a mouthful of axhandle."

The car bounced and jolted over the rocks. "This ain't the only road up, is it?" the other man in the back seat said.

"What's a matter," Ellis replied. "Too bumpy for you?"

"No place to run a roadblock," the man said. "It's a bottleneck. Some son of a bitch puts his finger in it and . . . shit, all them trees . . ."

"I seen you done all right weavin' around them telephone poles in the Figure-8 at Genesis Saturday night," Ellis said.

"Yeah. And I had a souped-up Merc, not a truck full of gallon lightning jugs."

"Well, we got you the best goddamn truck that ever raced down a fuckin' mountain," Pete said. "Besides, there's one or two more roads down if you ever need 'em. You won't have no problem."

They pulled to a clearing. On one side was a huge metal vat filled with slug-colored slop. Four men with tree branches taller than the men were pushed their way around the outside of the vat stirring it. They obviously needed tremendous effort to get the branches to move through the thick mash.

The Cadillac doors swung open. Ellis approached the vat with the others behind him. "Hey," he called to the men around the vat. "You can do that better gettin' back down inside." The legs of the men's pants were caked in mash, indicating they had already spent time in the vat.

"Gettin' too hot, boss," one of the men said.

Two other men came out of the woods carrying large tanks of butane, and set them next to other tanks that were fueling the deep blue fire under the vat. Now each of the six plugged-in tanks of butane forming the hot plate around the vat had a twin ready to be plugged in when its own gas was exhausted.

One of the men with the branches stopped stirring, caught a breath and said, "It get any hotter we cain't stay this close. Gonna have to let her bubble and go."

"Nobody tol' you to stop stirrin'," Ellis said. "Cain't make no whiskey with cold mash."

The man who had been on the right side of the back seat of the Cadillac, the race driver, was approaching a big, open-back truck parked near the edge of the clearing. The truck seemed about to split apart under the strain of its heavy pile of sugar sacks. The sacks were piled over the sides of the truck until it seemed that one more sack would have started an avalanche.

"That is one mother load of sugar," the man said.

"Cost enough," Ellis told him. "But we can easy sell five thousand gallons this week. All we can make." Then he pointed to the men at the vat. "They ain't even hooked up to the cooling cars yet," he said.

The other man, the race driver, saw the two junked cars sitting next to the vat. Their radiators would provide the cooling coils for the distillation process. "They ain't gonna be ready with no whiskey till close to dawn," Ellis said. "Wait till I get a security system set up, then you and me'll go back down. Pete can handle things till it's time for you to run a load."

The men who had been stirring the vat backed away with their branches. Two other men set the vat's heavy cover in position to be slid over the top when it was time to hook up the radiators. "Now, this is what you guys are gonna do," Ellis said, approaching them. Then he saw the man with the missing front tooth, wiping blood from the wound on his right cheek, and Ellis motioned the man over with the others. "You, too," he said, and then, after a moment's thought, added, "Shithead."

CHAPTER TWENTY-FIVE

I met Elan at the courthouse as he instructed. There was nobody else there.

"You think two of us are enough?" I asked.

"You and me? Hell, yes. If it looks too bad we can always come back and phone for help."

"You told somebody where we were going, didn't you?"

"Oh, a couple ol' boys I know. That damn ATF office in Nashville, they had already closed up by the time you left here this afternoon. You know how federal offices are. Tried callin' one or two other agents around here and couldn't find nobody home. They'll probably be home tonight, though—if we need 'em."

As we went out the door and headed for the parking lot, Elan kept talking. "You know, ever since the sugar prices took off in '73, we ain't had much still action. Used to be we'd bust up maybe ten a month. Nowadays we're lucky to see one. Kinda miss it. That's prob'ly why I couldn't get nobody today. They just don't expect the action."

"If times are so bad, why's Ellis taking this chance?" I asked.

"Well, lotsa reasons. One thing, sugar prices goin' down, I hear. 'Nother, they's still a lot a niggers grew up on the stuff and just like to drink it. Just prefer it." As if he could sense my unease with the word, he added, "Black guys, whatever you want to call 'em. That's mostly the market now. But the main thing, these ol' boys in Chattanooga were tellin' me, there's been a kind of change in the organized crime leadership down there. Used to be a fella name Horse Mawsley ran things out of Chattanooga. Well, they got Horse on gamblin' last fall. Funny thing, too, it was prob'ly the sugar prices that clipped him. We never did pay too much attention to gamblin' around here before. You know, numbers and them other games from up North. But when the moonshine market started dryin' up, they wasn't enough for us guys to do, you know, so the Treasury Department, they switched the gamblin' law enforcement from the IRS to the ATF, and they put a bunch of our boys in the cities. Used to be four or five guys workin' out of my office. Now they's just me and maybe sometimes one other'n, and that's mainly for illegal firearms. Same thing with the other courthouses around here."

Elan's car had left town and was cruising the highway at speeds that persuaded me to fasten my seatbelt. But somehow the belt had been jammed back into the holder so it wouldn't work and wouldn't buzz for not working.

"Well, anyway," Elan said, "what with all the new manpower workin' gambling, why they got ol' Horse down in Atlanta doin' a stretch now, and things are switchin' around in Chattanooga. Horse had some boys runnin' shot houses down there—shot houses, that's the places where the, uh, black folks go to get the lightning, you know. Anyway, couple of those boys were using the shot houses for numbers, and they went away, too."

"A power vacuum," I noted.

"And so there's this guy named Billy Moon," Elan went on. "Used to run shot houses all over the place, and now it looks like he's taken over, not just in Chattanooga, but even down into Alabama. And Billy Moon always used to buy a lot of Bardell whiskey, and that's what I figure happened now, you know? Billy took over the shot houses, and the first thing he does is call Ellis for some whiskey."

"Why is it just blacks?" I asked. "I always thought—"

"You always thought it was that good ol' white lightnin' that everybody in the South loved to drink. Well, it used to be, partner. That was back before the war when they used pure copper vats and copper coils and had pride in their work. That stuff'd come out pure white, at least a hundred ten proof, just as good as you could make it. Those days are gone, buddy. Copper got expensive, for one thing, so they switched to metal. They started using butane gas to cut down on the smoke, to try to keep us guys away. And the butane didn't work as well with copper, either, and that was all the more reason to switch to metal. Besides, white folks got to where they could afford government whiskey. It just ain't the same anymore. You know what they use for coils now? Automobile radiators. The radiators off ol' wrecked cars. Hell, they don't even take 'em off sometimes. Just drag the junked car right up to the still."

"Doesn't sound like it would taste too good," I agreed.

"Taste, hell. It'll give you a dandy dose of lead poisoning, that's what. People die all the time drinkin' that stuff. Prob'ly has rust, residual antifreeze and everything else in there. Hell, you want to talk about taste. Even in the good ol' days they used recipes that called for a few dead possums or some horse manure into the mash at the end to give it flavor. Nowadays, they don't even mind whether the animals are dead. I busted up a still once where they was a damn hog run into the vat and got boiled alive, or drowned, in that slop. They didn't even bother to take

him out. Hell, they all thought it was the biggest joke—
that hog was just gettin' distilled and comin' out whiskey
when we found him. Hell, those guys who make moonshine, they wouldn't drink it in a million years. Not nowadays. Shit, you find beer cans around them stills.
That's what they drink."

We were off the main highway now, headed up a hill
that Elan called a mountain, and getting jolted around on
a very rocky dirt road. Finally he pulled off behind some
trees and cut the engine.

"From here on, we walk," he said. "Here's a flashlight.
It's got a hell of a beam for such a little baby, so don't
switch it on unless you absolutely got to. We want to surprise 'em. So we got to be quiet and invisible. You got
your gun, don't you?" I nodded. "Okay," he said, and
started to leave the car.

"Just one thing," I told him (already we had started
whispering). "Remember, I'm here because of a four and
a half million dollar business swindle that's upset the
whole goddamn FBI and half the lawyers and insurance
companies in the country. I respectfully suggest that if
we can get Ellis Bardell to talk about how that check
business came down, that's what we're really after, still
or no still."

"Right, partner," he said. "We get an indictment on
him for this still and he'll sing like a bird. Oh, I want to
bust up that mother's still so bad I can feel it."

And so we set out into the forest, up the hillside. If this
was supposed to be moonshine, I wondered where the
hell the moon was. It was dark as pitch. How could those
guys be working up on top? Sticks kept poking me in the
face, somehow missing my eyes. I covered my eyes with
one hand, following the soft sound of Elan's boots ahead
of me, occasionally touching him with my free hand. I
had forgotten to ask him if there were snakes around
there, but I don't know what I could have done if he had
told me there were.

After an interminable time—I guess in point of fact it was about 15 minutes—we heard voices, the sounds of hissing butane, the crackling of underbrush from things moving around. Elan touched my arm, which at first terrified me. Then I realized he was telling me to stop. We waited there for another few minutes and suddenly, as if by some ethereal magic, the woods around us began to be faintly illuminated. The clouds that had covered the moon were blowing away. Through the thin trunks of trees, maybe only about thirty yards away, we could see the clearing, the shadowy shapes of men around a wide, low, blue fire that was covered by a broad black shape.

"That there's the vat," Elan whispered. "An' son of a bitch, that's Ellis himself. Right over there by that Cadillac!"

"How can you tell? All I see is shadows."

"I tell you, that's Ellis. First time I ever seen him right there at a still. You know what I'll bet? He was gonna drive back down, but the moon went under and he didn't want to risk it with lights. He'll be leavin' soon. We got to get him now!"

"But there's only two of us. I thought you said we could go back and phone for help."

"There's only five or six guys there. We can take 'em."

"What do we do with them when we got 'em? We can't march that many guys back down the mountain in the dark."

"They got that truck of sugar over there." He pointed, but I couldn't see a thing. "We make 'em dump that sugar and tie 'em onto that. The road down the other side's easier. Hell, it don't matter what we do about all the other guys. If Ellis gets away, we got to prove to a jury again that he knew this still was up here. I been through that. We got to catch him clean, now."

"But they could be armed. If they start shooting . . ."

"Look, we get killed, we'll have company. Jim Bob Adams, he was my first boss, they dug him up off this same mountain a few years ago. Had his own gun in the grave with him. That was the second revenuer they found on Bardell land, and they's prob'ly more. Now I want to get this son of a bitch good. We can do it sneaking. Now, we'll move just a bit closer, maybe ten yards away from the clearing, and you'll squat right there and wait. Don't even breathe. Just get your gun out and wait. I'm going to circle around this clearing to the other side, right behind that Cadillac. Right up behind where Ellis is standing. And I'm going to run out and get a gun on that son of a bitch, and when I do, they're all going to be looking my way, and you're going to come out into that clearing, gun in one hand and spotlight in the other, and tell them they're all under arrest, hands over their head, face down on the ground just where they're standin'. Got it?"

"Oh, shit."

"Come on, it's gonna work beautiful. He'll know he's goin' to jail for one thing or another unless he breaks that Portaquil thing for you. Now, come on."

We inched forward another twenty yards or so, careful not to make a sound, and Elan put his hand on me, gently pressing me into a squat, just as he had said. Then he disappeared. I put the gun in one hand and the flashlight—why all of a sudden did he now call it a spotlight?—in the other, and waited, just as I had been told. I could see the figures moving in the clearing. I heard the big guy near the Cadillac, I guessed it was Ellis as Elan said, and he called a thinner guy over. They started to open the doors.

Oh, my God, I thought. They're going to get in before Elan grabs him. Well, maybe that will change our plans and we can take time to go back and get help.

Then Ellis walked away from the Caddy, pointing a finger toward the vat. He started giving directions to a group of men. They were big, goon-looking guys in undershirts and blue jeans, and they were standing around the vat holding branches, I guessed for stirring the stuff. Then the big guys in the undershirts picked up a long flat thing—it must have been heavy metal from the way they were straining—and started to slide it over the vat.

Then I felt an awful blow in the back of my head and an incredibly powerful arm snapped around my whole body pinning both arms to my sides. I tried to raise my gun to aim behind me, but my assailant's other hand just pried it loose from my grip as if I were a child.

I felt myself being dragged into the clearing. The guy must have hit me with just his hand because I was still conscious. Where the hell was Elan? What was I doing here? Why wasn't I back in a warm, safe city room, writing about other guys doing things like this?

"Lookit, lookit, who the hell's this," my tormenter shouted. His right arm alone had me completely helpless and in pain.

Another big guy, but with a shirt on, was coming over with a light on me, and said, "He ain't no revenue man I ever seen."

All of a sudden there were guys appearing from everywhere, not just the five or six we figured on, but ten or twelve, and they were gathering around me trying to guess my identity. None of them actually asked me who I was. They were just barking around at each other. Then another big guy with a shirt on pried his way through the crowd. It was Ellis.

"Oh, fuck. That's the fuckin' FBI man," he said. "He was over at my house today."

The other man with a shirt on turned to Ellis. "What's the FBI doin' in on this?"

"It's somethin' else," Ellis said. "Never mind. He's down from the North. They ain't nobody else. Just this shithead. Come 'ere," he said, reaching a meaty hand around my belt and grabbing a tender hunk of flesh with it. He was pulling me his way, but this big goon behind me still had me tight. For a second I thought I would come apart in the middle. If they had just made up their minds which way they wanted me to go, I wouldn't have struggled. This whole time, nobody had said a word to me. So I started to talk, to try to come up with some sort of basis for negotiation, but before I had three words out of my mouth Ellis clubbed my face with his hand and yelled, "Shut up!"

Then I was being half-dragged and half-carried by both of them over toward the vat, and Ellis was growling, "You know where you're going? You know where you're going?" over and over. The rest of the crowd seemed to be following along behind us and around us.

"Wait," I said, and started to add that I was a federal officer and that other people knew where I was. I don't even remember how many words I got out before the guy behind me clamped his hand over my mouth. I was going to bite it for lack of anything else to do, but found myself biting my own lips instead. His hand was so big I could scarcely see over his fingers, but we were obviously going over to that vat. Ellis kept saying, "You know where you're going?" over and over, and I thought about the pig Elan had told me of, and I began to suspect just where it was that I was going.

"You gone be whiskey, boy," Ellis finally announced to general laughter.

I saw the vat up close and I felt myself being hoisted off the ground. Then there was a loud cry from the edge of the clearing behind the Cadillac: "There's another one!" And everybody began to look, so I did, too. And I saw Elan struggling with another one of the goons, and finally break free. Then Ellis shouted, "That's Warfield! Elan Warfield! A revenuer!"

There was a moment of confusion. I felt the guy behind me loosen his grip on me, and I started to twist away. But now it was Ellis himself who held me fast.

I began to wonder, irrational as it was, if Elan could just draw his gun and yell "Freeze, you motherfuckers," the way they do in the George V. Higgins novels, and everybody would throw up their hands and surrender. But

Elan was off and running across the clearing, headed the other way, back toward the road we had come on. The son of a bitch was leaving. "Thanks a lot," I thought. Then, as we all watched, he began to veer off across the clearing again. Suddenly I realized he was heading toward the big truckload of sugar. He opened the door and reached down.

Ellis realized before I did what was happening. His arm tightened around me as he yelled, "That's the sugar! He's got the fuckin' sugar truck!"

Elan had released the brake and the truck was slowly rolling toward a road that began at the edge of the clearing. Elan had one foot on the floor of the cabin. He was steering with one hand and holding on to the open door with the other, as if ready to jump off when it picked up speed.

"Get that goddamn truck!" Ellis was shouting. "That's ten thousand dollars worth of sugar! Before it gets to the cliff, goddamn it!"

Cliff? I thought. There were a lot of things nobody had told me about this mountain.

Then the people around us started to fly after Elan and the truck, a string of ragtag men in undershirts, terrifying only a moment ago, but now looking like clowns as they stumbled and tripped in the dim light.

I tried to break loose, but Ellis still had me. "You're goin' in. You're still goin' in," he said, and I felt myself being lifted again. Somehow I got an arm free. I hit him. It wasn't much of a punch, but that and further struggling got a leg free, too, and then at least the situation had become complicated enough to stave off an immediate distillation in the sour mash. He was twice my strength, but I had a leg up against his gut and was somehow holding him off. "Somebody stay back and help me with this mother," he yelled.

I thought they had all gone, and that maybe I could hold him off, and get away with just a good beating, a few broken bones maybe, but still alive. But there was one more of those goons around, a tall guy, strong looking, making his way over to us slowly, as if he enjoyed having me agonize first before being overpowered. Ellis and I were braced, as if trying to throw each other into that bubbling slop. Then this other fellow, who would surely put me away for good, arrived.

For a moment he just stood looking at us. There was an idiot's grin on his face, distinguished by a missing front tooth. Suddenly, for reasons I will never understand, the guy grabbed Ellis instead of me. Together we were hoisting Ellis up and over the lip of the vat. My own hands were still pushing on Ellis as he fell, yelling, "No, no, you shit—." And then his head went under.

Suddenly I realized I wasn't defending myself anymore. I was helping kill Ellis. My God, I thought. That's my witness! The other man was laughing a foolish, "Hee-hee, hee-hee," and with great effort was sliding the heavy cover over another foot or so across the vat to block Ellis's escape. "That's my witness!" I yelled at him, and tried to stop him, to reach a hand in for Ellis. But the goon with the missing front tooth shoved me aside powerfully. Ellis was trying to get out, but the lid had trapped his leg up over him, pinning him upside down. I watched until the leg stopped moving.

The next thing I saw was Elan running towards us from the other side of the clearing. "Who's this?" he said, pointing to the man with the missing tooth and blocking his path as the man turned to escape.

"Let him go," I said. "He just saved my life and killed Ellis Bardell, and he damn well doesn't know anything about any bank deals, or much of anything else. Besides," I said, as the man ran off in the direction the others had taken, "he could beat the shit out of both of us. What happened to your gun?"

Elan laughed. "He couldn't beat the shit out of me," he said. "And I'm the son of a bitch who saved your life. My gun's over there in the woods somewhere, where the guy knocked it down. Let's let that idiot go and get out of here before the others come back. We'll get a team up here to bust the still."

We had just made it to the edge of the clearing when we heard a noise and saw a flash from out of the woods, then smoke rising from the horizon. We stopped.

"Welp," Elan said, "the damn sugar truck must have gone over the cliff. Wonder what the fire is, though. Be the first time in history if those cheapskates put a full tank of gas in her."

We ran down the hill to where we left the car and the moon was now bright enough that I only fell down twice. I expected at any moment to hear that gang of men chasing us, but Elan said later, as we drove down, that once away from the still site, with the truck lost, they probably ran straight for home. The Bardells aside, those guys had nothing to gain but trouble by going back, he told me. The only two he got a look at were strangers.

We managed to clean me up pretty well at Elan's house, so when I got back to Sara there was no blood on me and fewer bruises then I would have imagined. I told her it had been a scratchy climb up the mountain, that the guys operating the still had run away, and that we had gone back to Elan's and phoned for a team from ATF to bust it up. All of which was true.

The next day Elan and I went to see George Hewlitt. He openly admitted to us that Ellis Bardell had offered him a $50,000 "fee" if he'd cash some big checks, a million or two worth, drawn off the account of some company up north. George didn't remember the name, said he'd flat turned the deal down because it sounded illegal. There was no mention of Fud Peerce or Hezekiah Portaquil or anybody else. He was probably telling the truth.

"Wonder why nobody ever asked me about that before," Hewlitt said.

I was about to inquire as to why, with all the publicity about the Portaquil case, he had never come forward before. But he solved that riddle with his next remark: "By the way," he said, "I hear ol' Ellis died in a moonshine vat you revenue fellows broke up last night. Hard to understand how a guy like that, with all his money, still hangs around stills at night. I would'a thought after he went away and all, he would'a learned his lesson and stayed out of that business."

"No kidding," Elan said. "How'd you hear a thing like that?"

"Oh, I'm worried as hell about it," Hewlitt said. "I got a lawyer checking out the estate situation already. Why, it was just a few weeks ago I lent ol' Ellis ten thousand dollars on his chickens."

PART THREE:

THE SCAM

CHAPTER TWENTY-SIX

1

Bent Morrison answered the phone with his last name. The voice on the other end asked for Frank Scanlon.

"Frank's out of the office. Can I help?"

"I gotta talk to Frank."

"Well, Frank and I work together sometimes. That's why they put you on my line."

"Can you get ahold of Frank?"

"Well—who's calling?"

There was a long pause. "My name's Fakazzi. Walter Fakazzi."

Jesus Christ, Morrison thought. "Hey, listen, where are you? Listen, I been working the Quincy thing with Frank from day one. I know all about you. What's up?"

"Man, I gotta talk to Frank."

"He's out of town. In fact, he's down in Tennessee on the Quincy case. I just talked to him a little while ago." There was no reply. "Whatever it is, you can tell me," Morrison said. "Where are you? Can I pick you up some-where?"

"Can you get a message to Frank?"

"He was just leaving his motel. He might not be back till late. You can tell me anything you can tell him." There was no answer. Morrison signaled to get the call traced. "Look, where are you?" he asked.

"Man, I been hidin' out for a long time. Ever since Christmas Eve. You know what happened Christmas Eve?"

"Of course I know. We thought you might be dead. Where are you?"

"You know how many people'd like to make me dead?"

"What do you mean?"

There was a long pause. "I mean, kill me. Richards's people are in this. You know that, don't you?"

"Richards. You mean Ruggiardo?"

"Just tell me when I can talk to Frank."

"What does Ruggiardo have to do with the Quincy thing? Was he running Carmody?"

"Look, I'm in a phone booth. I—"

"Where?"

"There's a couple a guys standin' here funny. I got to go."

"Can you tell us where the money is? Do you know?"

"The money. That's what Ruggiardo wants."

"Can you tell us where it is?"

"Look, man, I got wounds. I'm bleedin'. Tell Frank I think I can identify Portaquil for him if he can protect me."

"Protect you from whom? Who was Portaquil?"

"Shit. I gotta go. You got a number for Frank or not."

"He's flying back tomorrow. Look, if you can talk to him, you can talk to me."

"Tell him I'll call him tomorrow."

"Okay, okay. Here's a number for him in Tennessee. Have you got—" The line had gone dead.

2

Morrison went to the door of the assistant agent in charge and was waved in.

"I just got a call from Walter Fakazzi. Fakazzi's a very important missing suspect in the Quincy thing. He was Mickey Carmody's bodyguard—"

"I remember, for Christ's sake. This is a four and a half million dollar case. What did he want?"

"He wanted to talk to Frank. He said he wanted protection and that he might talk."

"Where was he?"

"He wouldn't tell me a damn thing, just wanted to talk to Frank. I had a tracer put on it that ought to come back in a few minutes, but I don't think I kept him on the line long enough to pin it down."

"What did he want protection from?"

"He said Ruggiardo was involved in this somehow. I kind of got the idea he was saying the Mob was after him. But he wouldn't open up with me. Just insisted on talking to Scanlon."

The assistant agent in charge got up from his desk and paced to the window. "What is it about that kid?" he asked. "He practically turns Tennessee upside down to get a wiretap order in some little hick town that the Nashville office has already combed over, so everything finally gets set up and then he comes through with a blank tape."

"Well, that was the fault of some local cop—"

"That's what Scanlon says. Maybe it's true. It doesn't change the way things look, though. I send some hot-shot down there, which is a slap at our Nashville office, and he comes up with a blank tape. Then he gets involved with an ATF man, and you know what kind of reputation they have, and he goes on a raid to break up a moonshine still and nobody gets arrested, and the supposed suspect—or witness, or whatever he was—in our case gets killed. And Scanlon now admits he hasn't got a case against anybody."

"He's coming back tomorrow, sir."

"And this guy Fakazzi won't talk to anybody else. Why?"

"I don't know. Just knows Scanlon from way back, I guess."

A woman appeared at the door. "You wanted the results of that trace right away?" she said. "It came from northern New Jersey. That's all we got."

"Thanks," Morrison said.

"Damn it," said the assistant agent in charge. "Get Fakazzi's picture out to the police departments in Hudson and Bergen counties."

"We've had his picture floating around all over the country."

"Yeah, but tell them now we've got reason to believe he's really there. Get 'em looking. I want that son of a bitch in tow. I want to get him before Scanlon comes riding in on his white horse tomorrow."

CHAPTER TWENTY-SEVEN

1

I remember very well the turbulent flight back from Nashville, seeing nothing but clouds the whole way, my hand clasped in Sara's, our seatbelts locked. And I remember feeling so rock bottom that it almost seemed fitting for me to have died in an airplane crash.

That morning, before leaving for the airport, I had talked to Bent. He made it pretty clear that the bosses weren't happy about my coming home without a case, especially after all the fuss I had caused. Worse yet, he told me that Walter Fakazzi's body had been found wedged into a telephone booth in Jersey City. Walter had got it nice and clean, three bullets in the head, apparently no witnesses. It was the kind of Mafia hit where the odds were a million to one it would never be solved. And the last thing Walter had tried to do on this earth was to come to me for protection.

Fuck. Why would they want to kill Walter? Surely *he* didn't have the money. At most, Mickey would have given him twenty or twenty-five thousand. Was that worth killing a guy for, when there was maybe four million around somewhere? Obviously it was. On the other hand, if Fakazzi had the money hidden, killing him was no way to find it, and if he had it on him they could have taken it without killing him. Revenge, that was the only explanation. He must have been holding out on them. Or maybe they only thought he was holding out on them. The poor shit.

And why was the Ruggiardo gang after the money at all? Where did the Mob come in? Did they own Mickey? They had made Fakazzi, all right. They owned him. But what had they ever done for Mickey that he owed them for? Timmons. The mob must have given him Timmons. All right, how? Timmons gambled. He got in debt. He met a shark. The shark bailed him out and Timmons welched on the shark. The shark belonged to Ruggiardo. Normally, Ruggiardo has Timmons killed. But somehow he senses that Timmons is a goose that can lay golden eggs. Ruggiardo needs a midwife to get the eggs out. Through Fakazzi, he finds Carmody. Perfect.

There's no evidence for it, but it's the only logical explanation for the whole deal. Only Carmody must have been holding out on Ruggiardo. Could even Mickey have been *that* dumb? Or maybe he just got killed before he had a chance to pass the cash. At any rate, Ruggiardo didn't have the money yet, or why would he have killed Fakazzi? Fakazzi didn't have the money, or why would he be hanging around Jersey City? Why wouldn't he just give Richards a few million and make everybody happy?

So the money was still missing. Maybe Mickey buried it. Maybe now nobody knew where it was. Who was Portaquil? We still hadn't found Bill Connally. Those were the missing pieces.

But the outlines of the puzzle were clear—clear enough that I could have written a hell of a newspaper story about the caper. I knew with moral certainty that Fud Peerce, Stanley Timmons, Vincente Ruggiardo and Bill Connally (if we ever found him) belonged in jail for a long time. I knew that Abner Bardell and George Hewlitt belonged there at least for awhile. I knew with moral certainty that Ellis Bardell and Walter Fakazzi would have belonged in jail if they had been alive. And yet I didn't have evidence to satisfy a court on any of them. Even if Mickey Carmody himself had come back from the dead, I would scarcely have had enough to indict him, and never enough to convict.

It was the same goddamned frustration I had felt as a newspaper reporter. I couldn't throw anybody in jail back then. Now I had my shield and my gun and I still couldn't. I couldn't even get the story into the newspaper to let the public know—as I used to—what crooks these were.

Well, some people were surviving the debacle. According to Bent, Sybil Manwaring had just taken a job at the Stanford University Medical Center, one of the best in the country. She and Don O'Neil got married over the weekend and were relocating in the San Francisco area.

Sara also seemed to be back on her feet. At one point during the airplane ride she told me, "You know, I think I'm not in love with Mickey anymore."

"A good thing," I said. I decided not to add, "considering the recent state of his health," but apparently my cynicism showed through anyway.

"Don't laugh," she said. "It's important to me. I really think I'm over it now. I just don't understand how I could have been so blind."

"Blindness is innocence," I said. "And innocence is something there's all too little of, Sara. I like you."

She clasped my hand a little harder and smiled. "Sometimes you're so deep I don't understand you. But I really do like you a lot. I really do. You know what I'm going to do when I get back to my apartment? I've got a whole box full of Mickey's things and I'm going to throw them all out, right down the garbage shoot."

"You've got a box of Mickey's things you haven't shown me?"

"They're personal things. Pictures, letters, little things he gave me."

"My God, Sara. That could be important."

"But they're personal things."

"There could be important evidence in there."

"It wasn't evidence of anything to me, except that he liked me."

"Sara, you were going to throw them out anyway. Let me look." Her expression was full of uncertainty. "You said he wasn't important to you anymore. This *is* important."

"You really think it's not—not—just low?"

"Low! Sara, how much lower can you get than Mickey? He lied to you, he used you, he stole from people, he—"

"Okay, okay." She looked out the window at the gray mist. "I just want you to know that I'll let you see them only because of you. Not because of anything else," she said. "I mean I wouldn't show them to anybody else. But you can look at them."

And that's the first thing I did after I drove us from the airport back to her place, finding a parking spot a few blocks away. From a closet in the bedroom she hauled out a cardboard box about the size that a ream of typing paper might come in. I sat on the bed and began to sift its contents. There were cocktail napkins and match books from Twenty One, the Four Seasons and half a dozen other restaurants. There were some postcard size handwritten notes that must have accompanied gifts. When I saw what they were, I didn't read them, except to note that they were all signed, "Love, Mickey." There were some pictures of Mickey, and one of Mickey and Sara together at an amusement park somewhere. And I was most surprised to find a photo of Donald O'Neil. I flashed it at Sara and asked what it was doing there.

"Oh," she said. "That's a man Mickey hated. Really hated. From some kind of business deal or something. Mickey sometimes sat around defacing pictures of him."

Sure enough, I could see marks drawn by a marking pen around O'Neil's eyes, as if trying to make them Chinese.

"Frank, please stop," she said. "It's just—it makes me feel bad. It really does." Her brow was furrowed, pleading. She had been changing clothes and was standing before me in a white lace bra and black bikini pants. I stuffed the papers back into the box and closed it without ever taking my eyes off her. I put the box on the floor by the bed. She said, "Thank you," and was going to say more, but I stood up and kissed her quiet.

We made love a couple of times, noticed it had gotten dark and decided we were hungry. Sara announced that there wasn't any food in the apartment, and so I announced that I would take us out. We dressed, and I carried off the box of memorabilia for later inspection. On the way down in the elevator, I remember Sara talking about how wonderful the trip had been, how much she had needed to get away, how glad she was that I took her.

As we had been coming in, Sara had observed there was a new doorman. The former one was a young Spanish-American who always had a cheerful hello and helped with bags, she said. This one was older, white and immersed in the *Daily News* while I hauled the suitcases in from the car. When I got the suitcases blocking the elevator door, Sara went back to check her mail and found a box, but the doorman was busy on the telephone and she had to carry it herself. Now, as we came out of the elevator, he again seemed to spot us out of the corner of his eye and turn away in surly fashion, as if to hide. He went out to the street, keeping his back turned.

It had begun to drizzle, so I went for the car alone and left Sara waiting at the door. About halfway down the block something in my memory of the furtive way the doorman had moved made me turn around to check that everything was all right.

I couldn't see Sara or the doorman. I took a few steps back toward where they had been. Then I caught a glimpse of struggling. I ran closer and saw a man in a trench coat dragging Sara away from the building. She was still on her feet and fighting to get free. Running faster, I drew my gun and held it out at arm's length, yelling, "Stop! FBI!" I couldn't shoot for fear of hitting Sara.

Then I saw a gun in the man's hand, saw it flash light and heard a clap and a whistle. For the second time in a few days somebody was trying to kill me. I started between parked cars for cover, wondering again why I had given up newspaper work for this. I heard another shot in my direction and saw that Sara, unlike me, was still struggling and impeding her abduction. I knew I had to try to help her, and began running forward again along the outside of the cars.

Suddenly Sara whirled free a few feet away from the man. I got a shot off. I know in the training schools they drill it into you that shooting at an armed adversary becomes second nature. Well, shooting at anybody is never going to be second nature to me. This was my first time firing a gun for real, and the lighting conditions were terrible. The practice range was supposed to have made me a good enough shot that I wouldn't hit Sara, but the awful possibility was on my mind anyway. Maybe that's why I missed. Still, the other guy was probably a professional, too, and he was missing me, and I was a lone target. God knows what innocent people we might have killed in a first floor apartment or on the street somewhere if luck hadn't protected them.

At least, though, I hoped my shot would convince the

man to flee, and he did start to go, putting Sara between him and myself so I couldn't shoot again. Then I saw him turn and take point blank aim at Sara. Surely, I thought, he wouldn't do that. But he fired directly at her. I heard the clap of the gun and saw her drop in a heap on the sidewalk. The man ran away and disappeared around the corner. I couldn't believe what I had seen. I ran to Sara and knelt by her. She was sobbing hysterically and blood was running from between those beautiful white breasts. I went to the doorway. The doorman was nowhere in sight. I picked up the phone and dialed 911 for an ambulance. Then I ran to the corner still holding my gun, but the block looked deserted. I hadn't paid enough attention to what the gunman looked like to be able to identify him if I saw him again. Sure, it had been night, but the street was lit and I could have done better. If this was real police work, then I had failed miserably.

I went back to Sara and she was still crying and clutching her chest. The blood was still running out of her onto the sidewalk. I didn't know what to do. I cradled her in my arms, but she didn't even seem to know I was there.

2

As it turned out, Sara wasn't as badly hurt as I had feared. The bullet had somehow missed her heart and she was expected to recover fully. In fact, within a day she was well enough to talk, and talk she did.

They had her well guarded in the hospital. I wasn't allowed near her, but other agents were. They managed to elicit the whole story of what they kept calling our "personal relationship," how we traveled together to Tennessee and stayed in the same motel room, and why we happened to be together on the sidewalk that night. Her goddamn priest was there to help them. As they relayed it, Sara blamed me for her having been shot—for involving her at all in this mess. I found it hard to believe she would turn on me so severely, but I was being treated like a man on trial.

There was a jury of one, the special agent in charge himself, and his verdict was succinct to say the least. I was discharged so quickly I didn't even have a chance to be suspended. By arrangement or coincidence, nobody much was around the office at the time, or said anything. As I headed for the elevator, a gunless civilian, my friend Bent did sidle over. Quickly and sort of on the sly, he told me to meet him at the Bull and Bear for a drink at six.

We found the same table and ordered the same drinks that we had years before. It was a pretty quiet conversation for awhile.

"Well, it's a shitty deal, I can't deny that," he finally told me.

"Yeah."

"But you can't say you weren't warned it was coming."

"Nope."

"So why'd you do it?"

"Sleep with Sara? She was pretty. I really liked her. I thought she wanted to."

"But you were investigating her."

"Not her—Mickey Carmody. And even so, even if it had been Sara I was investigating, the better I know her the more I learn."

"That's James Bond stuff, Frank. You could destroy a case if the defense lawyers find out about that shit. And it's soiling the reputation of the bureau."

I shrugged. "There's advantages and disadvantages to everything, I guess. We just disagree."

"You could fight it, you know. Appeal to Washington."

"I could go to court and sue," I said. He winced. I smiled and shook my head. "That's not my style. I don't want to be where I'm not wanted."

"So what will you do?"

"I don't know. Maybe write a novel about it all. Maybe

I ought to get out of the country for awhile. You think Ruggiardo was after me or Sara?"

"Ruggiardo? How do you know it was him?"

"I trust Fakazzi. And look what they did to him."

"So they were in on the Quincy deal and killed Fakazzi for holding back on the money. That's a whole long way from knocking off FBI agents—or pretty stewardesses Mickey was sleeping with. People get mugged on the street all the time, Frank."

"Mugged? Are you going to tell me that was a mugging? The goddamn doorman, the one they say they can't find now, set us up—you think just to steal her purse? The New York police don't think it was a mugging, do they?"

Bent shrugged and looked down, as if he didn't want me to hold his eye.

"That detective I talked to this morning," I said. "I told him the whole—hey, why didn't they hold me longer? I was a key witness. Hey, you're not telling me there's some kind of cover-up going on here?"

"If the New York cops can get the guy who shot Sara, they will. I promise you, Frank. If you got any more information, call that lieutenant and deal it out. There's no cover-up about solving that shooting."

"But it's not going to go down as an organized crime thing, is it? Because then it would come out that an FBI agent was screwing around with a witness. Right? And that's why that little story in the *Press* this afternoon didn't say a goddamn thing about me. Nobody's going to associate me or the Quincy caper with what happened to Sara."

Bent smiled. "You saw that, huh?"

"Bent, why are you here? Are you here to be nice to a friend, or did they send you here to make sure I wasn't going to ruin the whitewash?"

"Frank, there's no whitewash, and there's not going to be. There are just certain things that aren't going to hurt this investigation at all, that would be best not to come out right now. The New York police want to solve this thing and we want them to solve it. Maybe if we can find the gunman it will lead to the Quincy money. There will be no reluctance in this investigation. I give you my word on that."

"But what is your word worth? And what if Ruggiardo is trying to kill me?"

"Don't get paranoid, Frank. You got a shitty deal, and the bureau would rather not be identified with what you and Sara were doing. But we're not going to cover up for whoever fired that shot. If you can't trust my word any more, I'm sorry."

"So am I," I said.

3

After that conversation, I was all the more happy I hadn't told anyone about the box of mementos I had received from Sara. I had picked it up off the sidewalk the night before and left it in my car. It wasn't until I went home from the Bull and Bear that I got a chance to really sort through the stuff.

There wasn't just one photograph of Donald O'Neil. And what Mickey was doing wasn't defacing. There were several superimposed drawings of O'Neil, one with more hair and a Fu Manchu style mustache. If I had still been a law officer, I would have taken that picture back down to the bank in Caliquatta for identification. But I wasn't a law officer, just me again. And I already knew with moral certainty who Hezekiah X. Portaquil was, and had a pretty good idea what had happened to the Quincy money.

I looked at the picture and I looked at the wall. I rocked back and forth on a straight-legged chair for a good ten minutes. Then I went to the phone, called American Airlines and reserved a ticket to San Francisco. The woman asked me for my name. I thought for a minute, and decided to give her a phony one—Donald Moffitt.

Then she told me the round trip price, and I shuddered. I had barely that much in my bank account, no job, and it would be awhile till the severance arrived. Using Moffitt's name, I couldn't very well give her my master charge number. But I said I'd be down with the cash in the morning, and I was. Considering the money I was going to be coming into, such sums would lose their importance.

CHAPTER TWENTY-EIGHT

"Don't sit there," Ruggiardo said, shaking his head. "I sat there last night."

Danny Beethoven found another table. They took opposite sides. A fat man in an apron rushed over from behind the counter.

"Heya, Herky," Ruggiardo said, shaking the fat man's hand and holding it, but not getting up. "How's the business, all right?"

"Pretty good. Yeah, amazin'. Everybody's payin' regular. No trouble for a couple months now, you know? The economy's pickin' up. I read about it in *The Wall Street Journal.*"

"Fine, that's fine," Ruggiardo said. Still holding the fat man's hand, he turned to Danny. "He okay?"

"Best boy in town," Danny said. "They all like Herky, and we got no trouble."

"Listen," Ruggiardo said, addressing the fat man again. "Gimme a egg salad and coffee. What's for you, Danny?"

"Hamburger. Lots of raw onions. An' a Coke, Herky."

"Not so many onions," Ruggiardo said to the fat man. "I got to sit here. Seriously." The fat man nodded and left.

"What happened to your bacon and tomato?" Danny said.

"Me? Oh, it's been a long time. Ever since last August. You know, I grew so many goddamned tomatoes in that yard. We were eating tomatoes every day. Giving 'em away to the neighbors. I broke out in some kind of rash. So I never touch the things raw anymore. Only with pasta. Cooked, they don't seem to bother me."

"Yeah. Well, you look great, boss. Relaxed. Last time I seen you, you had a tie on and all that—"

Ruggiardo waved his hand. "Ah, it's good to be in town with people, you know?" He emphasized the word "people." "Sometimes where I am, everybody's a phony. You start acting like a phony yourself. It's the only way they'll respect you. Listen, you know why we're here."

Danny nodded.

"You know where Connally is now?"

Danny shook his head.

"No way to find him?"

"Them guys always turn up," Danny said. "Right now, he's hid. I don't even know it was him. How do you know it wasn't Willie Shutters?"

Ruggiardo shook his head. "It wasn't Willie. I know that. This really bothers me," he said. "I mean, I really don't like it."

"You're right. He shoulda killed her."

"Killed her! My God, Danny. She got on page five of the *Press* just getting shot up there on West End. This way, at least maybe they'll forget it after awhile. If she'd a got killed, they'd be all over town."

"Yeah, but this way she can identify him."

"Not if we identify him first."

"You mean hit him?"

"Danny, we got to stop thinking like that. I mean, get

him out of town, get him to cool off. Look, it'd be one thing if we had something on this girl. I mean, Fakazzi, that was one thing. He knew what he was doing. But this girl—we don't know anything on her, do we?"

"Just the phone."

"So she's some stewardess he was fooling around with. Carmody isn't going to give four million dollars to some stewardess. I mean, maybe she knows a little, maybe we talk to her, scare her. But to go shooting down stewardesses on West End Avenue—"

"They don't even know it was us, do they?"

"Yeah, well, there's something fishy about that, too. Those stories in the papers. I mean, if we know who that girl was, the cops must know who she was, right? The FBI?"

"So why would they keep it quiet?"

"I don't know, Danny. Look, all I'm saying is, I want that money, and whoever's sitting on it deserves anything that comes to them, but I don't want to throw up every racket we've got just to go chasing pie in the sky. We've got a lot of good businesses going, and you don't keep them by shooting down stewardesses on West End Avenue. Danny, I've got to deal with lawyers, I've got to deal with politicians, and top people. There's stuff you do and stuff you don't do. If a guy's got to get hit, like Fakazzi, then so be it. But not this."

Danny nodded soberly, and Ruggiardo went on with his lecture. "They got to suspect something. They're chasing that money as hard as we are. If we can get that girl's name out of the phone company, you know goddamn well they can get her name, too. The fact that the cops tell the papers maybe it was a mugging, that just makes me worry all the more they're up to something."

Danny nodded. The fat man brought the sandwiches and drinks, and waited a few seconds, as if expecting to be invited into the conversation. But the other two men avoided his glance and he left.

"You know what we got to figure out?" Ruggiardo said. "We got to figure out what Carmody would have done with that money."

"I don't know. Maybe he took it to Switzerland or someplace. We got any way of checking that?"

"Maybe. I thought about it. I got a lawyer knows everything going on at the airports. Through the unions. But if Carmody went overseas he probably did it under some other name. Besides, I don't know anything about Switzerland, even if I find out he went there. That stuff's out of my league. There's people who know. There's a lawyer out in Los Angeles handles all kinds of European business. But I can't go to him without going to those guys in Miami, and pretty soon the whole country's in on the money and there's none left."

Danny looked sympathetic. Ruggiardo smiled. "Well, that's my problem, isn't it," he said. "Hey, Danny, it's not your fault. Listen, you want a job playing the piano in Miami? I could arrange that. That wouldn't be any pain at all. Or out in Las Vegas—I know plenty of guys out there."

"Nah. Thanks a lot, but my knuckles been broke too often to think about showing off now."

"You sound okay to me."

"Nah. The pros'd know. Anyway, I got a good job at Luigi's. I'm good enough for that crowd. Besides, I can take off for business whenever I want. I better stick it out where I am."

"Still, it's something to keep in mind. A change of scenery." Ruggiardo finished his egg salad, cracked a grin and slapped Danny Beethoven on the shoulder from across the table. "Hey," he said. "You suppose maybe it really was a mugger? Wouldn't that be a laugh?"

CHAPTER TWENTY-NINE

Boy, were they surprised to see me. I wish I had a picture of those faces.

It took me the better part of a day to find out from various university offices where they lived. Beautiful new ranch-type house, nice lawn, looked freshly landscaped, just a walk from the campus. It stopped short of being ostentatious—people in their position had to avoid that—but I didn't doubt somebody had sunk a fair piece of change into it.

I hung around down the block until I saw Dr. Manwaring come home. I waited a few minutes, then knocked.

O'Neil answered the door and said I looked familiar. After a few seconds of silence I saw the shock of recognition. Then I saw Sybil through the doorway in the room behind him. She knew at once who I was, but quickly tried to recover her poise. "Come in, Mr. Scanlon," she said. "Has something happened?"

I looked at O'Neil who was dressed in a white T-shirt and slacks and was still blocking my passage. "Let him in, Don," she said, and he did. After the door was closed behind me, we just stood there looking at one another for what must have been thirty seconds. They were nervous, all right.

"Well, what's this all about?" Dr. Manwaring finally said.

"Aren't you going to offer me a cup of coffee?" I asked. "Show me the new house?"

"All right," she said. She started for the kitchen, then stopped. "We had just poured whiskeys," she said. "It is the end of the day, you know. Would you prefer—are you allowed?" O'Neil was following behind, glowering at me.

"I guess I'd allow myself some scotch," I said. "That'd be fine."

O'Neil made a move, but she said, "I'll get it, Don." We went to a buffet at one end of the dining room table. Each piece was a lovely and expensive-looking cherry wood. I caught a glimpse of a large, modern kitchen. The place could have been featured in House Beautiful. Even the booze was done up fancy, on a silver tray atop the buffet. An ice bucket was in the middle, flanked by two slightly different shaped decanters, obviously for scotch and bourbon. The glasses were stacked alongside.

As she poured, I heard the decanter knock against the lip of the glass twice. Some brain surgeon. God, they were nervous. I was getting high off of it. She handed me the glass. "So what brings you our way? You're still based in New York, aren't you?"

"Yes," I said, and headed nonchalantly toward the living room, which was on the other side of the hall from the dining area. "Really lovely place you've got here." It was. The living room was well furnished, the carpeting nice and thick, clearly wool, not nylon. "The house new?"

"It was built last summer. No one had lived in it till we moved in a month ago."

"You've done quite a lot of decorating in a month," I said. "Really beautiful, first-class job."

"Well—thank you. Actually, we had planned the move aways back."

"Before or after the Quincy caper?" I asked.

She shot me a glance. "We planned it when I got this job. We didn't say much about it, because we didn't want my ex-husband to know."

"Mickey didn't know? That's strange," I said.

"Well, not if you know my ex-husband," she said. They had both followed me into the living room. O'Neil was still glowering. I stood in front of a wing chair next to the white brick fireplace, facing the tufted sofa, and waited for an invitation to sit down. One didn't come, so I sat down anyway.

"Well," she said, "I presume this has something to do with him. With Mickey."

I studied the beads in my glass. "Not really," I said. I took a slow sip.

"Well, then what is this about?" O'Neil said, starting forward at me, annoyed. "You invite yourself into our house, you ask for a drink, you plop yourself down on our furniture—"

"Don," she cautioned, putting an arm in front of him to stop his advance. Then she looked at me. "I do think you owe us an explanation."

I smiled. "And you owe Cumberland Mutual Insurance Company and a couple of guys named Quincy about four million bucks," I said.

They were both grim and hushed, and trying to look puzzled. "What do you mean by that?" she finally asked.

"Mr. and Mrs. Portaquil—I know who you are. But the jig is not necessarily up."

"What are you talking about?" she said. "I get the idea you're accusing us of something."

"Maybe identifying would be a better word," I said.

"Isn't this a pretty odd way for the FBI to operate? I

thought even when you accused people of something, there were certain rights, that you had to—"

"I'm not with the FBI."

"Wait a minute. You came to my house once—I was at your office—you were at the hospital when Don was shot—"

"I was with the FBI then, but not now. And that's to your very good fortune. And mine."

"I don't understand any of this," the doctor said.

"What the hell's going on?" O'Neil asked.

"The FBI didn't like the way I operate. They threw me out."

"Then what are you doing here?"

"I'm here to offer you a deal."

O'Neil turned to Dr. Manwaring. "I think this guy has no business here," he said.

She looked at me. "I don't see what we have to deal with you about," she said. "I think you ought to put down that drink and get out."

"Then let me explain," I said. I got up from the chair. "If you won't sit down, I'll stand. I have a photograph of you, O'Neil—or Portaquil, whoever you are. It was doctored up personally by Mickey to match your disguise. I'm sure the employes of the bank in Caliquatta wouldn't have any trouble identifying it."

O'Neil and Dr. Manwaring looked at each other as if trying to decide what to do.

"Right now," I said, "that photograph, and an explanation of what happened and who you are, is in an envelope I sealed just before I came out here. The envelope is with someone I trust, who will mail it if I don't reclaim it within three days. If that envelope gets mailed, your ass is grass."

O'Neil seemed to hover between fear and outrage. "You think you can hurt us by going to the police with some photograph and a cock and bull story? The cops know where we are right now, if they want us."

"I'm not talking about the cops," I said. "I don't work with them anymore."

They were glancing at each other, glancing at me, trying to make up their minds.

"You know who Vincente Ruggiardo is?" I asked. "Well, Mickey was working for him. The Mob is hot after this money. They've shot two people already in New York. As it stands, we're probably safe. They don't suspect you've got the bank—any more than I or the FBI did. But if Ruggiardo gets that letter, they'll be out here in two seconds with an army, and they'll offer you a hell of a lot worse deal than I'm offering."

"Yeah, well who says we have the money?" O'Neil said.

"I'm making a bet on it, man. And I'm betting if you don't tell me, Ruggiardo will find out. Have you ever heard of Willie Shutters? He works for Ruggiardo. He's been indicted for five different murders. I think there's been a sixth. A couple of weeks ago somebody got Walter Fakazzi."

There was a gasp from Dr. Manwaring. "Walter's dead?"

I nodded. "They found him in a phone booth in Jersey City."

"But why?"

"They must have thought he was holding out on them. I told you, they think it's their money. Maybe you could tell me why."

She shook her head. "What's your deal?" she said.

"A million three," I said. "I'm not greedy. The way I figure it, there's probably about four million left. Mickey had overhead, and he's spent some. There's three of us. All I want's my one-third share. Besides, it's probably all I can carry back with me on the plane and I don't intend to make two trips. If I can't fit a million three into the two suitcases I've got in the car outside, you're just lucky. I'll take what I can. But I warn you, they're pullmans."

"You're crazy," O'Neil said, pointing a threatening finger. "How do we even know you're not with the FBI any more?"

"I guess you got to take my word for it," I smiled. "Unless you'd like to check out my story. I got kicked out of the FBI two days ago for having a personal relationship with a potential witness. Her name's Sara Rushington. She was one of Mickey's girlfriends. They found out because Ruggiardo got to her, too."

"Sara's dead?" Dr. Manwaring was startled again. "Is she the one on West End?"

"She's the one," I said. "Only she's not dead. Got a bullet in the chest, but pulled out completely and told them all about how she and I cohabited a motel room down in Crockett County, Tennessee. So they kicked my ass out of the FBI, just before I had a chance to tell them who Hezekiah Portaquil was. Now they'll never know, will they? If you're smart. Besides, O'Neil, it's like your wife already told you—this couldn't stand up in court. I haven't said a thing about your rights. I'm just threatening you, that's all. If you don't give me a million three pretty quick, Willie Ariolo's going to come out here and cut you into little pieces. Take it or leave it."

O'Neil's fists clenched. "You son of a bitch," he said.

"Don," she said, putting a hand on his arm. "It's okay." She was actually beginning to smile. "It's okay. He's just doing the same thing we did."

O'Neil came at me anyway. I started to resist, then realized he was just patting me down. "He doesn't have a gun."

"Of course not," Dr. Manwaring said. "He's telling the truth. He's just doing the same damn thing we did. He decided to take the money and tell the world to screw off." She began laughing, at first quietly, then out loud, until I saw tears come from the corners of her eyes. She ran up to me, locked her arms around my neck, kissed me on the cheek and squeezed me. "Scanlon, you're all right," she said. "You are okay." She was looking me square in the eye, still smiling broadly, her arms around my neck. I was expressionless.

"Where's the money?" I said.

"You go get your suitcases, and we'll show you something that'll knock your eyes out."

"Sybil—" O'Neil started.

"Don, it's okay," she said. She was still grinning away. "Go get your suitcases, Scanlon."

That's exactly what I did. O'Neil had me open them to see they were empty. Then he frisked me again, even more thoroughly, not missing a part of me. Sybil watched intently, still in the best of humor. "It's all right, Scanlon," she said. "I'm a doctor."

O'Neil stood back and reached into his pocket. He pulled out a gun. "You do one thing except what you said you were going to do—or if anybody else tries to bust in here—you're dead."

"Don—"

"Sybil, I got to do this. I don't want to be taken."

"Look," I said. "If I'm lying and I'm still a federal officer, then I'm not here alone and shooting me even by accident is just going to get you a life term. On the other hand, if I'm telling the truth, then shooting me cuts you off from your last chance to enjoy the money you'll have left. Put the gun away. It can't help you."

"He's right, Don," the doctor said.

O'Neil put the gun in his pocket and my heartbeat slowed back down to about one-and-a-half times normal.

The doctor resumed her good cheer. "Okay, get your drink and your suitcases, Scanlon, and come on." I had an armful. "Let me take one," she said, and grabbed it.

She led the way down the stairs merrily, like Dorothy on the yellow brick road. O'Neil followed behind me, glowering, and I looked back several times to make sure the gun was still in his pocket.

The basement was nicely finished. The usual furnace

and laundry room off to our left was unusually clean and spacious, and off to our right was a beautiful game room with blue carpeting, a green pool table, a glossy wood bar and a soundproof tile ceiling. The doctor clasped my shoulder when I got to the bottom of the stairs. "Welcome," she smiled. "Wait right here." She gave me a slow feel of her breast across my arm as she brushed past much closer than she would have had to.

She went to the fuse box on the wall of the little hallway. Inside, she messed with a couple of switches. "Okay, follow me," she said, and led us into the game room. O'Neil was still watching as if he wished none of it was happening.

Sybil scanned the ceiling tiles until it seemed she found the one she wanted, and stood under it. "Now, Scanlon," she said, holding her arms out to me. "I want you to stand right here."

I did exactly as I was told, which brought me close enough that I wished her husband wasn't there—and hoped, with that gun in his pocket, that he didn't mind. Sybil just waltzed away over to the cinderblock wall. Did the wall conceal a vault? I studied it and couldn't find a crack or gap anywhere. She reached for a particular block and pressed her hand against it. "It takes a few seconds," she smiled. "At this point, it's a matter of heat."

Suddenly the whole wall began to swivel out and I had to jump out of the way to avoid being hit by it. Sybil laughed. "One of the hazards," she said. "Come on."

She led me around the edge of the "door," which was in fact the whole wall. There was another cinderblock wall just a few feet behind the first. In that few feet were stacks and stacks of money. Paper money.

"The twenties, the fifties, the tens, they're all mixed in," she said. "It'd take forever to count. Why don't you just load up and we'll see if you get to about a third."

And so we did. It was like some sort of crazy dream. And when I got the first suitcase full and closed it and moved it aside, I realized for the first time that money is heavy. We didn't get a third of it in the two suitcases, not nearly. But it looked like enough to last awhile.

Then we stood back and she swung the wall shut.

"You could comb this place—you could even live here—and never know that was there," I said.

"I know," she replied. "That's the idea."

"How did you ever find a place with a vault like that?"

"Mickey had it built. Back in August he knew we'd need a storage place, and that I wanted to come out to Stanford with the kids. For awhile he was even acting like he had reconciled himself to the fact that Don would come with me. Anyway, he found this place being built and the architect was somehow a friend of his, or a friend of a friend—or maybe Mickey made him a friend—and anyway, he had the vault installed special."

"Then you put out the architect's eyes," I suggested.

She laughed heartily. "Exactly," she said.

"How the hell did you get all this cash out here, anyway?" I asked.

"I guess the same way you're going to get it back to New York," she said. "Mickey probably brought it on a plane. It's one of those things he wouldn't talk about much—he liked mysteries. All Don and I knew was that the stuff was arriving in Palo Alto. I flew out here twice myself to look it over—stacking up down here all nice and pretty. People sure thought I was doing an awful lot of double checking about the job." She was still laughing.

I shook my head and went up the stairs lugging my suitcases.

"Don, help him with one of those," she said.

"That's all right," I told her. "I can manage." Don didn't look any too eager. He was still glowering.

I set the bags down in the entrance hall. Sybil came over and put her hands on my shoulders again. "You're not going to rush off now, are you?"

"I figured I would," I said.

"Stay and have another drink. Why don't you stay for dinner!"

I started to say no, but O'Neil was faster. "Damn it," he said, giving Sybil a terrible look and heaving his body in front of me.

"When did Mickey bring you in on it?" I asked him.

O'Neil sputtered threateningly. Sybil put a hand on him, a moral rather than physical restraint, and again tried to wedge herself between us. "Back in August," she said, still trying to be cheerful. "Just a few weeks before it started. Mickey brought up the idea, and at first I thought it was crazy. Then I told Don about it and we got to talking. We decided unless there was some kind of settlement we were going to have to worry about Mickey the rest of our lives. And there were other things, personal things . . . You know, it wasn't easy. There were times it didn't seem like they were going to be able to ride in the car together long enough to transfer the money. A couple times we even had to get Walter to go instead."

"Don't say any more, Sybil," O'Neil interjected strongly, and reinforced it by moving her aside with his arm. "Now you've got your money. You get out of here," he told me.

"Wait," she said. "Hey, you guys. We're all in this together. The three of us. We have a secret now. And I think it's funny. We've all made the same decision. We're all perfectly respectable citizens, and we've all learned from Mickey Carmody that people who steal money have it better than anybody else in society. They don't have to work, they live well and they rarely go to jail. The only time they get into trouble at all is when they play with guns. And we all, all three of us, decided that here was some money we could steal that didn't really belong to anybody in particular, at least not anybody who couldn't afford to lose it. And so we stole it. And now we're all going to live happily ever after. I think that's really funny. The least we could do is all be friends."

I looked at Don and I looked at Sybil. They looked at

each other and they looked at me. "Well?" she said.

"You set Mickey up to get killed, didn't you," I said.

Her smile vanished into an expression of surprise.

I looked her straight in the eye. "That's why you went to the cops and why you came to me that day complaining about how he was threatening you. So we wouldn't be suspicious when it happened."

She was shaking her head. "You don't understand," she said.

"You knew what would happen Christmas. You set him up."

"You can't set up somebody who doesn't have evil in his heart," she said. "He thought he could just *use* Don. The way he used everybody. He was setting Don up that same night. Mickey had been setting Don up from the first time he suggested the deal. He knew I was coming to see you that day in your office. You talked to him afterwards, remember? It was all part of his plan. He said then it was just to throw off suspicion, so you'd never know who the other man was. But he wanted to *kill* Don. We didn't realize it then, but we realized it a long time before Christmas."

"So he had you tip me and the police off that he was going to do it."

"Mickey thought he could get away with anything. Nobody would have been able to prove it. He would have had the money, and in his twisted way of thinking he imagined he would have had me, too. The con man got conned. That's all that happened, Scanlon."

I just looked at her. I really didn't know which side I would have been rooting for in that shoot-out.

"Do you know what kind of person Mickey *was*?" she asked.

"I guess the human being kind," I said.

"Are you sure about that?"

I opened the door and picked up the suitcases. "Goodbye," I said, and struggled away to the car.

I flew to Buffalo just in case anybody was watching my comings and goings, and took a bus back to New York. I retrieved the envelope from my doorman, and right now I'm finishing off these notes. Someday this will make a hell of a novel. Maybe I'll even publish it as an autobiography. I read where Willie Sutton just finished his.

What I was really thinking I ought to do is, just before I leave the country, mail the envelope to Ruggiardo anyway. That would take care of the only two witnesses to what I've done. But I decided I'm just not that big a shit. So I put the idea out of my mind by burning the envelope.

Tomorrow I head for Mexico. They don't check your bags at the border. I've got a cousin down in San Miguel who says it's beautiful, and has been begging me for a visit. I could live like a king down there on what I've got. And my passport's up to date. I'll swap my goddamn Nova for a Mercedes. Just like Stanley Timmons. If I can ever figure a way to get all this money overseas, who knows where I might wind up?

CHAPTER THIRTY

Arthur Protter stared blankly at the litter of publicity handouts and news story carbons on his desk. Directly into his line of vision a copyboy dropped the late market edition of *The New York Press.* Its headline stared back at him:

NAB TWO GAYS IN PLAYGIRL SLAYING

He thought it would fit nicely into the collection of *Press* headlines he was building at home, in a scrapbook entitled "Things To Do On A Dull Day." Already he had pasted in such items as SAVE SIX INDIANS TRAPPED IN TRAIN and HOLD 23 CHI GANG BIGS IN FRAUD.

He got up and shuffled over to the locker in the small anteroom off the news floor, glancing out of the corner of his eye to see that no one was watching him. He opened the locker, reached in for a brown paper bag, unscrewed the top of the bottle and took several long swallows of vodka, screwed the top back on and closed the locker. He shuffled back to the city desk.

The late market was off the press and the deadline for the final had passed, unless Air Force One crashed or something. It was supposed to be time to plan ahead, talk to reporters about investigative pieces, read features that were being held over for tomorrow's paper because they needed a little more work.

But none of that seemed worth doing any more. The young women from Radcliffe or Columbia Journalism School who wrote features nowadays all knew too much, or thought they did, to want advice from him. The biggest investigation the *Press* had done in a year was when they sent some kid around to the massage parlors to report with feigned shock the competitive prices of blow jobs. In fourteen more months Artie Protter would be eligible for retirement, and the publisher and the new managing editor left no doubt that they wanted him to take it. Hell, they might make him hasten it.

There were so many things he could worry about— none of which would do any good. He settled into the swivel chair and sank comfortably back into his haze. He didn't know how long it was before he sensed a copyboy calling to him from over his left shoulder. "Mr. Protter . . . Mr. Protter . . . somebody to see you."

He turned and saw a familiar young man carrying two large suitcases. A surge of excitement pulled him awake. "Frank, you son of a bitch, how are you?"

"Fine, Artie." The young man set down the suitcases and they shook hands.

"How's the cops and robbers game going these days?"

"If you mean the FBI thing, not so hot."

"Well, I told you that life wasn't for you. You shoulda stayed here from the beginning. But if you're here about a job, I'm afraid it's been too long. We're just not hiring anybody these days. Maybe the M.E. could talk to you—"

"That's not it, Artie."

Protter's eyes began to focus better. "Hey, you really got your bags packed, don't you."

"Artie, I got to see you. It's important. Let's go into the M.E.'s office."

"What's this all about?"

"We've got to talk in private. It's important."

"Well, I just can't go in—you know we've got a new managing editor now. Gartner went to the *Des Moines Register*. This guy Harris is a real horse's ass. I mean, just between you and me. Why can't we do it here?"

"Artie, please, trust me. He'll appreciate it and you'll appreciate it."

"Harris, he's not even here this afternoon. He's at the dentist. Heh! I hope they take his gums out."

"If he's not here, then let's use his office."

Protter rose from his chair, wobbling. "Okay, if you're so all fired hot about it." He led the way to the office in a corner of the room, the only private place on the news floor.

A secretary gave an apprehensive look. "It's okay, Shirley," Protter said. It didn't make her look any less apprehensive.

Scanlon shut the door behind them and locked it. At the snap of the lock Protter looked worried. "You have to do that?" he asked.

Scanlon said nothing. He lifted one of the suitcases and dropped it on the desk, scattering some small objects. He unlatched it and flipped open the lid. It was stuffed with bills.

Protter watched, bug-eyed. "Jesus," he finally said. "What'd you do, rob a bank?"

"Nope. But you're close. It's the Quincy money."

"The Quincy money," Protter repeated, whispering, slowly, reverently, his eyes glued on the desk as Scanlon set the second suitcase alongside the first and opened it. The photograph of the managing editor's wife and children fell to the floor, but Protter seemed not to notice. "The four and a half million?" he asked in a hoarse gasp.

"Hell, there may not even be a million in here," Scanlon said. "But it was all I could carry."

"Where—were you working on the Quincy case up there on 69th Street?"

"I was. I'm no longer an FBI agent. They fired me almost a week ago. They don't know I've got it."

"Who does know?" Protter was serious now.

"Just you—and me—and the two survivors of the guy who planned it all. Artie, I got the whole story—who stole it and how. The FBI doesn't know a damn thing. They are so fucking stupid, Artie. You know, I almost went to Mexico. I swear I almost did. I got all the way to Wilmington, Delaware."

"Mexico? What the hell do they care about this in Mexico? You can't even write Spanish."

"Artie, what I mean is—"

"Sit down, right over there. Use Harris's typewriter. Nobody has got to find out about this. You locked the door, didn't you?" He checked it.

"I thought you said this M.E. was a horse's ass."

"Forget what I said. I'll take care of him. Are you sure the FBI doesn't know about this?"

"They don't know which end to shit out of, Artie. Ahh, I guess that's unfair. It's not true. Me and them, we just don't get along is all, not on the same side anyway." Scanlon sat down at the desk. "I guess I never should have—"

"You say you don't even know how much is in here. Christ, we've got to count it. You think it's almost a million? Maybe more than a million?"

"You know we can all get arrested, don't you?"

"Arrested for what?"

"We're harboring stolen money."

"We're not going to harbor anything. We'll turn it over to the FBI, just as soon as the story's in type. Hell, we'll have Henrietta herself turn it over."

"Henrietta?"

"Mrs. Jenkins. The publisher. Goddamn it, Frank, how long have you been gone from here, anyhow? Ol' Henrietta will eat it up. We'll go up there in her goddamn limousine with a couple of Brinks guards and some photographers. Those G-Men'll look so goddamned dumb! We'll have your story on the streets in the city edition tomorrow morning, and the half-page photo of her giving them that money will be right there under the headline by the time the noon market comes out. How the hell did you find it, anyway?"

"Well—"

"Don't tell me. Just start writing it. Oh, can you see the looks on those guys' faces. Do you think we ought to invite the TV people? We sure as hell aren't going to call the other newspapers, you can count on that."

"Artie, I just think we ought to call our lawyers."

Protter pointed a finger. "You got to work. Start writing. Does Harris keep any copy paper in this place? I'll go get you some."

Scanlon pulled a stack out of a drawer and held it up. "I've got everything I need," he said.

"Good," Protter told him. "Get to work. I'm going to have somebody get the clips on this thing. There ought to be some pictures of that bank they took down there."

"Artie, also get the clips on a hood named Mickey Carmody who got shot Christmas Eve out on Long Island. Also a hood named Walter Fakazzi, F-a-k-a-z-z-i, who got hit by the Mob out in Jersey City about ten days ago. And Vincente Ruggiardo, the Mafia boss." Protter was listening closely, taking mental notes of Scanlon's commands. "Also see if we got a picture of a young woman who got shot last Thursday, Sara . . . Sara . . . shit, Artie, forget that. Just have them get me Carmody, Fakazzi and Ruggiardo."

"What did they have to do with it? Never mind. Don't tell me. I'll get the clips. You'll need coffee, too. Are you hungry?"

"Yeah, as a matter of fact."

"I'll get everything you need. You just get to work." Protter sprang for the door and slid out, opening it only a crack. "Shirley!" he said. "Nobody goes in there. Nobody."

"But what if Mr. Harris comes back?" the secretary said.

"I'll take care of—Scanlon!" He opened the door a crack again. "Lock the door. Lock it! Don't let anybody in unless it's me, I don't care if he says he's the Marines."

There were footsteps coming over to the door and the lock snapped. Protter rushed off to his desk in the middle of the city room and picked up the phone. As he dialed, he shouted out into the room, "Copy!" Two teen-aged boys in dungarees began stirring around the water fountain. The secretary watched, puzzled.

Inside the office, Frank Scanlon hunched over the typewriter. He knew who the bastards were, on both sides. He would never again join them. The keys flew under his fingers and their rhythmic click was like a symphony. At long last, this time he was really going to get the bastards.